From the Canadian Arctic
To the
President's Desk

HMS RESOLUTE

And
How She Prevented
A War

Elizabeth R. Matthews

Auxilium ab Alto Press

An Auxilium ab Alto Press Book

Text Copyright © Elizabeth R. Matthews 2007

Cover design by Kim Orde Matthews ©
Front cover: HMS Resolute in the Arctic.

ISBN 978-0-755203-96-3

Auxilium ab Alto Press
19 The Cinques
Gamlingay, Sandy
Bedfordshire SG19 3NU
England

To Ted,
And to the memory of Eleanor Roosevelt,
Both of whom inspired in me
My life long belief in the potential of my country.

And to Kim, Scott, and William,
For instilling in me my belief in love.

"...Terrific! It truly is a fascinating story, and it [your book] deepens my already profound appreciation for this unique piece of American history."

-William J. Clinton-

The forty-second President of the United States (1993-2001).

"Elizabeth Matthews' research is thorough...[She has] a vivid imagination -that's a compliment! - to weave such a lively and convincing story around the historical facts. I have to confess that all the political machinations and tensions between Britain and the US were entirely new to me. I am really impressed."

-William Barr-

William Barr, holds degrees in Geography from the University of Aberdeen,, Scotland, and McGill University, Quebec. He has published 16 books, and is professor emeritus of geography, University of Saskatchewan, and is now a Research Fellow in residence at the Arctic Institute of North America, University of Calgary. He has published 16 books, and for the past 30 years he has focused his research on the history of Arctic exploration.

TABLE OF CONTENTS

N. W. Passage

Based on a map by
Lieu. S.G. Cresswell, 1854

Dealy Is.

Resolute's winter
quarters 1852-3

Melville
Island

— — — — Resolute's Route

. . . . Assistance's Route

Banks Strait

Bridport Inlet

*

Baring Island

Prince
Albert's
Land

Sea mostly
navigable

Cape
Parry

Dolphin & Union Strait

NORTH AMERICA

|———— 200 miles ————|

* Now known as Banks Island

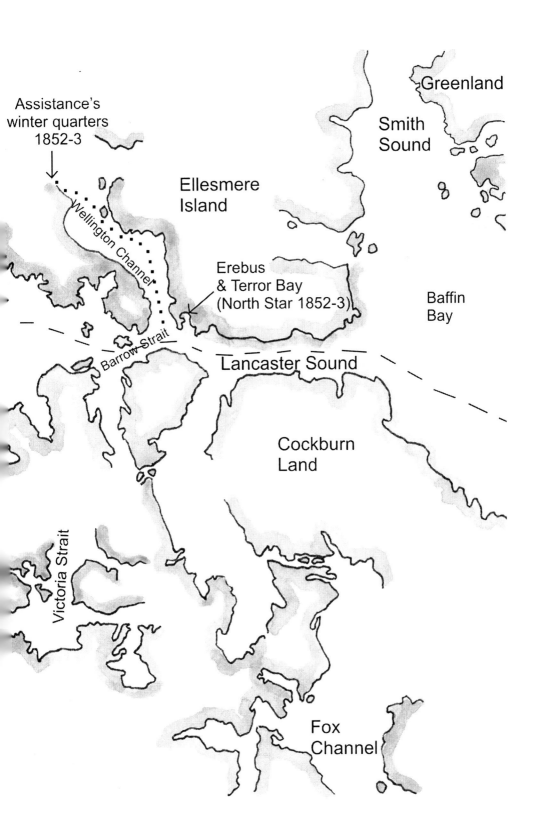

Assistance's
winter quarters
1852-3

Greenland

Smith
Sound

Ellesmere
Island

Wellington Channel

Erebus
& Terror Bay
(North Star 1852-3)

Baffin
Bay

Barrow Strait

Lancaster Sound

Cockburn
Land

Victoria Strait

Fox
Channel

PART ONE

SEARCHING

1852

CHAPTER ONE
APRIL 1852

Lieutenant Bedford Pim stood at attention. He glanced quickly to the windward side of the quarterdeck where his captain paced forward and aft. His hands clasped behind him, Captain Kellett's face was set hard. Pim could see the muscles in Kellett's jaws working and each step seemed to be imbued with anger. Pim looked straight ahead as Kellett abruptly turned. The captain announced he was going below and no one was to disturb him until the men were all on board. The sound of the captain's heavy steps resumed in his cabin in a matter of seconds.

Pim's shoulders sagged when he had the quarterdeck to himself again. He had never seen his captain so angry. Having served under him on board HMS *Herald*, he knew Kellett to be a firm, yet kind, commander. He could even admit to himself that he had a certain amount of affection for him. But, now he would rather be in a fierce storm being forced upon the rocks of a lee shore in uncharted waters than be here waiting for this storm to break. At least in violent weather he would know what to do.

Below deck Kellett swore at the bulkheads of his cabin, 'Is there no end to the stupidity of those fools at the Admiralty?' His dog, Napoleon, a spaniel and Irish red and white mixed breed, crouched under the desk, head lowered onto his paws, vigilantly followed his master with his eyes as Kellett continued pacing. He slammed his fist down on the table just above Naps' head, causing his dog to attempt the impossible of curling into a tighter ball in the hope of disappearing entirely. Unused to his master's anger, the dog's eyes showed his concern. Kellett swore again. 'If they had searched the whole of the Royal Navy, they couldn't have come up with a worse man to make squadron commander!' Kellett knew this better than any one else. How could the Admiralty order him to serve under Belcher again? They were demanding more from him than he felt able to give.

The expedition to search for the lost explorer, Sir John Franklin, was soon to set sail from Greenhithe on the Thames. For almost three hundred years, men had been prodding the northern ice with their ships' prows hoping to find a more direct and less dangerous way to reach the Pacific than the southern route around Cape Horn. The Legendary Northwest Passage. Franklin and his men aboard HMS *Erebus* and *Terror* had disappeared somewhere in the Arctic in 1845 while searching for it, and Kellett had been one of the first captains ordered to look for them and bring them supplies. Now, seven years later, the Admiralty, spurred onward by the loyal and persistent Lady Franklin, continued to pour money, men, and ships into the Arctic. Could it be possible they were still looking for live men?

Kellett sat at his desk to review again the list of captains, officers, and men sailing in the Belcher Expedition's five ships: Her Majesty's Ships *Assistance, Resolute, Pioneer, Intrepid,* and *North Star.* Naps tentatively put his chin on Kellett's knee. The captain stroked the dog's head affectionately and felt his anger begin to melt. Feeling a slight quiver in the beast, he smiled sadly. 'Sorry, old chap, for giving you such a fright. Not your fault, is it?' Naps' tail thumped against the wooden deck in acceptance of the apology. Kellett was in command of HMS *Resolute.* A good name for a ship facing the tasks ahead, he thought. He turned his attention back to the crew lists. There were some familiar names of men who had served under him before, but many of the names were new to him. Quite a few had seen prior service in the Arctic and that experience would prove valuable.

The sound of pounding feet on the deck above interrupted his thoughts. Kellett valued time alone in a new ship before having the men mustered in, but it was a luxury he could not now indulge. The men were arriving, and he was still in the grip of something between apprehension and anger. Whatever might happen he would not let the men see his feelings about their squadron commander, nor would he allow Belcher to affect the way he would treat his own men.

Kellett shook his head and thought of his wife as he usually did when he felt troubled. He remembered the first time he had taken her to Ireland after their marriage. She had been so quiet when Henry brought her home to Clonacody that he was afraid she wouldn't settle. During dinner parties at the neighbouring estates she had barely spoken. He had watched her walk the fields of their land and at night he had held her like a flower whose petals could be easily crushed. He had held her and engulfed her in his love. And he waited.

When her things had arrived from England, she began making Clonacody her own, joining together the relics of her life with those of the Kellett ancestors. As the months passed, she had made her presence felt in every room, making small but noticeable changes, blending their two lives into one. Henry Kellett smiled remembering the little things: the scent of her hair, the golden wheat colour when the sun shone on it; the quiet way she worked with the horses.

Gathering pen, ink, and paper Kellett started to write his last letter to Alice before the expedition's departure.

Greenhithe 20 Apr. 52

My Dear Alice,

I may not have another chance to write to you before we depart, and I write with a heavy and angry heart. You know too well my experience of serving under Sir Edward Belcher. After all this time I thought I would never have to suffer at his hands again, that I wouldn't have to watch him break any more good men. He is never at his best when he is under difficult circumstances, and he always makes others suffer for this.

I should not burden you, yet you know what we all lived through on the *Aetna*. May God preserve us from an Arctic *Aetna*! And may my fears be proven wrong!

Were you here I would hold you in my arms, but you are not and I must rely on these poor words to convey my love. Know that I am always your loving husband...

Kellett read what he had written, crumpled the paper into a ball, and threw it at the bulkhead. He began a new letter telling Alice of his love, leaving his fears unwritten.

He heard the bo's'n's call to muster and the quick steps of the men preparing to present themselves to their captain. With a sigh he rose from his desk, straightened his coat and epaulets, and squared his shoulders. This was not only the first time the men would see him as captain of the *Resolute,* but also his first opportunity to take the measure of them, the Resolutes. Napoleon followed him as he ascended to the quarterdeck and stood before the men and officers. His face showed no emotion, neither his recent anger nor his delight in seeing Richard Roche, his former mate from the *Herald.*

'We leave tomorrow at dawn. The Admiralty has entrusted us with the mission of finding the Franklin Expedition. Additionally, we are also ordered to search for, and relieve, Captains Collinson and McClure who have preceded us in the search for Franklin. It is my duty to inform you that this expedition is NOT being sent to continue the search for the Northwest Passage. We are to find and relieve, if they are still alive, Franklin and his men. If they are no longer alive, we are to report any signs we may find indicating what happened to them. I repeat: we are not searching for the Northwest Passage. The Admiralty has emphasised this point to our squadron commander, Sir Edward Belcher, in the orders for our expedition. He, in turn, has stressed it to me. If any of you have volunteered hoping you will receive a reward, I urge you to put away such hopes entirely.'

4

Kellett paused. He could see disappointment in the faces of several of the men. He knew that most of them were there to do what ever their superior officers ordered. For Queen and Country. He knew some had a genuine concern for the lost men. Money, however, always provides great motivation. Some of the men just needed the full pay of active duty and were glad enough in a peacetime Navy to have a ship. But, he also knew that some were looking to line their pockets with a share of the ten thousand pound reward Parliament had offered for the discovery of the Northwest Passage. He could not change the motivation of these men, but he could make certain they understood their mission.

'Many lives are dependent upon the success of our search. Men like you are struggling not to give up the hope that someone will come to save them from an icy grave. I know you will do your utmost so they won't hope in vain.'

The captain turned toward Lieutenant Pim. 'Dismiss the men, Lieutenant.'

✎

♂♂♂♂♂

Martha and Fairfax Abraham III stood on the steps of their New London, Connecticut home waiting for the carriage, their children gathering around them. The father looked with pleasure on his wife and seven children. More than his wealth or position, even more than being an Elder in his Quaker Meeting, Fairfax Abraham took pride in his growing family. Pride before the fall he reminded himself. Love certainly, but pride was too much. He made a silent apology to God as his driver appeared with the carriage. Samuel, the second oldest son, helped his heavily pregnant mother into the carriage. The rest of the children settled in and Father closed the door behind himself.

Baby Martha sat on her father's lap as they rode through town to the Religious Society of Friends' Meeting House. Even the baby was dressed in proper Quaker grey, all the girls wore their plain caps as did their mother, and the boys wore their wide brimmed hats just like Father's. It was First Day and the family began their preparation for waiting on the Lord during their carriage ride, as they did every First Day.

'God is Love,' Martha said, smiling at each of her children in turn. 'And His Light shines in each of thee. God's divine Spark is in every person. Remember this, and the Lord, and God will bless thee.'

Father said a short prayer, asking that his family be able to open their hearts to God's word during Meeting. They remained silent for the remainder of their journey; even little Martha quietly looked at her brothers and sisters.

Outside the Meeting House, there was the familiar First Day activity. Carriages waited in line to drop off the wealthy Friends; many other families arrived by foot. While all wore subdued grey, there was nothing subdued in their joy of seeing friends and extended families, most appearing early in order to have visiting time before entering Meeting. The children laughed and embraced playmates, burning off a bit of their energy before having to sit quietly. Men and women caught up on the week's news. As Meeting time approached, however, a quietness settled among them so by the time they began entering the Meeting House they were already in a reverent mood.

The Abraham family took their places on the family bench. However, because he was an Elder, Father did not sit with his family but on the facing bench with the other Meeting Elders. The only sound in the room was the shuffling of feet and the rustle of clothing as the congregation found their seats. A small baby cried and was comforted. A young boy whispered that he wanted to sit next to his mother. Baby Martha could not find enough room on her mother's lap to share with her unborn sibling so she held her hands out to Brother Samuel, who took her and settled her in his arms.

The town hall clock struck ten. The expectant waiting on God began; the quiet grew. The meeting gathered, centred down, and welcomed Christ to come into their midst.

The oldest son of the Abraham family, Fairfax Abraham IV, known as Fair Abe, prayed silently for the Word of God. He was greatly troubled and it took considerable effort to quiet his heart and mind this day. Yet, soon after settling, his spirit became agitated again. He breathed more deeply and slowly to bring back the feeling of serenity which he usually felt when waiting on the Lord.

The words of the Gospel Matthew came to him. He had never yet spoken in Meeting and had often wondered how someone knew whether they were being moved by God to speak or if they just wanted to stand up and say something of their own volition. *I just want to speak because of how I feel about slavery*, he thought to himself. *I must sit quietly and this urge will pass.* He breathed deeply again and tried to get his hands to stop shaking.

Martha looked at her son and saw his chest heaving and his hands trembling. She knew her son was being moved by the Lord, and soon he would rise up and give the message that was being pressed into his soul. This would be the first time God had called on Fair Abe to minister to the gathered Friends.

'The Lord saith,' the young man cried out. He placed his hands on the back of the bench in front of him and pulled himself to his feet. 'What has come into being in the Lord is Life, and Life is the Light for ALL the people. God's Light shines in the darkness and the darkness cannot overcome it.' He closed his eyes for a moment, and when he opened them, he looked at each expectant face, waiting on his next words. *No, not his words*, he reminded himself, *the Word of God.*

'Jesus said: "when the Son of Man comes into his glory, all the nations shall be gathered before Him." How shall they be judged? The righteous clothed Christ when He was naked, brought Him food when He was hungry; visited Him when He was sick and in prison, welcomed Him when He was a stranger. When did the righteous do these things, for they did not know they had tended Christ? "Verily I say unto thee: just as thou hast done these deeds to the least of these my brethren, thou hast done it unto Me", Christ said.

'Who are the least of our brethren today? To whom shalt thou give succour so that ye are not counted among the accursed and damned? Are not our Negro brethren children of the Lord? Wouldst thou keep Christ in chains and bondage? Are thy hands clean simply because thou ownest no slaves? Truly, thou art among the damned and shall not see salvation until this abomination is cleansed from thy midst! As ye free the least of these, thy brethren, thou freest Christ Himself.'

Trembling, Fairfax Abraham resumed his seated position. His words echoed through the Meeting room. Gradually the silence absorbed the waves of his intensity, the Meeting gathering the message into the folds of its expectant waiting. No other message was given that day.

'Thee spoke well in Meeting this day,' Martha said after the dinner table was cleared. 'There are many who know the abolition of slavery is what the Lord wants, but we do not know how it will come about. Thy father believes we should approach this gradually. Thou knowest he goes monthly to slave holders in Maryland and labours with them to release their slaves. He believes this is the best way forward.'

'Mother, should we not break the bonds holding Christ's own in slavery at once and forever? How can we say "just a while longer, Lord, keep thy peace"?'

'Friends did not give up their slaves instantly. We laboured mightily for many years.'

'But, Mother, that was ages ago. Decades have past and this evil is stronger than ever; who will be called to destroy it if we are not?'

Fairfax Abraham Senior, known simply as Abraham or Father Abraham since the birth of his eldest son, joined his wife and son after the youngest were settled for their afternoon rests.

'I understand thy urgency, Fair Abe, but do not forget the other cornerstones of our faith. We believe in peaceful methods of persuasion, not creating such strain that war is the only resolution. Our peace testimony is as important as relieving the suffering of the slaves, is this not so?'

'I do not believe that freeing the slaves would bring war. How could the South ever justify going to war over slavery?'

Abraham gently put his hand on his son's shoulder. 'Ah, my son, thy youth serves thee well in thy enthusiasm for justice, but the hearts of men have found ways to justify war over lesser causes than this.'

'Shall we go for our First Day walk?' Martha rose from her chair, sensing that now would be an opportune time for quiet reflection.

𝒞𝒞𝒞𝒞𝒞

Ship's Master George Frederick McDougall sat on the bunk in his cabin. He was glad to be on board *Resolute* again. He smiled to himself, remembering the frolics his friend, Osborn, and he had orchestrated within her wooden walls on their last adventure together. She was a good stout ship. Quite ugly, if the truth was told. She certainly did not have the beautiful lines of the fast and sleek Baltimore Clippers now being built in America. *Resolute's* builders, instead, gave her a broad flat bottom and a double hull so she could withstand the crushing action of the Arctic ice. And, at least the last time she was in the ice, she did what an arctic exploration ship was meant to do: she brought all her men safely home.

McDougall opened a leather-bound book to its first page and began to write:

> 'Greenhithe. 20. Apr. 52.
> We leave with the ebb tide early tomorrow morning. All the charts are in order and I have set up my navigational station. I am to meet with my new captain in less than an hour. I have not served under him, but some of the others on board have done, and they seem content to be here. We have some experienced Arctics with us and I am glad of it. Many of the old Assistances from the '50 expedition are here. They are mostly a good lot and know what lies ahead.'

McDougall set the book aside. Kellett had asked for a report on the sailing abilities of the *Resolute,* and the master thought about what he could tell his captain. She was as slow as an old, pregnant cow. No matter how well the men worked her, she lumbered through tacking and wearing ship. She did not point worth a damn. Her bow did not cut through the waves. Rather, because it was too blunt, she moved through the water by pushing it out of her way with the sheer strength of her will. With the right wind and all her sails set, however, she could move along at a reasonable clip. She was almost graceful. No, that was probably going too far...

The morning of departure dawned bright with a clear sky. The men's breath swirled away into the frosty air. At five o'clock, the bo's'n piped the hands aloft and the tops'ls filled with the fair wind.

'Brooke!'

'Sir!'

'Send for Lieutenant Pim to report to me immediately.'

'Yes, Sir!' Cox'n Brooke saluted.

Frederick Brooke ascended to the quarterdeck to relay the captain's message. Brooke was one of the old Assistances and he was happy that so many of his old shipmates were with him on this commission. At muster, he had noticed almost a dozen as well as a couple of old Resolutes from the 1850 expedition. Master McDougall was on board, too. Memories of McDougall's theatre performances made Brooke smile, and helped assuage the nervousness he felt at being cox'n to a new captain.

As Brooke followed Lieutenant Pim to the captain's quarters, Pim could sense the tension in the young cox'n.

'Don't be so uneasy about serving Captain Kellett, Frederick. I served under him on the *Herald*. He is a fair captain and he will treat you as you deserve. Just do your duties well, and you will have nothing to fear.'

'Yes, sir,' Brooke replied, wondering if there were other Heralds on board from whom he could get the real story. Officers and men usually had very different experiences of their captain's moods.

Pim knocked on the captain's door. 'Come in Lieutenant Pim!' He entered and stood at attention. 'Please be at ease, Lieutenant.' Naps gave Pim's hand a quick sniff in greeting and then settled back down at Kellett's feet.

Kellett looked kindly at Pim. The lieutenant had served as Kellett's mate on board HMS *Herald*, and remarkably, he had refused to leave HMS *Herald* for a higher commission on *Plover*. Kellett suppressed a smile as he recalled how he had had to force Pim's confession of why he would not leave, the loyalty the young man expressed, and how he had finally persuaded Pim to take the commission on a temporary basis. Kellett had recommended him highly in 1850 and he had subsequently received his promotion to lieutenant.

Kellett felt this man would continue to be a credit to the Navy and would have a distinguished career should he choose to remain in the Queen's service. Kellett was not certain, though, why Pim had decided to go to sea in the first place. He was an intelligent man and Kellett felt certain that almost any path he might have chosen would have opened itself before the promising lieutenant. He was a man with a keen mind and was an astute observer of the men and events that surrounded him. He never seemed satisfied with what he had already learned and was always seeking knowledge.

'Please sit, Lieutenant. I want to discuss the men with you because you are better able than most to see who shows promise.'

Pim removed his hat and sat before the captain's desk, relieved that the dark mood of the previous day had now disappeared entirely from his captain's face.

'We have several groups of men who have seen prior service together. You know the five Heralds, sir. Along with the Assistances and Resolutes from '50, they form a solid group of experienced Arctics.'

Pim made suggestions for promotion to the positions of bo's'n's mate and the captains of the hold and fo'c'sle, which were not yet filled.

'I shall think on your suggestions. Are there any other men you think I should note?'

9

'No, Sir.'

'Thank you, Lieutenant. I will consider what you have said about the men when I appoint the petty officers. We dine at five o'clock. You are dismissed.'

As he returned to the deck, Pim wished he had mentioned McDougall, the ship's Master, to Kellett. In addition to his own experience of taking an immediate liking to him, the old Assistances and Resolutes had already told him stories about their navigator. Underneath the surface of his scientific skill lay a bit of a wag and storyteller. He was a good man, and the men looked up to him. There didn't seem to be any one of his old mates who did not enjoy his sense of fun and theatre. He was someone Pim felt would be an asset to the ship's company during the long Arctic winters.

Pim reflected on the day that he had met McDougall. They had joined the ship on the same day, 16 February, each man immediately recognising a kindred spirit in the other. They were very different, yet similar, which seemed contradictory but was not. McDougall's humour was infectious and it balanced Pim's seriousness. They had quickly discovered that they were both writers, that they enjoyed observing and recording their impressions of surrounding people and events. Yet, they wrote with very different styles. Pim's mind, almost as though trained in the legal profession, worked in a very precise fashion. He picked up details and extracted symbolism and meaning from them. McDougall, though trained to think precisely in relation to his work as navigator, tended to focus on the broader picture, then he infused the details with his unique sense of humour.

McDougall had a sense of theatre that Pim lacked. Pim's feet were planted firmly on the deck, he viewed the world in a solid, and practical way, while McDougall's flights of imagination lifted him up to a level equivalent to the t'gallants. He viewed the world from that lofty perspective, laughing to himself all the while. Two men. Similar. Different. Complimentary. A friendship was growing between them.

⚓⚓⚓⚓⚓

At Clonacody Alice Kellett watched her daughter working the newest horse in their stable. The horses and Margaret seemed to share the same soul. Margaret had such an intuitive touch that, over the last two years, the stable hands had gradually had fewer and fewer horses to train. Now, at sixteen, Margaret was doing all the training and several of the Clonacody men had gone to neighbouring estates for work. The remaining staff did the mucking out and riding path maintenance, the feeding and grooming of the horses. They occasionally helped with the fields and gardens as well.

The estate, in County Tipperary, Ireland, was thriving under Alice's guidance while her husband was away at sea. Alice could hardly remember the time when Clonacody did not feel like home: that time in the distant past before this place of her husband's family became her own. Sometimes her thoughts carried her back to the days when she was happily carrying Henry's first child. She had taken the house in hand, beginning with the rooms on the top floor. Opening the long closed shutters, she had let the sun filter through the dusty air to reveal the nursery and day room where generations of children had been suckled and nurtured. She remembered smiling as she touched the cradle that had been her mother's-in-law.

When Henry had been called to sea for his commission as the commander of HMS *Starling*, she had filled her days with getting the nursery, children's day room, and nanny's room ready for the baby. First, the old curtains in the nursery had come down and the rugs were taken out and beaten. In the following weeks she had had the walls newly white washed and the wood trim painted while she freshly waxed and polished the old cradle. The staff had sorted, cleaned and ironed the linens, and placed them on the newly painted shelves with lavender between their layers. Alice had taken Great-grandmother Kellett's rocking chair into Clonmel to be repaired and freshly caned.

From the nursery, Alice had moved on to the day room. She had sorted the toys and dolls, and had the toys for older children put away in the steamer trunks that lined the wall in the room across the hall. Curtains had come down and been cut up for rags. Again, the carpet had been taken out for beating and airing. Then Alice and the staff went forth into the nanny's room with fresh white paint for the iron bed and cleaned linens.

Alice Kellett remembered sitting in the rocking chair at the end of all of it, looking out the day room window at the fields and mountain beyond, exhausted, happy, at peace. It was then that she had felt her child moving for the first time and she had known she was truly home.

Despite her inability to have more children, the years had been kind to the Kellett family and Clonacody was a happy home. Alice wondered how the years managed to pass so quickly, so that now, instead of holding her baby daughter, she was watching her riding in the north paddock, grown almost to womanhood.

⚓⚓⚓⚓⚓

On the first night sailing up the east coast of England Captain Kellett invited his officers to dine with him at his table. Dining with the captain was a tradition most officers dreaded. Most captains, too. Tradition and discipline dictated that no officer could speak until spoken to by the captain. Almost without exception, dinners at a captain's table were filled with awkward silences and discomfort. The officers sat stiff with fear that they would drink too much of the captain's good wine, that their tongues would loosen and they would speak out of turn. Kellett knew there were captains in the Royal Navy who found sport in trapping the officers into just such an act of insubordination and that in some cases it was justifiable fear.

Captain Kellett looked around his table at the assembled officers. The first course had been torturous. Even Pim had held himself stiffly upright in his chair. Every officer answered Kellett's questions with short and formal answers. Always agreeing with everything their captain said they kept their eyes down and stared intently at the food on their plates. The heaviness in the cabin was palpable. Kellett was struggling to keep his sense of frustration from showing in his face. He hoped the ongoing toasts and the well-prepared food would begin working on the men so that he could learn more about them. Of course, this could not happen unless they stopped feeling so afraid.

The silence grew and Kellett sighed inwardly, resigned to his failure to gain any insight into these officers. As he watched each man in turn, he caught Master McDougall's eye, and noticed an almost imperceptible look of amusement there.

Kellett recalled how much he had laughed when he read the newly published copy of McDougall's *Illustrated Arctic News* the commander of *Intrepid* had brought him just before they set sail. Perhaps McDougall could break the downward momentum of the dinner and save them all from any more suffering.

'Mr. McDougall, tell us about your experience on our good ship during your first voyage aboard her.'

'As a ship, Sir, you will find her a sluggish and lumbering beast. Mind, when you let her spread her canvas she'll always do better than the *Assistance*. You will discover that she is true to her name. Resolute she's named, and resolute she is. She got us through some tight spots before and always seemed stubbornly determined to defeat the worst the ice had to offer. Why, I can honestly say I've grown quite fond of her ugly self. I am sitting here, Sir, the living proof that she will do her best to bring us all back home again.'

'Didn't you find the winters long?' Young Nares asked and then he immediately reddened and looked nervously at his captain, realising he had spoken out of turn. Kellett gave a brief nod of permission. A conversation, not stilted questions and answers, is what he wanted.

'We had our ways of getting through,' McDougall answered, reading his captain's desire for him to continue. George Frederick began to tell the officers about the performances he had directed during the winter of '50. The Arctic Theatre Royale they had called it. Kellett watched the men relax as they became caught up in the web of McDougall's story telling. Within a quarter of an hour, McDougall had several of the young officers, Nares included, smiling as they listened to his description of one of the plays. Within half an hour they were laughing at the picture McDougall painted of the men playing the women's parts with mops for hair and with distinctively un-feminine swaggers in their walks.

With the easing of tension, Napoleon rose from under Kellett's chair and began a circuit around the table, putting his head expectantly in each man's lap, and gazing soulfully into their eyes. Fresh men who didn't yet know the rules couldn't be passed up. He just might get away with begging a few scraps before being caught out. Most of the men smiled at him and two slipped him scraps of food.

'Avast there! No begging!' Naps' reluctance and resignation to having to obey could be seen in his slow walk back to Kellett's place. 'You know better, my friend, although I can't blame you for trying!' Thank you, he said quietly to himself. Between you and McDougall the men are now much less stressed. Kellett was now able to observe a few of his officers without their noticing that they were being scrutinised. McDougall had the officers and the mate listening intently to the story of the former expedition's first sledging party. There was a clear laugh ringing around the cabin that Kellett recognised as Pim's. The young Nares laughed with Pim as McDougall continued.

'You should have seen us the first time we set our sledge's sail. We finally got us a favourable wind when we were between two ice hummocks. We had a long stretch of flat ice before us. This wind was only favourable, mind, because it was blowing in the direction we wanted to go. The sky was dark, low, and the clouds moving fast. It was as near enough a gale for us as we wanted it to be. Maybe it was too much, but we were tired and just couldn't see letting all that wind go to waste while we continued to struggle.

'At the end of the day we just exchanged one struggle for another. First, we had to step the mast and Sam'l almost sacrificed what brains he had to that endeavour, what with the bashing he received. The canvas almost took him next before we could get it hung. But, the chase really began after we got the sail up and the sledge set off at a run without us. We didn't catch her until she reached the base of the next hummock, which had a bit of a braking influence on her. Of course, our sledge crashing onto her starboard side and tipping her cargo all over creation helped end the race as well. I am willing to admit to you now our sledge got the better of us on that day!'

Young Nares laughed aloud, having completely forgotten for the moment that he was at the captain's table and that he was supposed to keep still. His pure enjoyment of the picture created by McDougall made Kellett smile. Nares, signed on as mate, had never served in the Royal Navy prior to this expedition. He had a broad expressive face framed by a shock of dark curly hair, and his brown eyes glistened with excitement and awe during McDougall's story telling.

The two mates on board Resolute would dine with their captain in succession, tradition dictating that only one at a time could join the officers at the captain's table. Dinner afforded an excellent opportunity for the young mates to observe the conduct becoming an officer and as such was a valuable tool in their training. However, it would never do to have the station of the officers diminished by the presence of more than one. Captain Kellett would have to wait until the next dinner to become reacquainted with his other mate, Richard Roche, who had served under him on the *Herald.*

13

After dinner, Captain Kellett took one last turn on deck, greeting the officer on watch whose duties had prevented his attendance at the dinner.

'All's well, Sir. Nothing to report, Sir.' The lieutenant saluted his captain. Alone in his cabin, Kellett lay in the darkness listening to the sounds of the ship, the creak of her timbers, the water rushing along side. His last thoughts before drifting off to sleep were of his ship's surgeon, Dr. William Domville. All Kellett had heard about him was, contrary to the common practice, he was not a drunk and he had a reputation for being fairly skilled with a knife. 'If he practices his art sober,' Kellett thought to himself, 'that will immediately make him be better than most!' Kellett could only hope that the long arctic winters would not drive his sober surgeon to drink.

CHAPTER TWO
MAY 1852

Favourable winds carried the squadron up the East Coast. As the ships neared Stromness in the Orkney Islands of Scotland, the wind shifted into the north, and the tide turned in their favour. It being a weather-tide, with the wind opposing the tidal flow, the ships were able to ride the tide toward Stromness, tacking port and starboard across the wind. Backing and filling they drifted broadside to the tidal stream with their topsails, jibs, and spankers set. The five crews worked as though they were one, keeping their main topsails backed, and the fore and mizzen sails full. To stay in line and to continue tiding into the harbour, the men brailed in the spankers or hauled them out as needed to keep their bows from falling off too far or coming up too much into the wind. Complementary action on the foredeck with the topsails and jibs kept the ships moving in concert. Fill and reach, tack and fill again. Back and forth. Back and forth.

The men were confident in their skill, yet this was the first time they had to perform this feat under Sir Edward's critical eye. The wind whisked away the crews collective sigh of relief when the squadron was finally safely at anchor.

With the Resolutes assembled on deck, Captain Kellett and Lieutenant Pim stood before the men. They needed strong men to quickly load the last of their supplies for the voyage. Efficiency was what Sir Edward Belcher had requested of his captains so they could be on their way with little time lost.

'Lieutenant Pim, we need volunteers to man the lighters. You may select additional men to make up sufficient crew if enough men do not volunteer. There will be no shore leave.'

A collective mutter arose from the men, interrupting the captain's orders. Kellett frowned and cleared his throat. The men quieted. 'However, there may be wives of our married crew who have come to Stromness to see their men this last time before we leave our Isle. Announce that they will be welcomed aboard tonight.'

With that the men staying on board seemed content. The following morning, the supplies loaded and the men happy from their last night with their 'wives,' all said a silent goodbye to their homeland as the ships set sail.

⚓⚓⚓⚓⚓

Martha Abraham gave birth to a son during the first week of May. He was blonde like his mother and arrived quietly in the early morning hours of the sixth. He looked a strong and healthy baby and they named him William.

The Monday following the birth of his son, Father Abraham left early to walk to his office. He always preferred walking, particularly on the first day of the workweek. The streets of New London were just beginning to awaken. The street cleaners were sweeping, shop owners washing down their windows, the bakery smelling of fresh bread. As usual, he was the first to arrive at the offices of Perkins, Smith, and Abraham, the whaling firm owned in part by Martha's father. He liked being the first in the office. He could tend to the work left on his desk from the day before while there was stillness all around him. Without distraction, he could get several hours' work done in half the time it would take once the office began to fill up. By the time the others arrived, his desk would be cleared and he could take a carriage down to the Perkins, Smith, and Abraham docks to check on the ships and dockside workers. His rounds completed, he would head back to the office to face the rest of the new day.

Some men would find it difficult to work for their fathers-in-law. But Father Abraham and Elias Perkins worked well together and were quite fond of each other. It had been helpful that Father Abraham brought his own firm to the table when he married Martha, which he had merged with the larger company. It had taken him years to rise from being a poor fisherman's son in the Chesapeake Bay to owning five fishing vessels and a whaler in New London. His father-in-law had quickly discerned when Martha introduced her beau that honesty and industry were an integral part of Abraham's character.

Now his son, Fairfax Abraham IV, had come of age and had begun working in the firm as well. He was still learning the business. And learning how to settle his restless spirit, Father had to admit to himself.

⚓⚓⚓⚓⚓

Fever struck Captain Kellett down on the first night out of Stromness. Kellett began to feel its effects at dinner when his cabin swirled around him after one glass of wine. Twenty days and twenty nights, the fever raged. Kellett knew nothing outside the world of his hallucinations. He did not even recognise his faithful Naps who kept watch beside his bunk.

Six days into the fever, on the fourth of May, McDougall recorded in the ship's log a strong SW wind with a cross-sea. The rising sea and the rapidly falling barometer forced the reduction of the ship's sails at 10:00 p.m. to close reefed tops'ls. By the following day, *Resolute* was lying to under close-reefed maintops'l, storm stays'l and reefed main trys'l, waiting out a violent gale with heavy cross-seas. For three days, the storm raged.

Waiting out the fever. Waiting out the storm. McDougall felt his ship being tossed about with the ship's company not yet pulled together into a working and harmonious whole. They needed Kellett now to bring them together, but the captain could only fight the battle raging within his own body. McDougall prayed this was not going to be one of those ill-fated voyages. They made for good stories and forebitters but were hell for the men involved.

⚓⚓⚓⚓⚓

On Sunday morning, Margaret Kellett accompanied her mother to services at the Anglican Church in Fethard. Most of the Anglo-Irish in the surrounding area of County Tipperary attended the transplanted Church of England. Most of the English families, though they had been in Ireland for generations, continued to exist almost entirely in a world apart from their Irish neighbours. Margaret, having been born in Ireland, thought rarely about the cultural divide. It was something that simply was a part of her daily life. She never focused on it, yet it was ever present like the weather, or the fields that stretched to the distant mountains. All but one of the people she knew abided by the unwritten law of the land that the two cultures simply didn't mix.

After services, the men and women gathered in groups to share news from the previous week. Margaret and her mother gravitated toward the group of men who were discussing the cattle market that would be held in Fethard the following Saturday. Being on her own, with Henry gone to sea so much of the time, Alice had taken over many of the duties that a male head of household in a country estate usually attended. As a result, she had become quite a good judge of both cattle and horses.

'This market will be a fine one,' one of the men said. 'There are going to be more cattle in this week's market than any time since last year: fresh stock from several counties.'

'How many head do you think?'

The men looked at Alice, some disapprovingly. The master of her neighbouring estate, O'Connor, had been heard to criticise Mrs. Kellett on numerous occasions, and he mumbled at her entering the conversation. Alice paid no heed to the men who looked at her with derision. They were, after all, fewer in number than the men who had finally accepted her, some even listening to her when she spoke of the quality, or lack of it, in a particular beast.

'There may be as many as 1,000 head.'

'What of their quality? That is, I suppose, the more important point,' Alice responded. Several of the men nodded in agreement. 'Have you heard anything about that?'

'My cousin is sending some of his best stock our way and I have heard from him that the quality of this market should be quite good. After all, the other estates will have to compete with him!'

Alice Kellett quietly listened to the men while they carried on their conversation about their herds and what they were looking to buy. She was naturally reserved and never did speak more than she needed to. That was one reason why most of the men found her presence among them tolerable. She never rattled on about inconsequential matters.

Nor, however, did she back down when she needed her voice heard. This measured but persistent presence won her more respect than not, among the women folk as well. She was usually helpful and most of the women had found through experience that they could confide in her without fear of Alice sending their private conversations into the gossip mill.

The Kellett's carriage stopped at the churchyard gate to take Alice and Margaret home. On their way Alice and Margaret talked about what they had learned about the up coming market, and Margaret talked of the new filly she would begin training on the morrow. Sundays were comfortably predictable. Sunday roast dinner followed church, and then the afternoon was spent quietly sewing or painting. Mother and daughter always ended the day with writing their letters to the man they both loved and missed. And so, this day followed the pattern of countless Sundays before, allowing the women to begin the week feeling rested and fulfilled.

⚓⚓⚓⚓⚓

Twenty days and twenty nights. Drenching his bedding in sweat, Kellett descended the maelstrom into a hell of visions. Visions that spoke to every fear. Visions pulling memories from their graves. Unconscious of his crying out, unconscious of the presence of his Cox'n Brooke, McDougall and Pim, unconscious of the ministering he received from Dr. Domville, the captain struggled to fend off wave after wave of nightmarish monsters and men. A rabid dog snarling in his face faded into the emaciated arms of his former shipmate reaching out to him, pleading for help.

Napoleon snarled at Belcher when he entered the cabin. 'Keep that mongrel away from me!' Belcher raised his cane to intimidate the dog. Naps snarled even louder and bared his teeth. Belcher cracked his cane across Naps' back; he yelped and retreated to a safe place out of the angry man's reach.

'I can't help you! I can't help you!' Kellett screamed, covering his face with shaking hands. 'No! God save us! No!' He struggled to turn away from the eyes that glared down at him.

The vision spoke, 'How long has he been like this?'

'A fortnight, Sir,' replied Dr. Domville. 'I fear for him if the fever does not break soon.'

'Bleed him. That's the only way to draw the fever out of him.' Dr. Domville did not respond.

'I am telling you, bleed him,' Belcher repeated impatiently, and abruptly left the cabin. 'Get out of my way, you bloody imbecile!' Belcher struck out at Brooke's shins with his cane when the two men nearly collided outside

18

Kellett's cabin. Brooke fell against the bulkhead wondering how he had managed to get into trouble simply by standing post. He fumbled a salute at the retreating figure, and then saluted again at the approaching Lieutenant Pim.

'How is our captain this morning, Brooke?'

'The doctor's worried, Sir. Commander Belcher brought his surgeon with him, and the two of 'em are in there now.'

'No improvement then?'

'Not as I can tell, sir. Nor the doctors neither. The captain seems to be more unsettled today, crying out like. Do you figure that could mean the fever's taking him, Sir?'

'I don't know, Brooke. I hope and pray not.'

Doctors Domville and Lyall could find no sign that the fever was ready to break, but both agreed that bleeding him would do harm rather than good. Domville called Brooke and Pim to their captain's bedside and gave them his directions for care; then, leaving the cabin with Lyall, he shook his head sadly. He hated losing a patient to fever, even though it was not the worst death the Navy had to offer.

'It seems a shame to lose a man so soon,' Domville muttered to Lyall.

'Give him time he may yet pull around.'

'Do you really believe that?'

'Perhaps yes. Perhaps no. Whatever I believe, we have done all we can and it is out of our hands.'

Twenty days and twenty nights, the fever raged. Almost a week after his nightmarish visions had made themselves manifest in the visit from Squadron Commander Belcher, the fever broke. Weakened and emaciated, Captain Kellett could not rise from his berth, but he was able to look around the cabin, recognition finally dawning in his eyes as he gazed on the grim faces of his cox'n, Brooke, and Lieutenant Pim. An almost imperceptible smile played at the corners of Kellett's mouth as Naps used his nose to nudge the weak hand that was resting above the covers. Pim's look of worry transformed itself into a broad grin and Brooke studiously worked to keep from laughing aloud with relief. Their captain had returned.

CHAPTER THREE
JUNE 1852

SHIP'S LOG: 6. Jun. 52 Dense fog
Anchored inner harbour
Lively, Disco Island
9 fathoms
Sandy bottom
Stern hawser ring on shore.

T he voyage was uneventful as the squadron made its way through Davis Strait into Baffin Bay. On a clear and bright morning the Resolutes, Assistances, Intrepids, Pioneers, and North Stars weighed anchor after their stop at the Whalefish Islands. They proceeded through Boat Island Passage toward Lively, a small Danish settlement on Disco Island, off the coast of Greenland. The five ships spread their canvas, *Resolute* quickly taking the lead.

The young mate, Richard Roche, smiled to see his ship, once again, out-sailing the others. This was his first expedition into the Arctic and it was all wonderfully new to him. He had delighted in the bustle their landing had caused when they had anchored at Whalefish Islands' Boat Harbour. Boats had been sent away surveying; *Resolute's* sheep had been sent on shore to graze; blacksmiths sent ashore to set up their fires so that necessary repairs could be made. 'In fact, a regular colony established,' he had written in his journal.

It had been great fun to see the Esquimaux continually round the ships in their kayaks, and to welcome their 'Aristocracy' on board to barter small articles. Roche had accompanied Master McDougall and several of the officers when they went out to explore the island. Even finding a small graveyard with the remains of an unlucky sailor buried in 1825 did not dampen their spirits. The whole ship seemed brighter now that Captain Kellett was well. The expedition no longer felt frightening to Roche, but rather like a grand adventure spreading out before him.

The approach to Lively went smoothly, until the ships neared the harbour, at which time the squadron quickly descended from five glorious ships in full sail into a seaside pantomime. The navigators could not distinguish the entrance to the harbour until five o'clock in the evening. The necessity of five ships tacking and wearing ship along the coast was destined to create trouble. *Pioneer* fouled an iceberg, her mizzenmast going by the board. In hauling off the berg by a whale line to shore, she blocked the entrance to the harbour. *Resolute* did not see this until she was almost upon her sister ship.

Resolute bore up from her stern, tacking three times, during which manoeuvres she did not prove remarkable for weatherly qualities. She finally anchored in twelve fathoms at the entrance to the outer harbour. In the mean time, *Assistance* had anchored, but she dragged anchor and had to make sail.

During the first watch *Assistance, North Star,* and *Intrepid* tried to work into the inner harbour, but they all failed. Both *Assistance* and *Intrepid* struck on a shoal in the centre channel and had to be hauled off. By midnight of the fifth of June, all hands were exhausted and no one could imagine that anything else could go wrong.

At 3:00 a.m., a dense fog rolled in and, during the morning watch, *North Star* struck on the outer point of the harbour. There she remained fast aground with a considerable list at low tide. She had to be hauled off. Finally, at the end of the first dogwatch, all the ships were anchored safely.

On board *Assistance* Belcher was furious, his anger lasting throughout the three-gun salute given to him by the governor. He knew they were all laughing at him. What a performance! What a show of incompetence! He would have to invite the governor to dinner. There could be no avenue for escape from that traditional courtesy. But, how would he ever sit through the meal knowing the faces around him all hid only mockery?

Belcher assembled his officers in his cabin. He paced back and forth, continuously clenching and unclenching his hands into fists behind his back, as if he was holding himself from striking out.

'That was a disgrace,' he shouted. 'Do you hear me? An absolute disgrace! How can you be so incompetent? I will not be made a laughing stock by the likes of you. I will not allow it. Use the starter or the whip if you can't get the men to work properly without them!'

'If you please, Sir,' Osborn began. But Belcher didn't give him the opportunity to finish.

'I do not please, Mr. Osborn.' He glared at the captain of the *Pioneer.* 'There is no excuse for the way these ships were handled coming into this harbour. I will not have that Kellett upstaging me! I am the leader of this expedition, and my ships will lead. If this ever happens again I will put the officers in charge under arrest, and the men will be flogged. For now, no grog, no shore leave, and no visitors. Dismissed!'

The officers left and Belcher gazed out of the stern window. How many more voyages would he have to be saddled with such incompetent officers and seamen? Christ! Some of the officers certainly knew how to present themselves to the Admiralty, conning positive reports from their superiors, oozing their way up the ranks. Belcher closely followed the careers of some of the men who had served under him in the past. Despite everything he had done to expose their unworthiness for higher rank, the Admiralty seemed to side with those that conspired to blacken his own reputation, rarely paying heed to his warnings about the defects in their characters and naval ability.

Was the Admiralty blind? Was he to be burdened his whole life with this lonely ability to see that wrong decisions were being made day after day, with the worst of the scum rising higher and higher in the Navy? He knew they did it to spite him. Even this commission bore evidence of their plotting. Here he was saddled with Kellett again. And to think he was being sent to rescue that damn Collinson! Oh, the two of them had been thick as thieves in China. He had warned the Admiralty about Collinson, repeatedly. Now, here the young usurper was captain of his own ship, sent off to find Franklin years before the Navy got around to commissioning Belcher. If this expedition was successful in discovering what had happened to Franklin they couldn't even use their position in the Arctic to continue looking for the North West passage. No! They had to go searching for Collinson and McClure! Always to Belcher the hard work, and to others the glory.

But he would show them, oh yes, Belcher mused as he ascended to the quarter deck. He would show the Navy he couldn't be pushed aside to make way for these younger upstarts. He would make this voyage the most notable to date. His expedition would...

'Damn it all to hell, man! What are you doing?' The men on deck flinched at the sound of their captain's anger, but carried on with their work as soon as they realised it wasn't one of them in the line of fire this time. Belcher was glaring at his second in command, George Henry Richards, the commander of his flagship, *Assistance.*

'Sneaking and skulking around me, are you? What do you want?'

Commander Richards saluted. 'I am sorry, Sir, for disturbing you, but is it your pleasure, Sir, that I call for your boat to be made ready to go ashore? The governor will be expecting your...'

'Do not presume to tell me what my duties are! Of course, I expect my boat readied immediately. Where is my damned cox'n? Fetch him to get the boat crew while I am below preparing myself to wait upon the governor. You are dismissed!'

⚓⚓⚓⚓⚓

Fair Abe started, realizing he had been staring at the same rows of accounting figures for almost a half hour. He looked around the office to see if anyone had noticed his inattention. Over his father's shoulder, he could see through the front window of the firm's office, and in the far distance, he glimpsed the masts of the ships in the harbour. Again, his thoughts wandered.

It was the first week in June. The smallest whisper of a sea breeze did nothing to move the dense air settling down among the buildings and streets, heavy between the sweating horses' flanks and the wagons they pulled, and between the men's stiff collars and their skin. The moist air clung to Abe's fingers as he sat fidgeting with his pen. It was unusual, this heat, so early in June. No one knew how long it would stay like this. This inert mass had been down pressing the New London citizens for almost a week, and the edges of even the calmest personalities were beginning to sharpen and fray. Could you call this heavy air apathetic? It seemed not to care whether it stayed or moved on. And yet there was tension. Fair Abe could not discern if the tension was within his own spirit, or if it was the weather, the steaming heavy air, contracting and pulling in on itself, preparing to leap into awesome rage and storm.

Fair Abe thought about the abolition meeting coming up in two days time. He doubted that he would be able to attend it, though several of the members of his Meeting for Worship were going to be there. Father won't go, Abe knew. He felt a sudden urge of shame, immediately followed by guilt. He glanced again toward Father only to find him looking at him.

'For a young man who is good with numbers, thou hast not accomplished much this morning.'

'I am sorry, Father. I cannot seem to concentrate. Dost thou feel a storm coming? Thinkest thou this heat will break?'

'I am certain, storm or no, the weather will change in its own time. I must go down to the docks. Our whaler, the *McClellan,* will be leaving tomorrow to go up into Baffin Bay to pick up the crew that wintered there. I want to check that the provisioning is going well. Wouldst thou come?'

Without answering, Fair Abe stood up and put his coat on, even though he could hardly stand the thought of adding another layer to his clothing. He placed his wide brimmed hat on his head and held the door open for his father. Having to wear hat and coat not withstanding, he was glad to have an excuse to get out of doors into the fresher air.

Fresh air? There was no freshness about it, but he hoped down by the water the slight sea breeze would make his breathing lighter. His father set a moderately slow pace and Fair Abe followed suit. He tried to remember what Father had said about the *McClellan.*

'Didn't she come home last autumn with about 300 barrels of whale oil?'

'Two hundred fifty eight, to be precise. And she also brought us a good haul of whalebone and sealskins. Buddington and twelve of the crew stayed up in the ice to trade with the natives and continue sealing, the first time any of our whaling men have wintered over without their ship and I have thought of them frequently through out the winter. We will know how they have fared when the *McClellan* returns. But first things first, let us see how far along she is in being made ready to sail.'

The docks were as busy as Fair Abe had ever seen them. Most of the whalers had left earlier in the spring for either the Arctic, or around Cape Horn to the Pacific. But the wharves were full of merchant ships. Some were loading and other unloading. Bales of southern cotton were stacked along one wharf waiting to be taken to the New Bedford cotton mills.

'Slave cotton,' Fair Abe muttered under his breath.

Father Abraham looked at his son and saw his scowling face. How his steady and even tempered first born had become such a firebrand for abolition he did not know. Their family, as well as all the members of their Meeting for Worship, were, of course, against slavery. What was beginning to tear the Meeting and families apart, however, was the method and means to be used in the struggle to end it.

⚓⚓⚓⚓⚓

Master George Frederick McDougall picked up his private journal.

> '6 June 52
> We are anchored in Lively Harbour, Disco Island. After an embarrassing entrance Captain Kellett decided the men deserved a repast, and has given permission for the local girls to visit *Resolute* tonight while he and the other officers dine with Belcher and the governor aboard *Assistance...*'

McDougall paused in his writing and went up on deck. He found mate Roche studying the shore and town.

'Now that the fog is gone you can really see how beautiful a spot this is, eh?'

'Oh, yes, Sir. I was just thinking what a very good little harbour this is, despite our difficulty in getting in. I must say I am proud of our ship being the only one to get in without accident.'

'It was not the ship, Roche, but you men that made that happen.'

Roche felt embarrassed by the compliment. Gazing out at the small town hugging the coast he said,

'I wonder what the locals are like. They must be a hardy breed.'

McDougall glanced at the town, with its chapel and two or three real houses amongst the dozen or so huts and nodded his agreement.

'We will discover tonight, Roche, just how hardy,' he replied smiling knowingly. Roche, unaware of his captain's largess, did not understand the Master's reference.

That afternoon a deep snow fell clearing the sky for a fine night. A cacophony of laughter and song got louder and louder as a boat, full of the local belles, approached the *Resolute*. Their enthusiasm for the night of revelry ahead was matched by the enthusiasm of the men on board who answered every line of the song the girls sang with a holler and a swig of rum. By the time the girls reached the ship the fiddler's bow had been amply supplied with rosin in the form of grog. Tuned up and warmed up, the fiddler got everyone dancing with a fast polka.

Roche and Nares both grabbed girls and twirled them along at a rapid pace. Everywhere the deck was awash with dancing feet and smiling faces, laughter, and rum. Napoleon ran and barked with excitement, weaving in and out around the dancing partners. The girls warmed by the dancing and the closeness of the sailors, and used to the cold arctic air, stripped down to their unmentionables. They were encouraged no doubt by the enthusiastic response the sailors gave to each rejected bit of clothing.

The sounds of revelry attracted the attention of the junior officers of the other ships, the lucky ones not suffering through Belcher's dinner. They came on board *Resolute* and joined in the dancing. The sailors' impromptu ball carried on for hours.

Young Roche and Nares, flushed with the effort of furious dancing, did not have the experience the others had, and did not know where the night's festivities were heading. In their innocence, they winked at each other and smiled, as if to say it can't get any better than this. However, the waltzes and polkas soon gave way to the dance the girls danced the best. Clara, Roche's dancing partner, grew tired of waiting for Roche to do more than dance. She took his hands from around her waist and placed them on her breasts.

Richard Roche blushed with embarrassment, but he did not take his hands away. Instead, he let the girl pull his face down to meet hers and let her kiss him full on the lips. Without a thought to what the other men were doing (as much as he and more), Richard pulled his jacket off and laid the girl down on it on the deck. Her experienced hands taught him what to do and guided him into her.

This was something he had never known. He was in love! In love with Clara. In love with the deck beneath her. In love with every Resolute timber, yardarm, sail and line. In love with the clear night sky and all the ice floes in the Arctic. In love with the contrast between the cold night air and the warmth of Clara's body and how it felt to be inside her. He was overcome with waves of love.

True, the feeling did not last, being somewhat dampened by her request for monies owed when the act was done. Even so, the young mate smiled for days afterward, wondering to himself why he had never tried such a delicious food before; wondering when the next opportunity would present itself, or rather herself, for another taste. Not any time soon, he correctly surmised. Not any time soon.

⚓⚓⚓⚓⚓

In County Tipperary the skies were low and the air heavy with mist on the day of the Fethard cattle market.

'Better than a dry day,' Mr. McCaffrey muttered to himself. As headman in charge of the Kellett stables he was rarely, if ever, challenged in what he said. About anything. Let alone the weather. He was therefore taken quite a bit by surprise when he heard a contradiction coming from outside the stable door.

'The cattle will raise no dust, but we'll have mud enough to contend with.' McCaffrey turned and saw Margaret standing in the stable courtyard, come to see if the carriage was ready.

'Yes, Ma'am.' McCaffrey smiled. Margaret was the only person he was happy with all the time, no matter what she said or did. He was in his fifty-seventh year of service to the Kellett family. Several generations of children had been born and reared during his time, but this one was his favourite.

'It was me, you know,' he liked to tell the lads from around, 'that held her up the first time she sat a horse. No more than two year old were she, squalling to break your heart until her mother and I set her there, up on Star Rose. And that stopped her good enough. Her baby hands twining in Star Rose's mane, she laughed and laughed. She didn't cry again until we took her down.'

Margaret had been a child after his own heart from that day on. Captain Kellett bought Margaret a pony named Bright, and McCaffrey made her a cart for the pony to pull. When she wasn't on Bright with himself holding her, she was in her cart being pulled by the pony around the stable yard or the front courtyard of the house. Horses were in her blood just as the sea was in her father's blood.

McCaffrey, having never married and with no children of his own, swelled with paternal pride every time anyone mentioned Margaret's name in conjunction with her equestrian skill. 'It was me what held her. It was me.'

McCaffrey drove the Kellett women to the market. By the time they and the Clonacody boys reached Fethard, most of the men from the neighbouring estates had already arrived and the cattle were being herded down Main Street. They converged along the north road into town, a broad river of hoof and horn squeezed between the canyon walls of the town's buildings. Soon, from one end of Fethard to the other, all that could be seen or heard were the cattle.

The bidding was brisk and there was some competition between Alice Kellett and O'Connor, but she won out in the end, and finished the day going home satisfied with the cattle she bought. Mr. McCaffrey and the other Clonacody boys herded the new cattle home, arriving at dusk.

The heavy mist of the morning had persisted all day and had indeed kept the dust down, but all and sundry in attendance at the market were fairly well covered in mud. Mrs. Kellett had tea and supper waiting for the men in their quarters so that, when they arrived and before they retired for the night, all they had to do was shed their caked clothing and boots, wash themselves at the back court yard pump, eat and fall into bed.

Alice could not sleep. The cattle market brought people from away. People from away brought news. News was an integral a part of market day, almost as important as the cattle and the bidding. News. News of Dublin and other cities, news of neighbouring counties, news of London and England, and sometimes even from her home in Durham.

But particularly since the Famine, news came from America. Most families had someone who had emigrated, even those in County Tipperary, which had been one of the least affected counties. Margaret's thoughts returned to that terrible time. Least affected. That was how it had been described by the official reports. Were the lives lost in Clonmel or the Cashel workhouses, or the Fethard Fever Hospital any less lost than those from the counties 'hardest hit'? Were the Tipperary emigrants any less far away?

Though Alice and the other landowners had not themselves gone hungry, the famine had left an indelible mark upon her. It had rocked her faith to its very core. Inheriting a very practical outlook on life from her mother, she grew up believing God will provide, but he does so through our human hands. If you set your hands to the task, then the task will be accomplished.

Rolling up her sleeves, figuratively and literally, she had joined forces with the Quakers. When Westminster had been slow to recognise the magnitude of the starvation stalking the land, the Quakers had set up soup kitchens and other relief works to ease the suffering of the local tenant farmers and migrant workers.

It was the eyes of the children that came back to haunt Alice at times like these when she could not sleep. Eyes dulled by hunger or bright with fever. Eyes that questioned the hunger pangs. Eyes glazed over with acceptance of something not understood. The eyes of the dead, open and staring, no longer windows to the souls, because those souls had departed.

Alice had worked and prayed as hard as she could, but it seemed that God had turned away. Though her hands never rested, God had not provided. No moment had seemed so desperate as the time when the Quakers had given up their relief work, acknowledging the need was beyond their resources.

The day Alice heard the Quakers were giving up she had collapsed in tears of exhaustion and rage. A hand had touched her shoulder offering a hot cup of tea. It had been one of the American Quakers who sat next to her, sipping her own tea, while Alice wept.

It was that American friend's face that was the last image Alice saw when she finally drifted off to sleep on the night of the cattle market.

⚓⚓⚓⚓⚓

For those who have never seen the Arctic it is difficult to imagine a world so harsh and brutal being simultaneously so stunningly beautiful. McDougall remembered the impact it had had on him the first time he saw it. Now on his second Arctic journey, as they left the Greenland coast to sail westward across Baffin Bay, the beauty still stunned him, so much so that the proverbial wag and storyteller's journal entry was imbued with a sense of the spiritual:

'12 Jun 52.

Probably in no part of the world does nature display more grandeur in her works than on the coast of Greenland. True, no towering pines crown the hill, nor are the valleys filled with verdure, but here, amidst desolation, grand in the extreme, nature may be truly said to reign triumphant.

Precipitous cliffs, themselves mountains, rise out of an unfathomable sea, and are surmounted by the snow of ages, never yet trodden by the foot of man. Deep chasms filled with accumulated snow, form the building-yards from whence are launched into the deep, those floating crystal towers, which are at once the fear and admiration of those who brave the dangers of the Arctic Ocean. The Psalmist could not have known these waters when he wrote the One Hundred and Seventh Psalm. Yet no truer words were even written than the words that say... those who go down to the sea in ships see the deeds of the Lord and His wondrous works in the deep.'

Fighting a full gale, intermittent freezing ice storms, and fog, the squadron made its way farther into the Arctic: through Waygate Channel, past Black Hook, Storoe Island, and Dark Head. McDougall sighted Sanderson's Hope through a thick fog on the 18th of June. By noon on the 22nd, the ships were abreast the headland of Cape Shackleton. Two days later, after she attempted to make headway in a dense fog, *Resolute* made fast to an ice floe in lat. 74°5'N, the same latitude she had reached the previous night.

Captain Kellett could see the crew becoming disheartened now that the realities of Arctic seamanship were hitting home. It was much too early in the voyage for a sense of futility to take hold of his men. He turned to Lieutenant Pim, who was standing next to him on the quarterdeck.

'Lieutenant, we must see to the men. Shore leave here won't be what it would be in a port town, but the men need a bit of fun.'

'What are you suggesting, Sir?'

'Games, Lieutenant. Games. For everyone on board, officers and men alike.'

'There is a place where the ice had melted and is now frozen, which would make a good playing field for a game of cricket, Sir. That is, if we could make equipment to suit a field of ice.'

'Get Mister McDougall to help you. Keep it quiet until you have something ready to use. I want it to be a surprise for the men.'

McDougall and Pim went below to search amongst the ship's supplies for the necessary kit. Two of the broken gig oars saved for the galley stove would do for the bats.

'How are we going to make a ball that won't roll to Kingdom Come over the ice?' Pim muttered.

'That'll be a challenge,' McDougall responded, 'at least we have plenty of bits and pieces for making the wickets and bails. What I do not understand is how the devil are we to set up the wickets in solid ice without the crew noticing? We will have to think of some excuse for cutting holes in the ice if the Captain wants to keep this a surprise.'

'Maybe Captain'll tell the crew about the games before we get that far. You know, we could make the ball softer somehow, and then it won't travel quite so far. Any ideas what we can use to make it?'

An hour later, Pim and McDougall stood before their captain in his cabin with bats, wickets, and bails. With considerable pride, they unveiled their pièce de résistance: the balls they had made for cricket, as well as football, constructed of cordage sewn round with bits of canvas.

Kellett burst out with a hearty laugh. McDougall and Pim looked at each other and then joined in their captain's laughter.

'If the equipment is anything to judge by, these games should be something to see.' Turning red with the effort to suppress his laughter Kellett continued, 'Thank you for your efforts. I will have Lieutenant Mecham assemble the men on deck.'

With their ship made fast, the men joyfully spread out over the ice floe. Brooke, Nares, and Roche started a game of leapfrog, and some of the younger ABs joined them. Naps jumped and ran around the men, giving each face a lick of affection as the men crouched for their leaping friends. The sound of their laughter carried across the frozen landscape, causing Captain Kellett to smile as he watched their antics from *Resolute's* quarterdeck.

In a short while, the chaotic play of the men began to transform itself into recognisable games of cricket and football. McDougall took charge of creating the cricket pitch. He delegated the work of setting up the wickets to Ice Quarter Master 'Stoneman' Wilkie, and sent Roche and a crew of men off to mark the boundaries of the playing field.

Captain Kellett organised the cricket teams choosing Pim and McDougall to head up the two teams. Pim won the coin toss for the first option and chose to bowl. He picked 'Stoneman' Wilkie, one of the strongest men from the crew as his first bowler and sent the rest of his team into the field. McDougall chose young Nares for his first batsman and his team mates left the field. Nares stepped in front of the wicket to bat while 'Stoneman' walked to the opposite wicket.

The fielders looked at each other when they saw who the first batsman was to be. Knowing the strength in his arms, they all simultaneously backed away from the original positions that they had taken.

'Stoneman' bowled his first ball. Getting the feel for this homemade ball was not easy and he pitched wide, giving the McDougalls their first run.

'Never you mind,' he said to himself. 'We will soon see bails flying.'

Nares tapped his bat in the crease chopped in the ice and shifted his weight several times, waiting for the next ball. Here it comes, he thought, in the split second before he hit it with all of his strength. Unlike the resounding thwack usually heard when Nares batted as he just did, all that the cricketers heard from this ice cricket ball was a dull thud. The speeding ball the fielders expected to see hurtling to the farthest reaches of the pitch and beyond was instead a rather reluctant traveller and ended its flight not far from the batsman.

No one was there to catch it. Nares and Wilkie began to run to the opposite wickets. Two gunners' mates were the closest fielders, and they set out for the ball at the same time. Getting their footing on the ice to start running was not nearly as challenging as being able to stop and they slid into each other as they neared their destination. One gunner's left foot collided with the ball. The ball, once reluctant to move, now seemed quite happy to skid across the ice, coming to rest in the middle of the pitch. It stopped at the very spot where the gunner had been standing before he left at a run to end in a heap. Napoleon, having been as unsuccessful at reaching the ball as the cricket players, now pounced on it and carried it away victoriously.

The foreyard men cheered their batters as they slid from one wicket to the other. Pim swore at his men.

'Get in there and get that dog, you buggers! For the love of God, get on your feet!'

However, no amount of cursing or encouragement could keep the ice from being ice. The harder the men worked at the game the more ridiculous it became until it was no longer the ice that made it impossible for them to catch the balls Nares hit, but rather their being doubled over with laughter.

Kellett stood on the quarterdeck with his hands clasped behind him. The bellows, the swearing, the laughter of his men cut through the frozen air and echoed off the towering pressure ridges that surrounded the floe. The rigging of the ship cast long black shadows across the blue-white ice where the men played their games. The long and dark arctic winter would come soon enough, he thought. The frostbite. The ice storms. Possibly hunger and death. The sun would rise again and the spring would follow, bringing with it the laborious sledging. Today the men would have this respite, and for this moment of joy, he thanked his God.

And McDougall and Pim.

CHAPTER FOUR
JUNE 1852 CONTINUED

Two days after the arctic cricket game, HM Discovery Ship *Resolute* made fast to another floe at half five in the evening, the wind being light from the SW. Miles of open sea lay before them. During the last dogwatch, Henry Bryant tuned up his fiddle and began to play. Some of the men danced while others watched or sang. Sail maker Robert Haile made use of the night sun and began repairs on one of the sails that had ripped in a sudden storm several weeks earlier.

Below deck in his cabin, McDougall wrote a letter to his friend Sherard Osborn, commander of *Pioneer*, the steam tender for Belcher's ship HMS *Assistance*. As long as the five ships of the expedition continued travelling together, it would be easy to get a letter to *Pioneer*.

McDougall and Osborn had become good friends on board *Resolute* during the 1850 expedition. Together they had edited The *Illustrated Arctic News* creating satirical reviews of the latest arctic fashions and theatrical performances. McDougall had some ideas for one of the plays he wanted to write for the upcoming winter season of the Arctic Theatre Royale, and Osborn was a good critic.

McDougall lost track of the time once he began writing to Sherard. What he thought might be a short note became a rather long epistle. In writing out the plot of his new play, he had been reminded of the humorous review Sherard had written about their last theatrical efforts. This had brought to mind the evenings they had spent preparing for the opening of the Arctic Theatre Royale's 1850 first season. In his letter, Frederick McDougall recalled the excitement of their opening night and asked Osborn if he planned to organise a similar event this winter.

These thoughts brought him around to thinking of their very different superior officers. He was struggling to find a way to ask Osborn if serving under Belcher was as difficult as he had heard it could be, when hurried footsteps rapidly approached his cabin.

He opened the door to find Brooke preparing to knock, the captain's cox'n breathless from his efforts to reach McDougall quickly.

'What is it?'

'Sir! Captain Kellett presents his compliments and asks if you can attend him on the quarterdeck. The ice is closing!'

Frederick McDougall grabbed his heavy jacket, putting it on as he ran after Brooke. When he reached the deck, Lieutenants Mecham and Pim were already there watching with concern as the open water to the port side of the ship rapidly disappeared. A large, wind-driven floe was approaching the ship from the aft quarter.

'Mister McDougall, is there enough open water for *Intrepid* to tow *Resolute* away from the edge of this floe?'

'At the rate the ice is closing I would say no, Captain,' McDougall replied, a sick feeling twisting itself about in the pit of his stomach.

'Lieutenant Mecham, have the ice quartermasters prepare equipment and teams of men for cutting a dock. Have the bo's'n pipe all hands and have the fo'c's'le watch captains and the lead stoker report to me. Lieutenant Pim, go to Commander McClintock on board *Intrepid*. Give him my orders to get out if he can, but tell him to send us any men he can spare. We will need all the men we can get to prepare *Resolute* for the coming nip as well as for cutting a dock in the ice.'

Mecham went below, bringing Thomas, Nisbett, and Miles with him to the quarterdeck where Kellett was pacing. Naps paced with him and occasionally looked up worriedly at his master's face.

'I need not tell you the urgency of our situation. We cannot avoid being caught in this nip. Thomas and Nisbett, you are to take the fo'c's'le watchmen and remove as much of the stores from the ship as quickly as possible. Get as much weight off her as you can. Miles take your stokers and shift whatever you can to starboard. We may be able to minimise how much damage we sustain by lightening the weight of our port side. If you need more men, take the marines. Go!'

Lieutenant Pim returned from *Intrepid*. Captain Kellett's face was calm, but his eyes betrayed some of the concern Pim knew he felt. Naps, feeling Kellett's anxiety, continued pacing and apprehensively looking from face to face. Kellett turned to Master McDougall.

'How much time do you think we have before the floe reaches us?'

'We may have an hour. Maybe more. Maybe less. The ice is closing rather quickly. It is difficult to judge how much force it will have once it reaches us, though, because that cannot always be measured by the speed the floe is travelling.'

'Lieutenant Pim, did Commander McClintock think he would be able to get up enough steam to get out in time?'

'Yes, Sir. He should be able to make the open water beyond it before the passage closes completely. I see the men McClintock is sending us making for our ship now, Sir.'

The floe reached *Resolute* at 11:00 p.m. The ice had shifted direction as it neared the floe to which *Resolute* was made fast and was now approaching from farther astern, fine on the quarter. The pressure created by the two floes meeting caused *Resolute* to begin listing to starboard and her stern to begin rising. There was not enough time for the men to finish un-shipping the rudder. Mecham called them away from the danger. There was nothing the men could do. Most of the Resolutes watched, helplessly, as their ship succumbed to the crushing ice.

'She has been nipped before and we came out all right,' McDougall reassured Pim. The two men were still on board, standing just outside the master's cabin.

'I know that she is built to sustain this sort of thing, but I'd rather not be subjecting her to such a test.'

'At least the other ships have a good chance of not being caught. The men are already preparing to cut a dock.'

'Listen!'

The ship's timbers were groaning with the strain as her port side and stern continued to rise. McDougall and Pim sat in the master's cabin and braced themselves against the bulkhead to keep from falling to the floor as *Resolute* tilted to starboard. They could hear the sound of wood splintering. The sound echoed through the bilge and the lower deck magnified a hundredfold by the anxiety both men felt for their ship, and for their personal safety.

The ice floe ground its way forward and *Resolute* began to shudder. All of her timbers quivered as if the ship was in her final death throes. Suddenly, a sound, unexpected and eerie, startled the ship's company.

As the vibration increased, the ship's bells started ringing. First, it was a small sound, like a funeral bell in a distant church tower. The ice pressed. *Resolute* groaned. The ship shuddered and heaved.

Troubled by the sound of this battle between ice and ship, and the frantic barking of a dog, an arctic tern rose from a nearby cliff. She swooped down toward the source of the disturbing sound, not knowing what manner of beast was disrupting her peace. The bird could not know that the dark form she swirled around represented the finest and latest developments in Arctic exploration. She could not know that within this hulk a whole human society tenuously clung to life, their grasp determined by the barque's ability to withstand the immense forces pressing down upon it.

The tern rose on the same wind that was driving the ice floe into the side of *Resolute*. The wind carried her aloft and she circled around and around. As she rose, the world of struggling life below receded, growing smaller and smaller, until it became a small bit of stick in a vast sea of ice.

The battle raged on. With a resounding rend, *Resolute*'s rudder carried away, smashed and splintered. Her false keel ripped timber by timber. Over this cacophonous din, the bells rang louder and louder. *Resolute* rose and rose. Now, the bells no longer tolled her death knell, but rang out deep and full, like the bells of Norwich: 'I will not be crushed. All will be well again. I shall not be defeated.'

Resolute rose up as the ice pressed in on her. Now her wide flat bottom, which made for her remarkably unimpressive sailing abilities, served her well. She came to rest, listing thirty-five degrees to starboard, with her stern seven feet higher than her bow. However, there was little time to assess the damage. It was midnight and the bo's'n piped all hands ashore, calling the men out onto the ice for the cutting of the dock.

⚓⚓⚓⚓⚓

With young William doing so well in his first month of life, Martha felt comfortable in writing to her friends about the newest addition to the Abraham family. She used this opportunity to invite her friend, Alice Kellett, to come across to America. She had not seen Alice since the Famine work, though they had kept their correspondence regular over the intervening years. She wondered how the Kellett's high-spirited daughter was doing in her transition to womanhood. She smiled to herself, thinking of the red headed girl galloping across the Clonacody fields.

New London was finally having a respite from the heavy early heat that had descended upon it. With the height of the summer yet ahead, Mrs. Abraham decided to take advantage of the mild air and take William for a walk. She would drop her post at the Perkins, Smith, and Abraham office and be able to spend a few mid day moments with her husband and Fair Abe.

Upon her arrival at the offices, she found the two Fairfax's working quietly side by side. Martha breathed a small sigh of relief. This month had not been easy in the Abraham family. Fair Abe had, against his father's wishes, attended the abolition meeting. The aftermath of the meeting had been similar in several of the Quaker family homes, as well as at the Meeting itself: inflamed and painful dissent.

Father Abraham was in the forefront of the Meeting's Committee on Abolition. This committee laboured with the nearest slaveholders about the manumission of their slaves. To Abraham, the resolution of the slavery issue was subservient to his commitment to the Quaker peace testimony. Above all, it had to be accomplished in a way that did not bring the country to war.

The abolition meeting had aroused the passions of Fair Abe, his fellow Quakers and others, who felt strongly that the sin of slavery needed to be swept away quickly, and cleanly, from the fabric of their land. He and his father clashed regularly in the days immediately after the meeting, their words imbued with anger. Martha did her best to intervene by proposing a period of Quaker silence when the atmosphere in the house became too over powering. This issue of abolition seemed immune to the Quaker principle: tolerance of difference!

In his exasperation, Father had said he would send Fair Abe out with the whaler *McClellan*. His stated reason was that he wanted Fair Abe to understand every aspect of the whaling business, and the trip would be an important part of his son's education. What he really hoped was that the threat of being sent to sea would frighten Fair Abe into quieting down. But he was ambushed by his son's immediate acceptance of the idea. Now Father Abraham could not back out without losing face.

The quiet in the offices was full of tension, but Alice welcomed it anyway. Both father and son looked up from their work at the same time and broke into smiles upon seeing Mother and William.

'Thy walk has done both of thee good!' Father Abe said, noticing the roses in both his wife and son's cheeks, and a brightness that the former heat had robbed from their faces in the last couple of weeks.

'Thy work seems to be doing the same for both of thee,' Martha replied. Father and son actually looked at each other and nodded without frowning.

'Would either of thee care to walk with William and me?'

'May I, Father?'

'I think I can spare thee for a while.'

Fair Abe closed his ink well, put on his coat and his wide brimmed hat, and held the door open for his mother. They walked silently down the tree-lined streets, happy in each other's company.

'I was hoping Father would give me the afternoon off so that I could purchase my sea trunk and kit. I have been to the dockside and some of the old hands have given me advice as to what I should take. But, Father hasn't said anything about it and I am afraid to bring it up.'

'The ship leaves tomorrow, is there no way thou canst settle thyself with thy father, make peace, and stay home?'

'Mother, I am as happy to go as Father is to send me. I will admit to having accepted Father's proposal in the first instance to spite him. But, in the past week, I have begun to realise I need the time to understand my heart and mind. I feel such turmoil inside, and have done so ever since giving God's message in Meeting. I feel such shame in my inability to keep my temper at moments when I argue with Father, and my inability to be a better Quaker within our family. And yet, I believe that by giving testimony to how I feel about slavery I am being the best Quaker I can be, even within our family. And Father is right about learning the whaling business. It would be a good experience for me. I know he never went whaling, but he certainly grew up fishing with Grandfather on the Chesapeake. He knew his business from the most practical level and it has served him well.'

'I fear losing thee. The Arctic is not so kind a place as the Bay was to thy father.' Martha paused and looked at her son. 'I had planned to tell thee that I need thee here. I was afraid of thy going away in anger. But now I must think on what thou hast said. Hast thou spoken of this with thy father?'

'I haven't been able to bring myself to admit I have any reason for going other than defiance,' Fair Abe replied with a shy smile.

'Thou art as stubborn as thy father!' Martha said, and put her hand affectionately through the arm of her tall son as they turned to walk back to the offices. 'And I don't think thou need worry about thy sea trunk,' she added with a don't-ask-me-any-questions look in her smile.

That evening Fair Abe knocked on the closed door of his father's library. Dinner had long since passed, the children were all abed and Martha was sitting in the drawing room reading by the fire.

'Come in. Ah, I thought, or rather hoped thou wouldst come to speak with me tonight.'

Fair Abe walked into the room and saw, immediately next to the fire an open sea chest with clothing folded in it.

'Oh, Father!'

'I cannot send thee up to the Arctic without making as certain as I can that thou wilt return home safely. Decent clothing is necessary. And Mother insisted on much more!'

They both smiled. Once again, Mother had found a way to bridge the gap between father and son.

'I have longed to talk with thee, but every time I try we get so angry.'

'I know, son. I would like us to sit in silence for a few minutes. Just the two of us. Wouldst thou be comfortable in doing this?'

'Yes Father.'

'I would like us to pray on our love and not our differences.' The two men bowed their heads. The antagonistic silence that had simmered between them for weeks melted slowly into one of peaceful love. Neither changed what they believed. The silence was not a magic wand that could take away their differences. But they both felt the focus gradually shift from that which separated them to that which bound them: the deep and abiding bond of father and son love.

⚓⚓⚓⚓⚓

The men of all the ships worked together to cut the dock in the ice. Before the whistle of the bo's'n's call had faded in the crisp air, *Resolute's* carpenters had begun measuring what would become the dock, chopping the outlines of it with axes. The boundary they marked encompassed a huge area, making a large enough space to accommodate all the ships. Two of the carpenters started at opposite ends of the eastern edge, working their way toward each other, while a second team did the same on the western edge. A third team of carpenters from HMS *Assistance* worked on the south edge, the edge farthest from the open side of the shore ice and closest to the cliff that indicated where land began.

The men were racing each other to see which team would finish marking their side first. The men preparing the explosives and the men who would be cutting the ice cheered them on, and Naps thought it was great fun as he ran from team to team barking and chasing the men. Captain Kellett came up on the quarterdeck to see what all the shouting was about and laughed to see the men making their fun from such hard work. The second team was far ahead of the other teams. Kellett glanced toward the other ships and could see

36

McClintock standing on the deck of *Intrepid* watching the men. Belcher was pacing on the *Assistance* and Kellett was surprised to see the commander so agitated. Could he possibly be that upset over a harmless bit of competition between the men?

Resolute's company was divided into three sawing crews of thirteen men each. Her ice quarter masters each led a sawing team. Their first job was getting the saws and tripods assembled. The saws were between fourteen and sixteen feet long. The men had to construct a pyramid for each saw, which would hold it in a vertical position. To do this a bolt was rove through the heads of three spars, the spars forming the pyramid's legs and the bolt forming its apex. The bolt supported a shackle, a gin block hooked to the shackle. A whip then ran through the gin block: one end attached to the saw and the other end pulled by the sawyers. The crew made and placed three pyramids, one on each of the dock's three edges, after the ice quarter masters finished marking them.

Now 'Stoneman' Wilkie, one of the strongest of *Resolute's* stokers and the best shantyman on board, stood in the middle of the soon-to-be-dock and bellowed in his resonant bass voice the shanty that would keep the men pulling in time. He called each line and the men answered, pulling down on the whips on the first beat of each call and answer, the singing making light work of their labour.'

'BONey was a Warrior'
'AWAY-ay-ya'
'A WARrior, a terrier'
'JON Francois'
'BONey fought the Pruss-i-ans'
'A-WAY-ay-ya'
'And BONey fought the Russ-i-ans'
'JON Francois...'

Each leg of each sawing tripod had a man dedicated to the delicate task of shifting it. It was essential to keep each leg in its proper place in relation to the other legs of the triangle, a detail Nares did not quite understand as his team began to move along the eastern edge of what would become the dock. He lagged just slightly behind the men who were handling the other two legs of his saw's tripod.

'Bloody hell!' one of the sawyers exclaimed as the saw jammed. Worse still, the saw buckled and snapped in two, leaving the lower half to protrude dangerously from the ice and the upper half to swing madly. The men ducked quickly as the broken bit swung at their heads. They let out a collective groan, several of them glaring pointedly at Nares.

Nares muttered an apology, which his team mates accepted with very little grace. A new saw would have to be fitted and the broken half, which was still in the ice, extracted. The men fitted a new saw, but gave Nares the laborious task of extracting the old blade from the ice. They used this opportunity to take a brief rest and to enjoy the satisfying occupation of watching Nares struggle. One of the men decided he had sufficiently paid for his inattention and got up to help him. Soon Nares' team was sawing again in time to the shanty singing, none of the men holding any ill feelings towards George even though they had now lost the undeclared race between the three teams.

While the sawyers worked their ropes, slowly but steadily making their way round the outside of the dock, the men composing the blasting party began boring holes in the centre. After making each cut, the men placed a small charge below the ice. When the sawyers finished their work, the blasting party would set off the charges by the use of Bickford fuses.

The men's voices rang out in a noisy, sometimes not quite musical, but heartfelt chorus as 'Stoneman' began singing a new shanty. Borrowed from the whale men, this shanty spoke directly to their condition as they faced the coming months in the harsh and demanding Arctic cold.

'Through many a blow of frost and snow
And bitter squalls of hail
Our spars were bent and our canvas rent
As we brave the northern gale...'

With a longing not one of them would admit having the men's thoughts turned toward the future and their own homeward journey...

'The horrid isles of icy tiles
That dot the Arctic Sea
Are many, many leagues astern
On the way to old Maui...'

Perhaps it was the thought of tropical warmth, or the girls in Maui they were singing about, but the last few yards of sawing seemed to go the fastest and the men began dismantling their tripods. Nares grabbed Napoleon by the scruff of his neck as the dog began sniffing around the Bickford fuses. 'Stay here with me, laddie, if you don't want to be blown to Kingdom Come!' Naps gave out a yelp when the blasting party set off the Bickfords fuses, and sniffed with suspicion as the ice cracked in all directions, from the centre of the dock to the now completed edges. The experienced Arctics knew the best part of their task lay ahead.

'Stoneman' Wilkie relinquished his role as shantyman and joined the rest of the men in the rush to get the best tools, boarding pikes, and handspikes, for levering the ice pieces out of the water. What a bustle commenced! The men began prying the chunks of ice up onto the floe. Not all the ice was willing to succumb to this prodding, so the men made recourse to dislodging it by jumping on it.

Mate Richard Roche was the first to jump. The ice block he was working on was quite large, but the force of his landing on it broke it loose and the maintop men, who were working along side him, helped to pry it out of the water. The men now began a competition to see who could balance the longest on the smallest bit of ice. The captain's hound joined in the fun and as soon as Roche jumped onto the next stubborn block he leapt for it as well. Then Nares leapt onto one just a bit smaller. Roche proceeded to see how close he could get to the edge of his bit of ice before tipping Naps and himself into the freezing water. He managed to get right up to its very edge before it began to capsize. He jumped nimbly to the solid edge of the ice floe, Naps on his heels. Nares, not to be outdone and cheered on by the other men, tried to do the same, but because he was heavier than Roche and the ice he was standing on much smaller, he was not quite so lucky and he ended in the water.

The men roared with laughter and began laying bets on the smallest bits and closest edges of ice that the men could stand on before being tipped into the ice-cold water. Many of the sailors could not swim and their predicament when they landed in the water was cause for even more mirth among the men, and served to keep the game alive.

When at last the entire dock was cleared of all the loose ice blocks, the men clambered back onto *Resolute* where Captain Kellett had ordered the ship's cook, Joseph Bacon, to lay a roaring hot fire in the galley stove. Napoleon immediately curled up beside the stove and fell fast asleep, occasionally running in his sleep as though he were still chasing the men. The sailors gathered around the radiant heat and the unfortunate ones who had fallen into the water stripped off their wet clothes. Captain Kellett sent Brooke to the galley with enough of the captain's private stock of whiskey for each man to have a tot to help warm him from the inside out.

Once the men were rested and clothed in dry gear Kellett sent them out to haul the ships into the newly finished dock. The men had to tow the ships into the dock stern first. Thus, the reinforced bows of the ships would withstand the worst of the pressure from travelling ice floes should they enter the outer edge of the dock.

HMS *Assistance* was the first ship to be towed into the dock. A team of men assembled along the eastern edge of the dock and took the warp from the port side of the ship. Another crew operated a skiff, hauling the starboard warping line. Now 'Stoneman' Wilkie resumed his role as shantyman and the men in the skiff rowed in time to his sonorous bass voice.

'Way, haul away. Don't you see that black cloud a-rising?
Way, haul away. We'll haul away, Joe.
Way, haul away. We'll pull for better weather, Tomme.
Way, haul away. We'll haul away, Joe.
King Louis wuz the King of France before the Revolu-ti-on
Way, haul away. We'll haul away, Joe.
But then they cut his big head off and spoiled his constitu-ti-on
Way, haul away. We'll haul away, Joe.'

Steadily, though slowly, *Assistance* entered the dock and made her way to the southern edge. The men secured her with hawsers and then repeated the whole process with *North Star.* The two tenders, *Pioneer* and *Intrepid,* did not need the men to tow them in and they made their way in under steam. Now only *Resolute* was unsheltered, unable to move, nipped and battered. The enemy floe, which had done so much damage to her, might actually serve as a protective shield if it stayed where it was. At least for the moment the ice seemed settled. The men could finally rest.

⚓⚓⚓⚓⚓

Alice Fletcher Kellett's strength was in her quietness. She had begun her life at Clonacody so softly, almost shyly, that her presence, both in the house and in the village, had been barely felt. It was in this unobtrusive way that she had woven her presence into her home and her new community. Being from away, she had not believed, and still did not believe, in the long preserved division between the Irish and the Anglos. She never argued about it with her neighbours. She did not even speak of it. Just in her heart, the division was not there.

After Margaret was born, and Clonacody had truly become her home, Alice had widened the circle of her daily life. The next time Henry came home, she had been more willing to go to the neighbours' dinner parties. And, before he had gone to sea again, she had hosted her first dinner at Clonacody. It had been a great success, with neighbours commenting positively on the changes she had made in the home.

She had then become involved in the life of the village. From her first days, she tended the families that farmed on the Kellett estate when they were ill or their babies were born. Gradually other Irish families had begun to call on her and she had responded. Word spread about her: she treated the Irish with the same respect and kindness as she did the Anglos. While she had been in attendance on them, the women began to trust her with small secrets. They felt that it was safe to entrust to her keeping the pains and joys too intimate to share with anyone else.

Alice Kellett had also silently woven herself into the fabric of the Anglo community. By the time the Famine hit, she had become the thread that was essential to the tapestry of their town and its surroundings. She was the first person the Quakers had been directed to when they came to offer relief. And the first American Quaker she had met was Martha Abraham from New London, Connecticut.

Now, in the summer of 1852, she received Martha's letter with joy. It would not be easy to leave Clonacody for several months. She would have to persuade Margaret to leave the horses in the hands of the men, the local midwife would have to rely on others for assistance, and she would have to make arrangements with the vicar for others to take up the work she did. In a crazy rush, the lists of things that would need to be delegated and organised almost overwhelmed her and made her want to say she could not go. Yet, she wanted to see Martha and meet her family, see America, and to have the chance to broaden Margaret's horizons. It would be difficult to extract her self from this world she loved, but it could and would be done.

Margaret Kellett was strong-willed, and she occasionally mistook her mother's quietness for a lack of strength. It was, perhaps, wishful thinking because deep inside herself she knew her mother was a redoubtable woman. In time of trouble she might bend, but never break. In good times, she was steadfast.

The two women were so similar physically, with Alice looking younger than her years and Margaret looking older, that they were frequently mistaken for sisters, sometimes twins, by strangers. This likeness was not simply skin deep. While she was growing up Margaret admired her mother, and when she was eight or nine, she had begun consciously trying to be as much like her as she possibly could. It was easy. She had inherited a very similar underlying character from her mother. But there was an edge to the girl's personality that made her fiercer, more quick-tempered. Mother and daughter had barely noticed this edge while she was growing up. And, while Margaret was still young, she was able to control the expression of this edginess when it flared up. This began to change as she matured: she suffered fools less gladly and her temper flared more quickly in the most recent years. Additionally, the similarities between them no longer gave Margaret comfort, rather they seemed to irritate her nerves, making her more likely to give vent to her temper than not.

Alice was not expecting the outburst that followed her announcement of the trip to America. Margaret had always been interested in new adventures and had her mother's love of learning. Going to America would be a great opportunity for both. Alice had been so certain Margaret would respond enthusiastically that she was completely taken aback by the force with which her daughter reacted.

'Did you stop to think of asking me if I wanted to go? You have made your decision with out even considering my feelings! We would be away for months. How would father know where we were? And what about the horses? Neither they nor I can go for months without training. And I wanted to ride in the hunts this summer. This would ruin all my plans!'

'I never thought for one moment that you would object to going. You have always wanted to travel and learn about new places. This is the perfect opportunity for us. For you. You don't have to worry about the horses; the boys will take care of them. They will ride and continue to train them while we are away. Don't turn away, Margaret, it is not polite. We can disagree with out being rude to each other...'

'Oh, Mother, how can you not understand?' Margaret was almost shouting, her voice trembling.

'You are correct, I do not understand. You must explain, but I will not tolerate disrespect and being interrupted. There is no reason for you to be...'

With a groan, Margaret interrupted her mother again. 'I can't explain if you don't try to understand!'

'Then I suggest you think on it, and we will talk again when you have the words for what you are feeling, and when you can give voice to those words with a great deal more self control!' Mother and daughter parted with out speaking further.

⚓⚓⚓⚓⚓

Resolute had endured her nip remarkably well and she was still structurally sound, but her survival came at the cost of her rudder and false keel. The carpenter's mates had replaced the rudder, but *Resolute* would spend the rest of her voyage without the protection of her false keel. Even though this loss left her more vulnerable to the possibility of the ice crushing her, the helmsman found that *Resolute* answered the better for it and she was the first ship to reach Melville Bay.

McDougall returned to his journal, when, at midnight on the 24th of July, the dense fog lifted unveiling a stunning view of Melville Bay.

'24. Jul. 52

A more beautiful or impressive sight could not well be imagined; not a breath disturbed the serenity of the glass-like surface of the sea, whilst the arctic midnight sun shone with unusual brightness, and even warmth, from a perfectly cloudless sky of the most intense blue, giving promise of a glorious day. The scene around was at once grand and desolate. To the eastward, the ice was bounded by the precipitous snow-clad peaks of Cape Walker, and other remarkable headlands tinged with gold and purple... The intense reflection of light from the ice prevented our distinguishing the sea horizon from the sky, except by distant bergs, which the mirage occasioned to take the most fanciful and ever changing appearances. Churches, towers, ships, etc., were formed for a moment, and as rapidly passed away, to give place to other equally strange and fantastic varieties of light and shade resembling the ruined remains of some mighty city.'

CHAPTER FIVE
JULY and AUGUST 1852

The morning after arriving in Melville Bay, the squadron had to cut docks again because the ice began closing. This time they were ahead of the ice and none of the ships suffered a nip. The ships were unable to leave the safety of the docks for several weeks, however, the ice pack thickening around them and closing off any stretch of open water as quickly as it appeared. Fog lay thick around the ships and the world contracted, collapsing around the men. And it was still summer.

The ice finally opened long enough for the ships to sail farther up the Bay. They hoped to have days, not hours, of sailing, but by the end of the first day sailing, the ice was closing in again. They anchored with a large whaling fleet of thirty-four ships. Thirteen ships flew British colours and eleven flew the Stars and Stripes. The Belcher Expedition docked immediately upon arrival. Again, the men made a sport of cutting the new dock, racing each other to see which ship could complete in the shortest time. *Resolute* completed her docking the quickest, finishing before the other ships by thirty minutes.

As the explorers disembarked, the whaling men met them with flags flying. Behind the flag bearers was a welcoming band, a poor excuse scraped together, consisting of men from each of the whaling ships. Those men who had real instruments played them with more enthusiasm than skill, any sour notes being amply drowned out by the percussion section, which seemed to consist of every pot and pan from every one of the thirty-four ships' galleys. To honour the Resolutes for their skill in docking, the whalers rewarded them with a welcome further warmed by an offer of rum, an offer no Resolute hesitated in accepting. When all the ships of the expedition were safely docked the whaling men (five hundred souls strong) surprised the Resolutes, Assistances, Pioneers, Intrepids and North Stars with a chorus of God Save the Queen and three hearty cheers.

On his first night in the Bay, Captain Kellett hosted a dinner for the captains of the whaling ships in *Resolute's* wardroom. It was thus he learned that the whalers had been in Melville Bay for a fortnight fighting the pack ice; the whaling men said it was more tightly packed than any of them had ever experienced this early in the season. It was the worst, the oldest among them said, in forty-seven years. The Belcher ships had come in on the only day in two weeks time when there was enough open water for passage.

The ice continued closing in during the night. The following morning all of the whaling ships were able to get into the safety of cut docks. All but one. The whaler, *McClellan*, out of New London, Connecticut, was the unfortunate. Everyone worked to salvage as much of her as could be saved. One of her crew had tears in his eyes when the ice broke her back. But the other, more experienced whalers stood motionless, sucking on their pipes as though they were wizened philosophers, watching her being swallowed by the ice. All should be philosophers who venture into this pitiless world, McDougall wrote that night.

One whaler, which was on its return trip, added many of the McClellans to its crew, promising to drop them in New London when the ice let them go. They also took letters from the Belcher expedition and the other whalers. No matter how long it would take them to get back, they would be the first to get the letters posted to the loved ones on both sides of the Atlantic.

⚓⚓⚓⚓⚓

Fair Abe had not been able to keep the tears from running down his face as the ice crushed his ship, the *McClellan*. He could not believe how his home away from home could be so complete one moment, and so completely gone the next.

The voyage had been a good one. Rather than having him join one watch, and learning just a few tasks, his captain had moved him from watch to watch so he could be taught as much as possible about the running of the whaler. He had even spent two days working along side the cook.

The men had been wary of him at first. None wanted to be bothered with the owner's son. A rich boy dabbling in men's work, that's how they saw him. But he was honestly eager to learn and showed a great respect for the men and their knowledge. When it became obvious he would put on no airs of superiority, the whole crew took Fair Abe under its protective wing. He worked as hard and as long as the rest of them, and he claimed no privileges. The men thumped him on his back when he did a job well, and just before the ship was caught in the ice the first mate had told him he would be 'without question, one of us' whenever he took his first whale.

They had not had bad weather on their way into Melville Bay, but as they progressed farther north the men muttered about how thick the ice was for this time of the year. Still, Fair Abe's heart remained unclouded by fear. The trip was the grandest adventure of his life and he could not understand why his mother had been so concerned. Of course, the actual killing of the whales could be dangerous. Perhaps that was what worried her.

Despite the hard work and daily regime, Fair Abe felt freer than he had in quite some time. He loved Father, but was wearied of their almost constant arguments. Fair Abe knew the disagreements had begun when he started questioning the gradual emancipation both Father and the Meeting favoured. The more strongly he felt that the evil needed to be eradicated quickly, the more frequent and heated the exchanges became.

Fair Abe had to admit that he started most of the arguments. He didn't really know what prompted him to keep needling Father. Part of it, he supposed, was built into his Quaker upbringing. He couldn't count how many times he had heard the phrase 'Speak Truth to Power'. Respect for someone more powerful than you should neither stop you from speaking out for what is right, nor against what is wrong. This speaking truth to power was as strong a pillar of his Quaker faith as the belief that the spark of God's Light is within everyone. These two concepts were the very rock upon which Friends based their concern for social justice and equality.

In reality, Father and Fair Abe weren't so different in their feelings about slavery. But something kept drawing Fair Abe toward the more extremist views on its abolition. The more he moved in the radical direction, the more he felt Father trying to restrain him. The more restraint Father exerted the more constricted he felt. The more constricted he felt, the more he felt compelled to argue the radical view of immediate and full manumission. They seemed to be caught in a vicious circle. The restrictions of working a whaling ship felt, by comparison, like unfettered freedom.

When the ice blocked them in with the other whalers from the United States and Great Britain, it began to feel like a magnificent party. The men did not act as though they were from different countries at all: they were all part of a grand band of whaling brothers. Competitive about the stories of their exploits, yes, but they drank and played music as though they all came from the same village.

The most exciting day had been when the Belcher Expedition from England had joined their multinational whaling fleet. All the officers and men grabbed instruments, and pots, and pans to create a marching band. Fair Abe pulled his fife from his sea trunk and joined the parade. It was rather difficult to tell, with the varying degrees of skill involved, whether they were all playing the same tunes, but everyone jumped into the fun, body and soul.

And the explorers had loved it! There were five ships on their way into the Arctic to search for Sir John Franklin. Every mariner on the North American Continent knew about Franklin and the many expeditions sent out to find him. But Fair Abe had never thought he would actually meet a British expedition at work! The most amazing thing was having the chance to talk with the sailors, to learn of their former exploits, and their hopes for this expedition.

Fair Abe was glad his days in the Arctic were just barely begun. As he rested in the afternoon sun, he dreamt about being on the British Expedition and sledging through the ice fields. *In his dream, he became the world's hero when he found Franklin still alive. Trudging back to his camp through the ice and snow, Franklin told Fair Abe that he had indeed discovered the North West Passage. It was through Fair Abe's timely rescue that this knowledge would be shared with the world! In the last scene of his dream he was stepping down onto the Perkins, Smith and Abraham wharf in New London to the tumultuous cheers of the crowd.*

Fair Abe awoke from his dream to the sound of a familiar name. The Resolutes around him were talking about their captain, a man named Kellett. Fair Abe asked the master if this Kellett was from Ireland. 'County Tipperary, son,' McDougall confirmed. Fair Abe began to wonder if he was related to his mother's friend, the one she still talked about meeting during her Famine work. He wanted to talk with the captain, but didn't know if he would be allowed the opportunity.

Once the *McClellan* was gone, her men had to find room on the other ships while waiting for the ice to clear. They also needed to decide if they were looking for berths on the outbound whalers or hoping to return home early. Most did not want to lose their chance to earn, but many of the outbound whalers had full crews. They were understandably reluctant to take on more crew than they needed because the profits of the trip were split between all the men. Unnecessary extra hands meant less money for all. Yet, the brotherly feeling that had developed during their icy incarceration endured. Each whaler shared the burden and took on one or two McClellans, but no more.

Some of the *McClellan's* men weren't bothered by the prospect of heading home early. They were the ones that had signed up for this trip as a last hurrah before retiring from the sea. For the captain and the officers the choice was easy. The *McClellan's* captain had to head back to New London, being duty bound to return to his employers with the news of their lost ship. The company could immediately send another ship in the lost ship's stead to pick up Buddington and the other whalers who had wintered over in the Arctic. The replacement ship would also carry on the interrupted whaling trip of the *McClellan*. The other officers had a choice: either they relinquished their commissions and became ordinary seamen, or they could go back to New London, sail on another ship, and keep their current rank. To a man, they joined their captain in finding berths on the returning whalers. The homebound McClellans had no problem finding berths, but the men who could not afford to go home struggled, and had to compete against each other, to find berths on the outbound whalers.

Fair Abe did not want to go home. Even through the terrifying moments when the ice swallowed the *McClellan,* he still felt the Arctic beckoning him. The temptation to extend his new found freedom also called him. The prospect of returning home to the ongoing disagreement with Father was particularly unappealing.

Where did his duty lie? Should he return home with the captain and resume his duties in the company office? Or should he honour the stated reason for his being amongst the whalers? Should he go on to learn the trade through which he and his family earned their living? If so, was staying in the Arctic and learning the ways of the whaling ships the way to do that, or should he go back to the New London office? Fair Abe tried to cleanse his desire to stay in the Arctic from his deliberations, the more readily to discern where his true duty lay. In true Quaker style, he sought the solution in silent meditation. Even so, he found himself no closer to knowing the correct course to follow.

Thinking if he went home now he would be going back with only the little bit of whaling knowledge he had gained so far, he asked around the fleet of outbound American whalers for a permanent berth. But after several days, he was still unsuccessful. The decision seemed to be taken from his hands, and he resigned himself to returning home. And it seemed such a short time ago that the Arctic and months of freedom were stretching out before him!

Day after day Fair Abe put off looking for a homebound berth. One of the ways he avoided the task was by spending hours on board *Resolute,* listening to Master McDougall's stories, and making friends with the two young mates, Nares and Roche. One afternoon, when he was in his temporary berth on one of the whalers writing to his mother and telling her of the lost ship, he was surprised by the approach of the cox'n from the *Resolute.*

'Sir, with Captain Kellett's respect, he would like you to attend him in his cabin on board HMS *Resolute,* at your earliest convenience.'

Fair Abe looked at his crewmate, wondering what do to.

'That's officer talk for right now, son. Best get you scrubbed up. And fast. Officers of the Royal Navy don't call on the likes of you or me very often.'

Fair Abe brushed down his coat and dressed himself as smartly as a whaling man could with the clothing he had for keeping the bitter cold at bay. He followed the cox'n to his ship and his captain's cabin.

⚓⚓⚓⚓⚓

Captain Kellett rose to greet Fair Abe upon his entering the cabin, Naps got up from under the table to sniff this new person. Fair Abe reached down to pet the dog's head, Naps wagging his tale in approval.

'I understand that you are the son of the *McClellan's* owners, is that so?'

'Yes, Sir. My father is a partner in the firm Perkins, Smith and Abraham.'

'Do you know a woman named Martha Abraham?'

'She is my mother, Sir.'

'And did your mother go to Ireland during the Great Famine?'

'Yes, Captain Kellett, she went to County Tipperary.' The captain pumped Fair Abe's arm as he exclaimed, 'I am so glad to meet you! My wife speaks of your mother frequently and with much affection. You must tell me how Mrs. Abraham finds her self, how your family is faring. My Alice would never forgive me if I didn't tell her about meeting her friend's son in this most unlikely of circumstances! And I certainly wouldn't dare go home without a full report about Martha. Sit, my boy, and talk to me.' Naps dropped his head into the lap of his newly found friend.

Henry Kellett and Fair Abe talked for more than two hours. Fair Abe told the captain about his family, his brothers and sisters, the new baby William; about his father growing up fishing on the Bay, meeting and marrying mother; about their Quaker faith and practice.

Fair Abe heard about his mother's work in Ireland during the Famine, of how Mrs. Kellett and his mother met. Fair Abe had always known his mother was a woman of considerable strength and depth of feeling, but the great respect with which the Kellett family apparently held her made him see her in a new way.

Captain Kellett asked the boy about his time on the *McClellan*. Fair Abe spoke about what he had learned so far, but became the most animated when he talked about wanting to spend more time in the Arctic. Somehow, late in their conversation, Fair Abe began talking about his reluctance to return home to the strained relationship with his father. And about slavery.

'It has always struck me as the deepest irony,' Captain Kellett said, 'that your country, which fought so gallantly for freedom, continues to accept slavery as an institution. Whereas the British Empire, so tyrannical in the American view, stopped slavery and the slave trade decades ago. It is a particular shame that this issue has created a wedge between you and your father when you both believe the same thing: slavery is an evil, which must be abolished.'

'I don't understand how Father can labour month after month with the Maryland slaveholders without condemning them out right. It is very difficult to be obligated by faith to see God's Light in persons who don't see it in others. I just don't see how he can speak to That of God in Godless plantation owners. Tell me, how was the struggle to free slaves in thy country won?'

'It didn't happen quickly. I am certain you know that the British Quakers were very prominent in our anti-slavery movement. When the Society for the Abolition of the Slave Trade was formed in 1787 most of the members of the committee were Friends. We abolished Slavery in Britain in 1772, but we were still very active in the slave trade until we made that illegal in 1807. Even though the slave trade itself was abolished, that didn't stop unscrupulous slave captains from carrying on. If they were in danger of being caught, they threw the slaves overboard. Still manacled together, they died a horrible death. The slave trade wasn't going to end as long as slavery was legal throughout the Empire and in other parts of the world, but it still took decades longer for Britain to abolish slavery in the rest of the Empire. That didn't happen until almost twenty years ago.'

'It may have taken years of struggle, but thy country is still ahead of mine. I wish our government would learn from Britain!'

'Our countries don't have the best history for seeing things in the same light! I don't think you should use that argument for the purposes of persuasion!'

Captain Kellett said goodnight to his young guest after their discussion about slavery. Fair Abe returned to his adopted ship in a quiet and reflective mood. He fell asleep brooding over what he should do once the ice opened, where his true duty lay, and what path he would take. By the time he awoke the following morning he had made his decision.

𝒸𝒸𝒸𝒸𝒸𝒸

A taut silence reigned in the Kellett home after Alice broke the news of the proposed trip to America. Alice wrote to Martha Abraham to tell her she was excited and very interested in the opportunity to visit, but needed some time to organise her affairs and the estate before making any sailing plans. Alice needed all the time she could get to get things, and most importantly her daughter, in order.

Margaret spent her days in the stables, and she began working with the new young filly the day after her quarrel with her mother. The first day of building a relationship with a young horse started with Margaret going into the field and sitting down. Then she waited. The individual balance between a horse's flight instinct and inherent curiosity determined the amount of time it took for that horse to come to her. To calm its fear she sat very still and made no sudden movements. Given no reason to take flight, the horse always gave way to its overwhelming sense of inquisitiveness.

Margaret did not break her horses by using fear and intimidation. Instead, she built a bond of trust. Other people who worked with horses either thought she was touched in the head, or gifted. She spoke the language of the horse; and rather than demand that the horse give her the behaviour she wanted, she chose initially to do nothing but give of herself to the animal. All she did during her first encounter was sit. When the horse finally came to her, no matter how long it took, she spoke praise softly and touched the horse in a calming way.

When Margaret came into the training field, the young filly reared up and bolted far away to the fence on the field's farthest edge. She was very frightened. Margaret didn't worry. She would take advantage of the opportunity to sit and observe the young horse so that she could think of an appropriate name for her. At least with horses she was patient!

Her thoughts turned to her mother and how strained their relationship had become since their argument. Margaret did not know why she had responded so strongly. In thinking about the possibility of going to America, she found herself torn between a reluctance to leave Clonacody and excitement at the prospect of exploring the New World. She wasn't opposed to the idea of going as much as it had initially appeared. What she really resented was the way her mother assumed she would want to go as a foregone conclusion, yet she could not deny that she found the prospect exciting.

It took hours of patience before the filly began circling around Margaret. Gradually getting closer and closer, she still bolted whenever Margaret looked at her. However, each time she ran she came back, then stopped, nearer to the girl. 'Bess,' Margaret whispered and the filly whinnied softly. 'I think I'll call you Bess.' A few minutes later Bess was close enough for Margaret to stroke her nose.

Weeks passed and the distance between mother and daughter grew, while at the same time Margaret and Bess continued getting closer. Exploring Bess by gentle touch, patting, and pressing, Margaret was able to find the places the horse liked best to be touched. The more Bess enjoyed Margaret's touch the less tension and fear she felt. The girl and horse began bonding, with Bess returning Margaret's affection. It was only after the trust and communication was established that Margaret began the actual training. Because of Margaret's approach, this was a time of enjoyment for the filly, not a time of being frightened and broken. Horses loved being worked by Margaret so much that they rarely wanted to stop when a session ended. Bess was no exception. She was showing herself to be an affectionate and eager student. Margaret's temper could be fiery when she was with her fellow human beings, but never when she was in the field with her equestrian friends. The young men in the parish, for whom she had no time, often wished they could get her to touch them as gently as she touched her horses.

While Margaret's presence was calming for Bess, being with the filly was also soothing to the young woman. It was thus, after several weeks with Bess that Margaret quietly apologised to her mother for her display of anger.

'I would like to talk with you about the trip, if you can forgive me. I would love to go to America if we can wait until Bess is more fully trained.'

'Thank you for your apology, I accept it, and I would be delighted to discuss visiting America. Why don't we talk over tea?'

Alice put her arm around Margaret's shoulders and they walked together into the kitchen.

'Mrs. McDonald, we would like to have tea on the back terrace, please.' The two women sat in the afternoon sun. 'While you have been working with Bess I have been getting my affairs in order hoping we would have this conversation! It is always helpful to be certain that the estate accounts are up to date. I have also made visits to the expectant mothers I am attending. I made a chart of their anticipated confinements, which has helped me to see when I might be able to leave with the least amount of disruption to them. In fact, I have made another chart for Clonacody of the works in progress so I could begin to straighten out the staff needed to run the estate while we are away.'

'I guess you knew I would want to go as soon as I calmed down. You have certainly been busy with preparations. I have just been spending all my time with Bess.'

'Other than packing, getting her trained is all you have to do to be ready to leave. I was watching the two of you yesterday and I am so proud of how you work with her. She is coming along very nicely. You must tell me how much time you think you will need to complete her training and to help in establishing a working relationship between Bess and Mr. McCaffrey. It wouldn't do to have her feel abandoned after all the work you have done.'

'How long can I have?'

'We should sail by the end of August to err on the side of caution. That gives us five weeks and enough time for us to send a letter to Mrs. Abraham accepting her offer and giving her the arrival information. Is that enough time for you?'

'I think so. Bess is being very responsive and I can start introducing her to Mr. McCaffrey this week. Oh, Mamma, I am so glad we are going, and that we are talking again!' Margaret gave her mother a warm hug and bounded up the stairs to her room. She really must begin deciding what to take. Once she began that process, the trip would become a reality to her.

⚓⚓⚓⚓⚓

In the first week of August the squadron was finally able to break free from the ice in Melville Bay to continue its journey into the Arctic. The explorers bid a fond farewell to the whaling fleet. Two days later *Resolute* made fast to an iceberg to replenish her water supply. The berg stood tall with its peak sixty feet above the water. When the crew completed gathering water, the men and officers led by young Nares took cask staves and bound them together, and then hauled them up the steep slopes.

Sliding down the side of the berg was exhilarating; many of the sleds came right to the water's edge before stopping. Some of the men had to 'abandon ship' to avoid crashing at high speed into the icy water. Several near collisions on the slope heightened the perilous excitement. Hours later with their work and play completed the men returned to their ship rejuvenated. Their spirits were renewed and they were ready for the challenges that lay ahead.

It was summer. In the face of all the weather: the gales, the tightly closed ice pack, and the thick fog, the experienced arctic explorers knew this was as good as it was going to get. The squadron laboriously worked its way farther and farther into Lancaster Sound, farther and farther away from the homes and the homeland the men loved.

The ships moved inextricably toward their destinies. What their fate was to be not one of the officers or men involved knew. The exploration and adventure were still new, the horizon opening indefinitely before them. In the night, as they lay in their cabins, did the truth ever come to them in their dreams? Could any of them see the failures, or the successes, that lay ahead? If they could, would any of these officers and men exchange the parts they would play in the drama unfolding around them for any other part in any other play?

51

CHAPTER SIX
AUGUST 1852 CONTINUED

'What are you doing on my ship?' On board the *Assistance* Sir Edward Belcher's face was red with anger, but his voice was soft. The young man standing before him did not see the warning sign that was in the captain's face and responded to the kindness in the voice.

'I wanted to...'

'You must take off your hat when you speak to me. And you are to address me as 'Sir'. Now, you were saying?'

'By faith I cannot take my hat off to thee, Sir. My religion...'

'Are you refusing to do what I have said you must? What are you playing at?' Crispness crept into Belcher's voice though it was still benign. A slight smile appeared at the corners of his mouth. He was going to enjoy this game. The boy, again misreading his interrogator and thinking the smile was encouragement to explain, said, 'Sir, I am a member of the Religious Society of Friends. We do not recognise the superiority of any man over another. We are all equals in the eyes of the Lord. Therefore, as no one is required to take off their hat to a more 'lowly' man, we do not take ours off to anyone.'

'Ah, I see. So these quaint customs we observe in the Royal Navy have naught to do with you.'

'I mean no disrespect, it is the way we have of showing each person the same respect.'

'Or lack of any respect to everyone?'

Fair Abe frowned slightly. How could he explain this so the commander could grasp it?

'So, you are what we call a Quaker, is that it? Aren't you also disallowed from taking part in wars?'

'That is true.'

'Then explain to me what you are doing on a ship of the British Navy? Do you not realize that, by and large, the navy's purpose is to wage war?'

'But you are not here to do battle, you are an exploration expedition. I wanted to join you because...'

'Hold your tongue, boy!' There was no longer any question that the captain was angry. Fair Abe understood too late that Belcher had only been goading him. 'Do you think I give a damn about what you want? This is a vessel of the Royal Navy and you are a stowaway. We are going into the Arctic, possibly for years. We have a full compliment and our supplies are limited to the number of officers and men with which we set sail. Do you comprehend how you have endangered the lives of all of us on *Assistance*? I am not concerned with what you want or don't want. My sole concern is for the safety of myself.' Belcher added as an after thought: 'and my men.' Belcher rose from his seat behind his table and strode to Fair Abe's side. He saw too late that this put him at the disadvantage, being four inches shorter than the boy he was attempting to put down. His anger boiled over. 'And what makes you believe I will allow the principles of your heretical sect to determine your behaviour while you are my uninvited guest? Naval justice is the law here, and I am its only administrator.' He looked up into the now fearful eyes of his stowaway. Yes, that was better. Give the boy a moment to understand his vulnerable position before making an example of him to the men.

'I am putting you under arrest. Take him below!' The attending Royal Marine sergeant grabbed Fair Abe by the arm. 'Dismissed!'

Belcher sat in his cabin and poured himself another tot of rum. There were two men in his crew he could rely on. Not trust, no one fitted that category, but two he could use without any concern for betrayal. He had their secrets, so they would keep his.

When he had discovered the stowaway, he had summoned these men to his cabin. He instructed them to rouse the boy as though they were the ones to find him and to bring him to the cabin inconspicuously, bound and gagged, in the dark of the night. Only the three of them knew he was on board.

What an innocent the boy had been! He really appeared to think Belcher cared about his reasons for stowing away! And he apparently expected to be considered noble for doing so! He closed his eyes and savoured the memory of the moment the boy had realised he was not his friend. It was the look in their eyes, the look of understanding, apprehension, and fear all rolled into one, which made him shiver with delight. Belcher experienced an almost sexual pleasure whenever he saw the comprehension that they were at his mercy. No. This was not a game that involved mercy, though he enjoyed seeing them beg for it. No. It was the power that excited him.

The Royal Navy gave him so much opportunity to explore the many ways he could exert this dominance. Nothing was ever so powerful on earth as a captain or commander on his ship. The punishments set out by the Admiralty for the captain to employ were severe. Discipline must be maintained at sea, and as the men greatly outnumbered the officers, the danger of mutiny always lurked in the shadows. The fear of grave consequences was one of the ways the men were kept in order and the work was done.

There were others in the Navy, not many, but some, who found meting out punishment the most gratifying part of the job. Belcher had a gift for finding a man's vulnerability and knowing how to exploit it. He was so adept at exciting the men's petty jealousies and resentments that he was frequently unaware that he was doing it. It was only when he found himself revelling in the ensuing conflict that he knew he had been at work. He always felt the most alive when he was in the centre of the tempest. The pure joy he took in inflicting even the most inconsequential atonement was like a drug for him. Yes, he was going to relish playing with his newfound prey.

⚓⚓⚓⚓⚓

In the depths of HMS *Assistance* Fair Abe huddled in the dark, trying to keep warm. For five days, he had seen no light and had neither the room to stand, nor space to lie down. No light and no heat, no blanket and very little food. He could only count the time passing by hearing the footfalls above as watches changed. He knew another day was almost gone when the shorter dogwatch occurred. During the second dogwatch, he was brought his one meal for the day: a cup of water and two hard tack biscuits.

Without movement, blankets, or adequate food Fair Abe struggled to keep from succumbing to the cold. He didn't dare sleep for fear he would not wake up, that he would drift away to a frozen death. When he felt himself dozing, he beat his arms about, slapped himself, and kicked his legs, anything to keep alert and to keep his blood moving. Second to his fear of freezing to death was the very real anxiety of losing his hands or feet to frostbite. As the days wore on, sleep stalked him like a hungry beast, circling ever closer to its prey.

How had he come to this? The moment after he had decided to stow away with the expedition everything had gone wrong: from *Resolute* sailing before he had the opportunity to get aboard, to finding this captain on *Assistance*. Fair Abe had never experienced cruelty for cruelty's sake. He had no inner defences with which to protect himself. Not only was he suffering physically, but also emotionally. He felt defeated. Crushed.

Fair Abe now understood how little he had considered the consequences of stowing away on a naval vessel. He was utterly astonished at being deemed a criminal. After a certain amount of surprise and consternation, he had envisioned the captain welcoming him as another pair of strong hands to share the work. Even accepting that what he had done was an arrest-able offence, he still had not anticipated that the squadron commander would punish him with so much gratuitous savagery.

The worst cruelty he could imagine was slavery, yet even that did not seem as capricious as the actions Belcher was taking against him. The men who owned slaves had a rational reason for their brutality. Fair Abe, while disagreeing vehemently with the institution, could at least see that there was a logical belief system that underpinned it. Men owned slaves for economic profit. They found nothing wrong in owning Africans because they thought

54

them inferior and barely human. Most slaveholders only punished their property when the slave had done something the owner considered wrong: something that put their person or finances at risk. Refusing to work or running away for instance.

Belcher's actions were different. The young man could find no rationale for the captain's degree of barbarity. His mind numb with the cold, his muscles cramping, his body shivering, he began wondering if the squadron commander took pleasure in the pain he was inflicting. Perhaps he had forgotten him? Maybe that was what happened. He might have meant to drive home the lesson with a few hours of distress, but then his duties required so much of him he had thought no more of Fair Abe. If this was the case, all he had to do was remind Captain Belcher that he was still captive in this freezing black hole and he would move him to a place with warmth, light and the company of the men. He might even get more food!

This thought came to Fair Abe on the third day of his confinement. It had lifted his spirit until that day's meal had arrived. Belcher must be ordering his continued feeding, and therefore his confinement. It was then that Fair Abe realised that Belcher wanted him to suffer *in extremis.* Did he mean to kill him slowly? If he didn't find a way to escape this could very well be his end. Help from any of the crew was impossible. No one seemed to know he was there. Or if they did, they didn't care.

Fair Abe was too weakened to think of a way of saving himself. The darkness deepened around him and entered his inner being. He suffered the true loneliness inherent in having been completely abandoned and he began to collapse into despair.

⚓⚓⚓⚓⚓

When the month of August was half gone McDougall sighted Beechey Island at midnight, from *Resolute's* deck. The squadron was to reassemble here in Erebus and Terror Bay, each ship retrieving its share of winter provisions from HMS *North Star. North Star* had already cut into a dock and was waiting for her sister ships when *Resolute* arrived in the bay. The men hauled in beside the depot ship and started the transfer of provisions. After they had finished the loading, Captain Kellett, the officers, and most of the men set off to explore the island.

During the next several days, McDougall revisited the cairn he had built while on the island as part of the 1850 expedition. He extracted the documents from within to see if there was any indication that Franklin, or any one else, had visited the island in the intervening years. His hopes of finding some written evidence that Franklin may have made his way back to this site were dashed by the discovery that no new documents had been added to the cairn.

The officers and men combed the island and the remnants of Franklin's first winter encampment, and the rest of the island, each with the ambition of being the one who could return victoriously having found concrete evidence of the direction Franklin had taken after leaving winter quarters in the spring of '46. In this desire, they were all to be disappointed. Richard Roche, with Naps at his heels, joined a small party to explore the high cliffs of the island where dovekies and gulls nested in abundance. It was here that Napoleon found traces of a Franklin hunting party. On a sheltered rocky ledge under one of the cliffs, he discovered a number of empty discarded meat tins and several small piles of birds' bones. Roche was attracted to the clank of the tins being moved about by Naps' nose. A feeling of melancholy so profound struck him that he sat without noticing the time passing, stroking the soft fur of Naps' head and ears, while Naps laid his head on Roche's lap, occasionally looking longingly at the bones and tins. Somehow, the sadness of his companion overrode his desire to sniff about and he stayed beside Roche until he returned to the ship. In the evening when Roche returned to *Resolute* he remarked upon his sadness and pondered the fate of the lost men in his journal. Could any of them still be alive, surviving, perhaps, because of the kindness of local Esquimaux? If they were all dead, were their deaths painful ones of lingering hunger, cold, and illness, or were they mercifully quick? What chance was there now of finding any of them alive?

Why didn't Franklin build a cairn and leave an itinerary of his intended proceedings? This question crossed many of the men's minds as they searched the abandoned workshops of the encampment site. Richard Roche and several of the men from the fo'c'sle watch inspected a hut, about twelve feet in diameter, built and paved with stones. One side was recessed and had apparently been used as a fireplace for it was there that they found ashes and the remains of feasts consumed long ago. Nearby they found pieces of iron around the spot where the Franklin men must have set up an anvil. The northern shore of the island revealed another stone hut and two buildings with debris indicating that they had been used as armourer and carpenter shops. Not one man was successful in finding any written word, however. There was no indication when the Franklin expedition abandoned the encampment, or in which direction they may have gone.

Commander George Henry Richards had begun to suspect something was amiss upon HMS *Assistance*. Twice he had come across Royal Marine Sergeant George Roberts acting as though he had been caught doing something wrong when he saw him coming up from the lower hold. There were at least two men on board *Assistance* whom he did not trust and Roberts was one of them. McCoy was the other. They had been too quick in their acquiescence to anything Captain Belcher requested of them. There was the respect and compliance due a superior officer, and then there was unnecessarily obsequious behaviour. Richards suspected that these two were not just being obedient seamen, but he could not say exactly what gave him this impression. He couldn't point to any one act that had triggered his distrust of them, any more than he could put his finger on what made him suspicious of George Roberts now, other than a vague impression of furtiveness in his behaviour the nights he had accidentally come across him. But, if Roberts was up to something, Richards was certain McCoy would be in on it with him. He decided to keep an eye on both of them.

Not content with having Fair Abe to abuse, Belcher vented his spleen on his officers. He did not trust them any farther than he could spit. Already he had seen the signs of their conspiracies in the way they looked at him when they thought he didn't notice. If he didn't crack down now the winter ahead, when they would be locked in the ice, would be insufferable. The insubordination had begun with Lieutenant Cheyne.

Despite Belcher's orders that all officers were to present themselves on Sundays in full dress uniform, spotless and in top order, Cheyne had had the nerve to appear on deck with a frayed collar. Belcher could hardly believe his eyes.

'Mr. Cheyne, please step forward,' Belcher commanded. 'Explain yourself, Sir!' Cheyne looked blankly at his superior, not knowing what he had done wrong. 'This is despicable behaviour! How dare you insult me, and disobey my orders, by coming on deck with your uniform in this state!'

Cheyne looked down at his spotless coat, confused by the reprimand. He looked at Osborn who ran his finger along his own collar, indicating to Cheyne what the problem was. Cheyne was embarrassed, but then made the mistake of trying to justify himself. 'Sir, my father gave you my funds in trust, and I did ask you for some of them to replace this collar before we left England. But you refused, Sir.'

'You dare to speak to me in this way, and in front of the men and your fellow officers? Did I ask you for lame excuses? Showing such disrespect and ignoring my orders is insubordination and I will not tolerate it. Do you understand?' Belcher waited for Cheyne's acknowledgement. 'Mr. Richards, place this man under arrest! Perhaps some time in solitary confinement will give you the opportunity to consider your actions and will bring you to your senses. And you can utilise your time well if you repair your collar while you think about your attitude, and whether or not you intend to be the proper example officers must be for their men. Take him below!'

Richards reluctantly ordered two marines to escort Cheyne below, where he would remain in solitary confinement at Sir Belcher's pleasure.

⚓⚓⚓⚓⚓

The day after she and Margaret began talking to each other again, Alice Kellett wrote to Martha Abraham. Mother and daughter spent most of August preparing to set sail. Margaret continued her work with Bess, and began introducing her to Mr. McCaffrey. McCaffrey had never seen horses trained the way they were by Margaret. He had no idea where she acquired her notions, no one in County Tipperary worked with horses the way she did. When asked, Margaret couldn't explain it herself. She said she just listened to the horses and always knew what the correct thing was to do.

At first, McCaffrey had joined those who thought she was a bit touched. But then he remembered how Margaret had always had a special relationship with the horses at Clonacody, ever since that first ride when she was a baby. It didn't take him long to see the merit in her technique, the horses were calmer and were trained more easily. So, the old hand learned from the young lady, and the more he learned the more he respected her. His pride in her grew with the years and now all the horses at Clonacody were trained by Margaret's method.

Bess had, by mid August, lost her fear completely. She was comfortable with bridle and saddle, and Margaret was able to give her daily grooming and work out to McCaffrey. During her last week at home, Margaret saw Bess only twice; the filly was not pining for her first friend though she was glad to see Margaret each time. With Bess settled, the young woman began to look forward to the voyage with eager anticipation.

$$\mathcal{LLLLL}$$

On Beechey Island, during the late evening of August 14th Captain Belcher assembled and addressed the officers and crew of his Expedition. Kellett was barely able to concentrate on the words Belcher spoke, being absorbed instead in watching his commander as he strutted before the men, his chest swollen with self-importance. Such a display of pomposity! Was it really supposed to motivate the men?

In this new phase of the search, the squadron was to split. Captain Kellett was to take command of the western branch, instructed by Belcher to reach Melville Island with HMS *Resolute* and *Intrepid* before taking up winter quarters. Meanwhile Squadron Commander Belcher would take HMS *Assistance* and *Pioneer* north through Wellington Channel, and *North Star* would remain at Beechey Island as a depot ship.

Kellett's orders were to proceed if possible to Winter Harbour on Melville Island, where Sir William Edward Parry had wintered in 1819-1820. Here he would deposit provisions for HMS *Investigator,* the ship captained by Robert McClure, which the Admiralty had sent into the Arctic from the west. Kellett's orders also directed him to build cairns as depots for supplies for his own ship's company along his route so that they would be well supplied should an accident befall *Resolute* and the men have to return to Beechey Island by foot.

Captain Kellett was further ordered to dispatch travelling parties the following spring to the north by way of Byam Channel and west over Melville Island with an expected return to Beechey Island during the autumn of 1853.

During the evening, after Captain Belcher's speech to the men and his meeting with the officers, Sherard Osborn walked with his friend McDougall. It was the first and last opportunity they would have to be alone together and to speak freely with each other. Osborn, serving in HMS *Assistance's* steam tender, *Pioneer,* would be sailing with the half of the expedition that was heading North through Wellington Channel while McDougall would be going West on *Resolute.*

George Frederick McDougall was trying to cheer up his friend but Sherard remained immersed in gloom.

'Come on, Osborn, things can't be as bad as all that.'

'He is already insufferable and we haven't run into any serious difficulties yet! I am not looking forward to seeing him when he really has any justifiable cause to be upset. You should have seen him a week ago when he berated one of the officers in front of the men, right there in front of them! Can you believe it? Lieutenant Cheyne's collar was fraying and Belcher called it an act of insubordination! He completely lost control of his temper, shouting about what kind of conduct was becoming of an officer and what kind was not. Then he barked at Cheyne about the sort of example all the officers need to be for the men. I know I should not talk about my captain this way, but all he did was undermine Cheyne's authority by giving him such a serious tongue lashing within the hearing and sight of the men!

'You know, I think that is why he did it. He seems to be jealous of his junior officers, including me. Anything we do well angers him and sends him into a temper tantrum, yet he is even more unbearable if we don't do everything perfectly. What a dressing down we get every time *Resolute* beats us to a port! Nobody knows what to do to make him happy, and we all walk as gingerly as though the decks were made of glass. Each one of us is trying to avoid being caught in the cross fire the next time he lets loose his anger. I am telling you, George, it has already demoralised the officers as well as the men on both *Assistance* and *Pioneer.* And our voyage has just begun! Until now, he has at least been attempting to keep his temper under control when all the ships are in harbour together. Once we split and go our separate ways who knows what will happen!'

'I have heard plenty of stories about Belcher, but it's always a knotty bit trying to tell what's true and what's exaggerated. However, you are correct in one thing, my friend: we have not seen anything yet. If he is this distraught already, what is going to happen when something goes seriously wrong or the men need to rely on him through real difficulty? You and I both know how hard it is to get through the long dark winters up here. The men's morale is one of the most important ingredients to their survival. If your gloom is anything to judge the rest of your ships' companies by, all I can say is I wish you were all sailing with us. And I am sorry you got stuck like this, Sherard.'

'I think he is particularly jealous of me. He knows I have more experience than he does up here, and that the men like me. He seems to take it as a personal insult, rather than seeing me as an asset. I really don't know what to do to make him happy!'

'I don't think that can be done. I think you have to just try to do your duty and stay out of his way as much as possible. Of course, with what you tell me you're sort o' damned if you do and damned if you don't. Just try not to make an enemy of him if you can avoid it. He seems to have a fondness for stripping his officers of their commissions, putting them under arrest, and having them court- martialed. So be careful!'

'I'm trying to be, George, but I can't seem to stay out of his way...even though I am on *Pioneer* and not on his ship, *Assistance.* I'm afraid he could be the death of my career in the Navy no matter what I do.'

They walked on together up the high cliffs and back down along the shore, but McDougall was never able to lift the cloud of despondency from his friend's shoulders. Both men spent their last night on Beechey Island tormented by nightmare after nightmare, waking in the early morning exhausted despite their hours of sleep.

McDougall, nearly always able to bring his unsinkable sense of humour and fun to bad situations, found his heart heavy when he parted company with his friend on the morning of the 15th. He thought of their joint efforts during the last expedition when, as an indomitable team, they had written their *Illustrated Arctic News* and produced the plays for their Arctic Theatre Royale. At least George had found a new kindred spirit in Lieutenant Pim, but whom did Osborn have? No one. Not one compatriot to help with the coming storms, the icy gales that seemed quite likely to prevail both above deck and below.

CHAPTER SEVEN
AUGUST 1852 CONTINUED

On the evening of Belcher's speech to the squadron, Commander George Richards' vigil bore fruit when he followed McCoy and Roberts as they crept down to the lower decks of HMS *Assistance*. Below the stored supplies, the stalls of animals, to a small locker beyond the sheep pens the men edged along the shadows. They stopped frequently to check if they were being followed, and at least once Richards was certain they had heard him, but they carried on without searching for him. *I have you now*, he thought, as he watched the two men haul a bundle from the locker. *Whatever it is you are hiding here, whether it is stolen or not, it must be against regulation or this secrecy would not be needed.*

Richards heard a groan and saw McCoy kick the heap they were dragging between them. It groaned more loudly. It was not something they were taking away, but some one! What nefarious undertaking was he witnessing? George Richards pressed himself back into the shadows behind the sheep as the men carried past him what was revealed to be an almost naked man. He could think of no crew that had gone missing, so who was this unfortunate being? Richards decided not to confront the men but to follow them to their new destination. He could learn much more by staying hidden. Whatever transpired now, he was certain there was evil intent involved and he wanted to know as much as he could before arresting George Roberts and McCoy.

To the commander's utter dismay, after trailing them through a circuitous route that avoided all shipmates, the men hauled their captive up in front of the squadron leader's cabin! Belcher is involved! Richards was certain he could write up and punish his men, but what exactly could he do about Sir Edward? He would have to tread very carefully; he would need strong corroborative evidence before he could end this wretched man's suffering. Because to end the suffering without being able to punish the wrongdoing would only be half his job done.

Assistance's commander crept closer to the captain's door after the three men had entered the cabin. He could hear voices but could not distinguish what was being said, until Belcher raised his voice.

'So, our stowaway Abraham still refuses to show proper respect, does he? Take off your hat!'

Scuffling ensued, then the sound of fists striking a yielding body. A few minutes later Richards heard George Roberts' protest.

'Captain, Sir, I think he was trying to lift his arm to remove his hat, but he couldn't raise it.'

'Did I ask you to think? You are here to do what I tell you to do, nothing less and nothing more. Take him away! We will see what twenty four hours with no food does for his beliefs!'

Richards scrambled from the door and quietly slipped into his own cabin. They called their captive Abraham. Could he be that young Abraham boy from the *McClellan*? If this was so, did the men involved in his maltreatment realise Captain Kellett was an old friend of the Abraham family? He was not some nameless youth being used for Belcher's pleasure, but someone whose harm would certainly be avenged, not that this consideration made any difference to Richards in his resolve to free the young man. However, his being known to Kellett gave Richards an idea about how he could go about rescuing the unfortunate captive. Certainly it could help him bring to justice those involved in his captivity. What harm did these men intend, anyway?

He lay in bed awake until the morning: until he knew what he had to do.

When the sky had just begun to lighten, George Richards made his way silently to HMS *Pioneer*, and woke Sherad Osborn, telling him what he had witnessed.

'I need your help,' the commander confided. 'I have thought long and hard about what to do. Before I make any attempt at a rescue I must have at least a second, possibly a third, witness to this disgrace. Perhaps Captain Kellett would be willing to be a part of the rescue, and we can smuggle Fair Abe off *Assistance* and onto *Resolute*. At the end of it all, we must make an official record of this and report it to the Admiralty. I will discuss with Captain Kellett what we should do with Roberts, McCoy, and Belcher in the meantime. If you are willing to help in this adventure, you must be willing to make a report to the Admiralty. It is as important to me that these men receive a just punishment as is it to rescue poor Abraham. What do you say, Lieutenant?'

Sherard was silent for a moment. His thoughts raced quickly from his concern about what the consequences could be for his career to realising he could only do the right thing, irrespective of the possible repercussions.

'Of course I will help you. What should we do first?' The two men consulted in low whispers, and parted a half hour later with their plan in place.

Captain Kellett sat in silence, a look of distress on his face. He had feared Squadron Commander Belcher would do something like this on the expedition, yet had been hopeful that the man may have changed in the years since he had served under him. He was not completely taken by surprise like George Henry Richards, but he was alarmed none the less. For Belcher to do this to such a young and inexperienced boy who wasn't even a sailor in the Royal Navy, and to have it happen to the son of a family friend, was completely outrageous! Fair Abe's innocence probably acted as a stimulus to Belcher's sadistic streak, unwittingly bringing out the worst the man had in him. Not that it was Fair Abe's fault by any means.

'There is no question that I will join you as a witness and agent to get the boy out of Belcher's grasp. This is an unconscionable abuse of power. What is your plan, Mr. Richards?'

Richards disclosed what he thought they should do and he and Osborn departed from the *Resolute*. The men would meet again after dark.

After dinner, Captain Kellett sent word to Captain Belcher requesting a meeting with him onboard *Assistance* and Belcher agreed. The two men met in Belcher's cabin and talked about the upcoming split in the squadron, when Kellett would command the western arm and Belcher the northern arm of exploration. After their meeting Kellett descended unseen to the lowest deck, where he met Richards and Osborn. They hid behind the sheep and waited.

Roberts and McCoy came for their prey and it was all Kellett could do to stay hidden while he watched the men beat Fair Abe, and drag him away. The three officers followed the men silently, and then listened in the shadows outside the cabin door. They heard another beating taking place and the faint cry for mercy.

'I will show you mercy when you show me respect.' Belcher smiled coldly. He found a strange excitement seeing the bruises and blood on the boy. His hands moistened with sweat and he only just restrained himself from giving into the urge to touch the boy's swollen face. He lost himself for a moment in the sweet fantasy of kissing the blood away, but quickly regained control of himself.

Fair Abe swallowed hard. Quaker belief not withstanding, he could take no more. He was hungry, tired, wracked with pain. He was certain one of his arms was broken, and possibly a rib or two. He mumbled through his swollen lips, 'Please, Sir, if I could raise my arms I would take off my hat to you.'

Belcher pursed his lips. 'Very well, for that you may have food tonight. Roberts, get him blankets and water. Make sure no one hears or sees you, though, I do not want anyone finding our friend.'

Outside the closed door of the cabin Roberts and McCoy showed a small glimmer of humanity. Instead of dragging Fair Abe, they actually carried him below. Kellett, Richards, and Osborn followed them. An hour later, after Roberts and McCoy delivered food, water, and blankets to their captive, Osborn crept out of the shadows, spoke softly to Fair Abe to reassure him, and broke the lock.

⚓⚓⚓⚓⚓

Having passed out from the pain when leaving Belcher's cabin, Fair Abe could not tell if the voices he heard were real or imaginary. He slowly surfaced through the fog and blackness to hear the lock being broken, but the darkness overtook him again when the men tried to move him. When he opened his eyes again, he was in Captain Kellett's cabin.

'I am so sorry this has happened to you,' Captain Kellett said. 'When you are better, I hope you will tell me about it, but for now, Brooke will clean you up and then I want Dr. Domville to see you, and dress your injuries.'

'Thank you, Sir.'

Brooke came to the bedside, and gently peeled away what was left of Fair Abe's old clothes. He gasped when he saw the state of the injuries. With the greatest of care, he sponged Fair Abe from head to toe, combed and braided his hair and replaced his tattered clothes with clean replacements from his own sea chest. Naps watched with interest. Brooke left Fair Abe for a few minutes so that he could recover from having been moved about. Then Brooke returned with a savoury broth to feed the invalid. He smiled to see Napoleon keeping watch next to the bed. He had not yet finished his administrations when the doctor entered the cabin. Brooke excused himself and closed the door.

Abraham's injuries were extensive. His right arm was broken in two places, and three ribs were cracked. Dr. Domville had to clean a festering wound on his leg before he could stitch it, and he had to ply his needle again on Abraham's scalp. He then made poultices for the bruises and cuts on his face and torso. When Captain Kellett returned to his cabin latter he found Fair Abe propped up on his pillows, trussed up like a Christmas turkey, Naps faithfully sitting with his head on the bed next to Abe's bandaged hand.

'The question of how you are feeling need hardly be asked, but are you at least feeling somewhat better?'

'Yes, Sir. The laudanum helps with the pain, but it makes me sleepy.'

'I would think the ordeal you have been through would be tiring as well. When you are better we need to talk about what exactly did happen, and what we can do about it, but for now you must simply rest and regain your strength. Know that you are safe now and you will be sailing with us on *Resolute*. No one will harm you any more. For the immediate future, you will share my cabin with me. I have decided to keep your presence here known to the fewest people possible. Richards on *Assistance,* and Osborn on *Pioneer*, who effected your escape, Dr. Domville of course, Brooke and I are the only ones privy to the knowledge of what has happened here and to your being on board *Resolute.* Though this may be inconvenient at certain times, I must insist that you do not leave this cabin, nor make any excessive noise. Until the squadron splits, we are still in danger.'

'I will do whatever you say; I am in thy debt and will never forget what thou art doing for me.'

'Don't worry, son, I just want to keep you as safe as I can so that we can say with confidence that your nightmare is over.'

When the captain departed, Fair Abe drifted into a drugged sleep. He lost track of time: sleeping, being fed by Brooke and being treated by Dr. Domville merged into a kaleidoscopic dream. At first he felt as though he was a small speck in a dark sea of pain, almost overwhelmed by it as it came in upon him in wave after wave. Whenever he cried out in pain, he felt the warm soft muzzle of his constant companion nudging him to let him know he was not alone. Gradually he felt himself growing stronger as he regained his health. Soon, rather than being contained in the pain, the pain was contained by him. He was finally able to tell Dr. Domville he could do without the laudanum and he began walking about the cabin with Naps at his side. The same morning he stopped taking the medication Captain Kellett came to him with a request.

'You are safe now, young man. We left the *Assistance* and *Pioneer* two days ago. You have no obligation to do what I am about to ask you, but I want you to give it due consideration. Misters Richards, Osborn, Domville, and I are writing up a report of what has happened to you. We intend to submit it to the Admiralty upon our return to England. We have enough evidence for courts martial of Belcher, Roberts, and McCoy without testimony from you, but the case against them would be much more damning with it. The Admiralty is prejudiced toward the superior officer in cases involving discipline or the possible abuse of power. You have the advantage of not being in Her Majesty's service, even though being a stowaway puts you in a bad light. We cannot deny that Belcher had the right to put you under arrest, but arrest does not give license to abuse. We can talk about this again later, but please give some thought to making a report.'

'I don't have to, Sir.'

'No, you don't...'

'What I mean is I don't have to think about it. If by giving a statement or being a witness I can prevent this from happening to anyone else, then I will do it. I don't know if I am the first, but I want to be the last. Commander Belcher took great a pleasure in what he did. He won't stop on his own. If he can't stop himself, we must.'

'I can tell you that you are not the first; I was on board *Aetna* when he destroyed a man. In a navy where there is nothing on earth so much like God as a captain on board his ship, Belcher was actually court martialed for the way he treated his men. When I discovered I was to serve under him again, I feared he would still have the same sadistic streak that causes him to take pleasure in the suffering he inflicts on others. This brutalisation confirms my worst fears. A man like Belcher cannot change. I only hope the Admiralty does more than slap his hands this time.'

⚓⚓⚓⚓⚓

Resolute and *Intrepid* had left Beechey Island at 2:00 p.m. on the 16th of August, spending their first night in Assistance Bay. For two days they progressed slowly westward accompanied by beautifully clear weather, though without wind, so *Intrepid* had to take *Resolute* in tow. They encountered loose ice and numerous walrus and seal. At midday on the 19th, when they were working against a strong tide running from the West, a SW breeze sprang up with every sign that it was freshening and the ships were able to make sail. By 3:00 p.m., however, the weather had thickened and forced the ships to beat slowly to windward, tacking frequently to avoid the large bodies of ice. Though the weather cleared by 9:00 that evening, their passage west was now almost entirely blocked and they made fast for the night.

That one night became many. Every day Kellett climbed to the highest pinnacle on the floe to check the state of the ice. Every day he could see no lead. On the fifth day, Kellett busied the men with watering the ship from a pool of water they found. He instructed Pim to have them work watch and watch, night and day, getting all the casks full as quickly as possible so that they would be able to take advantage of any opening as soon as it appeared. It took two days to complete the watering of both ships and still there was no passage to westward. Every day Kellett sought the highest pinnacle and every day he returned without joy.

No passage. The young ice was forming quickly now, trapping pools of water, which in turn froze solid with a smooth surface. Kellett, always keen to take advantage of an opportunity for the men to have fun, sent the men out of the ships and onto the frozen pools for an afternoon of sliding about and skating. Pim and McDougall organised a rather ridiculous game of tug of war and a game of crack the whip. And even Naps tried to join in the fun, skidding on the ice as he chased the men.

It was not until the early morning of the 28th, the ninth day of being ice bound, that Kellett returned from the high bluff with the news that he saw passage to Griffiths Island and, beyond the island, a way into a large expanse of open water. The ships made sail at half seven with a fine westerly breeze and reached open water at half two after pushing their way through heavy pack. They then hauled up to the wind and lay the course for Point Sheringham.

By 6:00 p.m., they found they could do no more by beating to windward so they furled the sails and *Intrepid* took *Resolute* in tow. They steamed their way between Browne and Somerville Islands. Soon they were able once again to make sail. In a short time the ship was on a starboard tack with fore and aft sails drawing, the wind NW and fresh at about 17 or 18 knots with occasional showers of snow. After passing Browne Island, the ships ran into a heavy swell from the NW, which proceeded right out of the sound named after *Resolute's* own Master McDougall. It was a curious phenomenon, too large to have been caused by the tide and no one could quite explain it until Lieutenant Pim smiled at George Frederick and said, 'I think your sound is welcoming you back!'

The spirits of the officers and crew lifted with the change in their fortune and their ability to make passage. Captain Kellett was aware of the way their temperaments had been affected by having been ice bound and having to work so hard for such negligible progress, but there was little he could do other than offer encouragement. Sailing in the Arctic Ocean always seemed to go from one extreme to the other, more so than in any other sea with the exception, perhaps, of sailing in the deep Southern Ocean. Even the experienced Arctics were not immune to the effects of that uncompromising harshness. He was glad to see that they were just as susceptible to the beauty of the place and the joy of sailing free as they had been to the gloom caused by their difficulties. The men were cheerful again. Fair Abe was mending in body and spirit. Even *Resolute* seemed happier as she met each wave. Kellett, walking the quarterdeck alone, smiled to himself and savoured this moment of contentment.

⚓⚓⚓⚓⚓

Alice and Margaret's crossing of the Irish Sea was smooth and uneventful. The *London* was due to leave Liverpool Dock for America on August 28th, weather permitting. However, after they arrived in the city the weather took a turn for the worse and they arrived in their stateroom cold, wet and tired. Upon entering, they found vases of fresh roses and a telegram from Henry Grinnell, the ship's owner, welcoming them aboard. Before even having a chance to unpack, they were surprised by a knock on their door. The steward asked if all was satisfactory and then extended to them the captain's invitation to dine with him the first night out of Liverpool.

It was not until their sixth day aboard, the morning of September third, that the steam tender towed *London* down the Mersey. Margaret was keen to meet the captain and to see with whom they might be dining on their first evening at sea. Despite her father being a sea captain, she had never sailed before and every thing about the ship fascinated her. She was also looking forward to meeting her fellow passengers, to see if there were any young women her age she could befriend. She wanted to discover why others were making this trip to America.

Margaret did not usually care that much about her dress, spending most of her time as she did with her horses, but this night she took some care to choose her moss green dress with the black velvet collar and cuffs. It flattered her so, complementing her colouring: her auburn hair, blue eyes and fresh complexion.

Alice Kellett looked as stunning as her daughter, her red velvet dress highlighting her thick blonde hair, braided and wrapped around her head. Both women enjoyed the appreciative glances they received from the men in the dining room. Their life in Clonacody was devoid of this kind of attention. Most of the men they knew at home still struggled to accept these two headstrong and independent women, beautiful though they were.

'You are most welcome aboard, Mrs. Kellett and Miss Kellett.' Captain Hulbut greeted his first guests to the table. 'Do you find your rooms sufficient unto the day?'

'Yes, thank you,' Alice Kellett replied. 'We were most delighted with the flowers and the telegram from Mr. Grinnell. Does he always welcome his passengers thus?'

'I must confess that he has asked me to treat you as his personal guests. He is very keen, is our Mr. Grinnell, to honour your husband. He has an avid interest in exploration, above all exploration in the Arctic. Did you know that, in 1850, he used his private funds to underwrite an expedition to search for the lost Franklin? He keeps abreast of the news regarding anything Arctic, particularly the expeditions that are continuing the Franklin search. Therefore, you see, when he established that yourselves were none other than the wife and daughter of Captain Kellett, of HMS *Resolute,* he ordered me to treat you as his very honoured guests.'

'We certainly appreciate his personal interest in our well-being on this voyage. It is our first time crossing the Atlantic, and, though we both enjoy adventure, we admit to a certain amount of anxiety. Strange for a sea captain's wife and daughter you may think!'

'I say it is quite natural to feel some fear, or at least apprehension. The sea can be a formidable foe should she chose to rise up, but you are as safe as any can be. Our firm, Grinnell, Minturn and Company, is among the most powerful and wealthy of the American shipping firms, you know. I am proud to say we hold the record for the fastest clipper ship sailing time between New York and San Francisco, a record we established last year with our ship *Flying Cloud.* We ply the waters regularly between Great Britain and the United States, bringing immigrants and wealthy passengers to the New World. I've been at it many a year myself, and our master, Mr. Fredrick Hebard, has been with this very ship since she was launched in 1847. We know our ship, we do, and the waters we are sailing on. We will do our best to take good care of you.'

Two elderly sisters and a very serious looking young man soon joined the Kelletts. The captain introduced him as Mr. Carl Schurz, a young aristocrat from Germany.

Mr Schurz kissed the hands of Alice and Margaret in greeting, and looked into their eyes with a piercing, searching gaze. He was a very handsome man, with dark moustache and brown curly hair, aquiline nose and strong chin. He spoke little during the main course, but listened attentively to all that was said. Margaret felt herself flush each time she glanced toward him.

Margaret had never been shy, and had been looking forward to asking Captain Hulbut more about the ship and his experiences. Yet, in the presence of this quiet man she found herself at a loss for words. She studied her food instead, watching her hands as she ate. Alice Kellett, having discovered that their female companions were Quakers, was talking about her American friend and their work together during the Famine.

'The ship we sail in tonight was built in 1847 and was in service with the firm through those dismal years. While other shipping firms used that disaster to pursue solely financial gain, our firm's partner Robert Minturn, a devote Quaker, insisted that the steerage class have greater room, ventilation and provisions.' The captain paused to motion the waiters forward to clear the table for pudding. 'I felt we should have used the space more economically, but have to admit the percentage of Irish dying en route was significantly lower with Grinnell and Minturn than with any other firm.'

'Surely you cannot mean that you would have preferred sailing a 'coffin' ship? I have heard that some ship's lost ten to twenty percent of their steerage passengers,' Alice replied.

'With all due respect, madam, from what I have heard most would have died anyway, being sick with fever.'

'I, and many like me, worked hard to keep body and soul together for many of these unfortunate poor. My husband helped to pay passage for the families that lived on our estate who wanted to leave. I hate to think, through the selfishness of others, that they all could perish before reaching America. They left us with such a painful mixture of despair and hope that one could only wish the best for them.'

'Please, Madam, I did not mean to offend you; certainly I also wished them the best. Either way I got paid. And the firm still added considerably to their fortunes during those years.'

'I, too, have seen suffering,' the quiet man spoke haltingly. 'I thought our conditions bad in Germany until I read about Famine. Our...how do you say...difficulties were man-made, liberty held for ruling class. I was born in castle, but do not feel free if brothers are not.'

'You sound like an abolitionist,' one of the Quaker sisters said.

'I do not know this word.'

'An abolitionist is someone who believes the slaves in America should be freed.'

'I do not wish to say bad against new country, but I flee my old for zis beliefs. Zis Abolitions, are all Quackers such?' Mr. Schurz did not understand the barely suppressed laughter that went round the table. 'Did I speech wrong?'

'Just a small mispronunciation, but with a very big difference in meaning,' Alice spoke kindly. 'Quakers are members of the Religious Society of Friends, who work to relieve suffering and to help peoples be equal, and free. A quacker is a duck!'

'I sorry, Quaker, Quaker. Danke, danke. So much to learn vis zis English speaks.' Carl, having finished his dinner, and being embarrassed by his deficiency in the language, stood, asked to be excused from the captain, and with a bow to each woman, left the dining room.

'Mother, what did he mean by that, about fleeing Germany?'

'Margaret, I believe our young man is more than he may seem. You may not remember, but during the height of the Famine, there was great unrest in Europe. There was much republicanism bantered about after the French drove away Louis Philippe and proclaimed a Republic in 1848. This sparked an uprising in Germany, primarily among the students. Judging by the age he appears, our Mr. Schurz may have been one of those students.'

Margaret blushed and then was immediately angry for doing so. Could this aristocratic gentleman really be a rebel? He did not look like someone who would scream in the streets for… 'What were they fighting for exactly?'

'Perhaps you should ask him yourself,' her mother replied.

'I could hardly do that!'

Several days later, Margaret did pluck up her courage to speak with Carl Schurz when they were both taking air on deck. He seemed interested in talking with her but his frustration with the language barrier was evident.

'I could give you English lessons! Why not? We have days and days ahead of us, it will help me to pass the time. And you will have to learn it sooner or later if you plan to stay in America.'

'It is kind off you. I vould like very much.'

So they began their lessons that morning. Carl was quick to understand names for things, and the more he learned, the more Margaret learned about him.

'Zis is difficult for me; I speak very good in German. Many listened to me when I speech.'

'Spoke,' Margaret corrected him. Speech is a noun. Speak is the present tense of the verb, spoke is the past.'

'When I spoke, thanks you.'

Carl told her about his time at the University of Bonn, the idealism he and his fellow students felt, the excitement of knowing a new Germany was theirs to create. They had optimistically talked of an end to oppression: freedom of speech and press, the right to assemble freely, free elections. They wanted nothing less than a Constitutional government, democracy.

'What happened?'

'I vas in prison put. At Rastatt. I escaped, to Switzerland. The Germany I dream is not yet being. My family help me with many monies there. I come to England, now I am going America.'

For Schurz his idealism was as strong as ever and Margaret felt it in every thing he said. What made him a radical in his homeland was the desire for things she took for granted everyday. She was beginning to admire him for his principled life. He could have isolated himself from the trouble with his money and privilege, in that respect he reminded her of her mother. She began to tell him about her mother's work, how she did not accept the class distinctions at home, midwife to any woman who needed her care.

Margaret really hadn't thought much about these issues, she had always lived through and for her horses. But getting to know Carl forced her to examine herself, and when she did she saw a self absorbed and shallow young woman. She did not like what she saw, and worried that Carl would see her in the same light. She wanted more than anything for him to like her, but the only way she could talk about the issues that were so important to him was by telling more stories about her mother. She thought he was very polite to ask so many questions about Mother's work and beliefs, and to speak with such admiration.

Every day Margaret brought anecdotes about her mother to Carl, and brought her mother stories about her student. Alice heard an enthusiasm in the young woman's voice that had never been there before when she talked about a man, and she wondered if Margaret was attracted to him. Through her daughter's eyes she began to share the admiration and affection Margaret felt for her pupil. A week into their voyage Alice and Carl were in the library looking for something interesting to read.

'I vas wishing there to be a book in German,' Carl said in greeting. 'It vould be better for me to read in English, but harder working!'

'Margaret tells me you are progressing rapidly with your study of the language, but it must be so frustrating for you.'

'I have many things I vant to say, but I sound stupid struggling vis words. I no stupid, but you can't tell zis.'

'Oh, Mr. Schurz, I do not for a minute think you are anything less than a very intelligent man. The stories Margaret tells me about your student days, your struggles, political ideals, the way she describes how so many listened to you and followed you when you protested the old ways of privilege and tyranny…why, without having spoken to you a great deal myself, I have grown to admire you very much.'

Carl listened without embarrassment to Alice speaking; he was not troubled with a false sense of modesty. But was she only responding to his ideas, he wondered, or to him as a man? He watched her face as she spoke, not hearing her words so much as watching her lips move, seeing the brightness in her eyes, and the curve of her cheek. He listened to her breathing, saw her breasts rise and fall, felt the cadence of her lilting voice surrounding him. Several minutes later he realised with a start that Mrs. Kellett had stopped talking and was looking at him, as though in expectation of an answer to a question he had not heard.

'How foolish of me speaking so fast when you must be struggling to understand my words! I was asking about your family, is someone waiting for you in America? Or will anyone be joining you later? What are your plans once you arrive?'

'No family is coming with me, but many of students and families are in state of Wisconsin. I think I going there. I vant to study law: to be a part of justice in my new country. You say you like my idealisms, but for me they are like the stars. I do not believe I will ever be able to touch them, but they are my guides. Just like stars for the ship's mens. By the light of my idealisms stars I hope I will reach my goals. I only struggle along, and sometimes the struggle is, how do you say, lonesomeness.

'Margaret tells me about your workings in Famine and the peoples, the womens. You do not keep separate, keep a distance, like the other English, though your...mm... is the word...position...would allow you to. It must cause difficults amongst your English, treating the Irish as Margaret says you do. I think you are very much like me.'

'I believe all people are equal in the eyes of the Lord. My Quaker friend refers to it as "God's light is in everyone." I do cause resentment on occasion, I can tell you, but I just don't believe I am better than my neighbours, whatever their situation. Actually, I experience the most difficulty when I am managing our estate in my husband's absence. My neighbours believe I should have a man overseeing it, but I enjoy doing it myself. I think the men don't know quite what to do with me!'

'Why are you going to America, Mrs. Kellett?'

'We are visiting my Quaker friend, the one I spoke about at dinner the first night, and her family in New London, Connecticut. This is the first time we are visiting the United States. We may even do some touring, but for now we plan to spend a few months with the Abrahams. I have not seen Martha for many years, but she has just had her eighth child, though they lost one baby a long time ago so now have seven living. Now there is a strong woman!'

'Do I understand your husband is in Arctic exploring? Will he come to you?'

'No, I will not see him again for a long time. It may be two or three years before he returns from this expedition. If they do find the men they are looking for I suppose it could be sooner, but he was expecting to have to winter over at least once and probably more. We will be waiting for him at our home Clonacody in Ireland.'

Alice could see Carl's look of bewilderment. She knew it was difficult for people who do not come from a naval family to understand how a wife could be content with her husband's long absences. He must be completely baffled by me, she thought. Alice and Carl continued reading the titles of the books on the library shelves, a companionable silence between them.

On the twelfth of September the *London* encountered an ominous sky. The glass started dropping and the wind picked up. At first the passengers were allowed to go on deck, but Captain Hulbut saw all the signs that this was going to be a severe storm. During breakfast he warned the Kellett women to get some air on deck while they still could as he would soon be asking all passengers to return to their cabins. Margaret and Carl decided to cancel their English lesson for the day.

Alice and Margaret went to their rooms and bundled themselves up for a brisk walk on deck. The air was invigorating under the threatening sky and Margaret whooped with excitement. The wind whipped her face as she ran along the deck. Alice cautioned her to be careful, but the girl felt as wild as the weather. The sea began to rise, however, and the deck pitched and rolled. With the salt spray stinging their eyes, both women thought it prudent to go below. Alice Kellett lost her footing going down the stairs. Margaret tried to catch her, but Mother fell to the bottom of the steps, knocking herself unconscious. Margaret ran for help and the first person she found was Carl Schurz who was coming up on deck. He quickly followed her and picked Alice up, carrying her in his arms to her cabin. He sent Margaret off in search of the ship's surgeon.

Carl gently laid Alice on her bed and loosened her cloak and blouse so that she could breathe more easily, then soaked a flannel in cold water and placed it on her head. Waiting for the doctor, he held her hand. The short time it took the Doctor and Margaret to return seemed like an eternity, and yet they came too soon. For in that time the young man realised he had deep feelings for Alice. The awareness of this came as a shock to him. A married woman who was how many years older than he was? What did he really know about her? The daily stories he heard made him feel he knew her quite well, but why didn't he feel this way for the daughter? He spent so much more time with her and she clearly fancied him. What an impossible situation! He ruled his life with his intellect, yet here was his heart beating rapidly as he watched her face, looking for any sign of consciousness. Waiting for her to waken, he felt an overwhelming desire to kiss her, but as he bent over her to press his lips to her forehead Margaret returned with the doctor.

Carl stepped away so that the doctor could examine the patient and Margaret caught his eye. He looked away, guiltily, said he should leave them now, and turned to go. Margaret caught his arm.

'Thank you, Carl, for helping us. Mother will be thankful as well when she recovers. Shall I let you know what the doctor says?'

'Yes, please. Danke. Thank you. I was pleased I could help, and I hope she will be good soon.' Carl looked away, unable to meet the young girl's eyes. Margaret closed the door quietly after he left wondering what had made him act so strangely.

Alice awoke while the doctor was examining her. 'Mrs. Kellett, I am afraid you have bruised yourself badly but there are no broken bones. We must watch you to see if you are concussed, but I believe you will mend! Keep to your bed for a few days so your body can heal, you have sprained your ankle and bruised several ribs. Keep your ankle elevated on cushions, and I will give you some laudanum to ease your pain. I will let the captain know you are to receive your meals in your rooms and I will check on you in a few hours. If you begin to see double images send your daughter for me at once. Miss Kellett, please, if your mother should fall asleep, do not let her sleep longer than an hour and if you cannot wake her come and find me immediately. Good day, ladies.' The doctor packed his bag and took his leave.

'Oh, Margaret, I feel such a fool! With this weather I am not too unhappy to be tucked up under the covers, but I just hate being waited on.'

'Never mind Mother, I am happy to stay with you. I can read to you and we will weather the storm together.'

Margaret sat in the chair that Carl had placed next to the bed and opened the book her mother had been reading the night before.

'I am sorry to interrupt you, dear, but how in heavens name did you get me back to our rooms?'

'I ran into Mr. Schurz and he carried you. He is very kind. Mother, I don't know what is wrong with me, sometimes I feel so stupid when I am with him. I stumble over my words and am certain he thinks I am a silly girl for the number of times I blush when we talk. Sometimes I feel so shy around him, but other times it is easy to be with him. I do feel confident I am helping him with his English, and he listens attentively to the stories I share about you. I can't help feeling I am a shallow person compared to him. I am just realizing how little attention I have paid to the issues that inflame him so. I want to understand and feel the same passionate indignity over injustice, but all I have ever done is play with horses!'

'Firstly, my darling, you do much more than play with horses! You have an unusual gift and I have always encouraged you to use your talent. Do not denigrate what you can do and have done just because you are beginning to see that you want to broaden your self and your understanding of the world. You are a very sensitive and deep young woman, and you could not do what you do with the horses if you were not. Secondly, this single focus you have had does not make you shallow. You will bring your depth of feeling to everything you encounter. Now is the time, perhaps, for you to learn about social issues. I did try, perhaps too efficiently, too shelter you from the horrors of the Famine, but you were very young, too young I felt, to see such suffering. I believe your Mr. Schurz is an excellent teacher in this regard and that you are both benefiting from your daily lessons. Maybe you are a little in love with him?'

'What I feel is so tormenting it can't be love! Love should feel good, shouldn't it?'

Alice patted her daughter's hand. 'Yes, it does feel good, but it can be tormenting at the same time. Love is very difficult to pin down to any one definition! Don't worry; your feelings will sort themselves out in time. Let us read for a while.'

Margaret read to her mother until she fell asleep. Doing what the doctor had told her to do she did not let her fall into a deep sleep, but woke her every hour until the steward brought them their dinner.

𝓮𝓮𝓮𝓮𝓮

McDougall recorded a thick fog in the logbook on the morning of August 31st that lifted by midday. When it cleared, the ships were two degrees off Cape Gillman. They had hoped to make passage around this point but the ice was set close in and there was no chance of a passage round. The ice was fast from Point Langley to Graham Moore Bay, but finally clear passage opened through Byam Martin Channel. They cast off the towing ropes and *Resolute* made sail.

A T'gallant watchman spotted Melville Island from the crow's nest. Many of the men eagerly climbed the rigging to see the land that had only been approached through this channel once before by ship many years ago. The knowledge that they were the first to follow in Parry's wake filled many of them with pride in their captain and pride in their own service on this mission.

On the 2nd of September, the ships landed near Point Palmer. It was a beautifully clear and calm evening. Mates Roche and Nares went for a short walk after the hawsers were secure and the sails re-furled to Lieutenant Mecham's satisfaction. It was unusual for the two mates to be off watch at the same time, and they were enjoying each other's company. To the West they could see Cape Bounty so distinctly that every object on the shore stood out in bold relief. As they walked up to the top of a small hummock, Nares grabbed Roche's arm.

'Look, Richard! What're they?'

Half a dozen large animals were slowly moving along the ice toward the land. 'Those, my friend, are muskoxen, and I believe we just found some fresh meat for tomorrow's dinner!'

The two mates returned to the ship with their news and Lieutenant Mecham informed Captain Kellett. He gave the task of assembling a hunting party to Mecham, an undertaking that turned out to be much more difficult than it seemed it would be. The excitement of a hunt spread quickly through the crews, and too many of them wanted to join the sortie. The men were so eager for the kill that McDougall noted wryly in his journal that evening...

> '...This feeling must be attributed partly to the imperfection of human nature, and partly to a longing for fresh beef. Indeed the observation which originated in the last expedition might safely be applied to this, viz., 'That every man would shoot his own father if he could be converted into *fresh* meat.''

The party went out, returning to the place Roche and Nares had been when they spotted the animals, and found the oxen grazing quietly along the ridge that formed the edge of the land. Four of the muskoxen quickly fell to the hunters' marksmanship and the men brought the fresh meat on board. The crews of both ships savoured the evening's meal and felt rejuvenated by the feast. Even Napoleon enjoyed the treat of the fresh offal.

Resolute and *Intrepid* continued their journey along the coast of Melville Island and their expected winter quarters. There were days when the ice opened and the breeze was favourable; on these days, they were able to make good progress under sail. On one such day, a strong North wind opened a lead all the way to Cape Bounty and *Resolute* sailed through it. Other days the ice closed in, sometimes making it necessary for the men to cut a dock to prevent the ships from being crushed. Fog, cloud, and storm beset them, and then they were blessed with the clearest of skies. At every stop, they set up cairns of supplies with details of their log and their expected itinerary.

The ships were working their way up toward Winter Harbour.

Eventually, with the thermometer dropping quickly and the danger rising of the ice closing in around him, the ships headed for Dealy Island. Her Majesty's Discovery Ship *Resolute* and Her Majesty's Steam Tender *Intrepid* reached their winter quarters on 10 September 1852: Lat. 74°56'N. Long. 198°53' one half mile ESE of the eastern most Point of Dealy Island. The preparations for the coming months of darkness began almost immediately.

CHAPTER EIGHT
SEPTEMBER - NOVEMBER 1852

The ice quartermasters and the men from the fo'c'sle watches began cutting the dock, and 'Stoneman' Wilkie resumed his role as shantyman to the sawyers. After the dock was finished, he continued singing in his deep bass voice as the men hauled the ships into the place that would be their winter home. The men answered his call in chorus.

Cutting the dock and making fast the ships were just the beginning of the work needed to prepare for the months of inhospitable darkness that lay ahead. In the following days, Kellett divided the overseeing of the preparations between Lieutenants Mecham and Pim. Under Lieutenant Mecham's direction the sawyers cut blocks of ice, and the gunners dragged the ship's boats on shore and unpacked the travelling sledges. As the sawyers cut the blocks of ice, the gunners and the fo'c'sle men loaded them onto the sledges and hauled them to the ships' sides. The men lined the blocks up outside *Resolute's* wooden sides. The Irish and Scottish contingents of the ship's company worked on the starboard side. Working like bricklayers the men built a wall of ice around the ship, joining the top of it to the rail of the upper deck. As the men completed each section of the wall, they also shovelled snow into the space behind it created by the curve of the hull. *Intrepid's* men did the same for their ship. The winter homes began to look increasingly like igloos, with the five feet thick walls of ice and snow insulating the ships from the wind and extreme cold of the coming months.

While Mecham's men laboured with these tasks Lieutenant Pim's team of bo's'n's mates, top men, mizzen men, marines and carpenters were working aboard *Resolute.* At the sound of the bo's'n's call the foretop, maintop and mizzen men ascended the rigging of their respective masts. The men furled the t'gallants tightly to their yards and, at the bo's'n's command to cross the yards, they hauled the yards square using the lower lifts and upper braces until the upper yardarm was level with the crosstrees and the men in the tops could reach the lower yardarm. Once the yards were vertical, the call was given for them to be sent down: the fore and mizzen yards going down to port and the main to starboard.

The men worked quickly, efficiently, and silently. The work was completed when all the yards were sent down and the t'gallant and topmasts housed; the jib and square sails, the driver and trysails unbent and stowed; the trysail masts unshipped.

Work then began on roofing in the upper deck. The carpenters used the trysail masts & studdingsail booms as ridgepoles for the housing stops. They measured and cut the wood for rafters as well as the end frames that were to be placed at the fore and mizzenmasts. A couple of the marines then carried the lumber to the carpenter's mates and their two assistants. The air filled with the sound of sawing and hammering and the smell of newly sawn wood. When the carpenter's mates completed the construction of the roof, six of the marines spread and secured canvas over the rafters.

Lieutenant Pim sent the now idle top men below to retrieve lanterns. They filled, trimmed, and hung them from the rafters of the new roof while the carpenters tightly caulked the forward hatchway. After all these preparations, the sawyers, long since done with their job of cutting blocks of ice, spread a thick layer of snow on the upper deck. Some shovelled the snow and others trod upon it until they had covered the deck with nine inches of tightly packed snow.

All the preparations made sense to young Nares, but this last activity confused him no end. When the icemen began topping the snow with a layer of gravel and water, he gave up trying to understand it at all and turned away. McDougall noticed the puzzled look on the mate's face.

'We use the upper deck for exercise. The water will freeze and the gravel in it will give us good traction. We will be less likely to break our necks while we're trying to stay fit.'

'But why spread the layer of snow in the first place?' Nares queried.

'Same reason we hauled all that ice and snow to *Resolute's* sides. It helps keep the heat inside below deck where we'll be doing most of our living.'

Nares just shook his head. It seemed to him that an awful lot of effort had just gone into keeping the snow off the upper deck. It still did not make much sense to him to spread so much of it around after all that work.

On the fourth day in their winter quarters, Captain Kellett met with Francis Leopold McClintock, commander of HMS *Intrepid,* Lieutenants Mecham, Pim, Hamilton, and DeBray and Mates Nares. The men assembled in the captain's cabin.

Commander McClintock had just celebrated his thirty-third birthday. He had a thoughtful face with high cheekbones and deep-set eyes surrounded by dark curly hair. Francis was the oldest surviving son of Henry and Elizabeth McClintock. His father, a former dragoon guard, and a poor man with a large family, had not been pleased when his son said in 1830 that he wanted to join the Royal Navy. Though poor, the family was closely knit by a deeply felt and often expressed affection. Francis would be dearly missed. Besides, a peacetime Navy was not the place to create a career and Henry had hoped, before he died, he would see his heir distinguish himself and bring honour to the family name in a more promising profession. The young man was bright and showed considerable promise. It seemed a wasteful mistake for him to be buried in the Navy, a Navy that still had men at the head of the captain's list who had reached post-rank after the battle of Trafalgar.

However, Francis had been doggedly tenacious and determined to go to sea. Despite his father's reservations, Francis had his wish and entered the Navy in 1831 at twelve years of age, to serve on HMS *Samarang*. He passed his examination in 1838 to become an acting mate. Henry McClintock's fears for his son appeared proved true because Francis became a mate at a time when promotion in the Royal Navy was slow and uncertain; he remained a mate for almost seven years.

Francis had finally received promotion to lieutenant in 1845 and had first served in the Arctic in 1848 in HMS *Enterprise* under Captain Sir James Clark Ross. During his second Arctic voyage, as a member of the Austin Expedition of 1850, he had served as first lieutenant in HMS *Assistance*. It was at this time that he had started gaining a reputation for being a noteworthy arctic traveller. The demands of Arctic seamanship seemed to utilise the same personality traits that had occasionally exasperated his father: indefatigable tenacity and strong-willed perseverance. In the winter and spring of 1851, McClintock had completed a precedent-setting sledging journey, covering a staggering 760 miles in 80 days. Promoted to commander upon his return to England, he now served in that capacity under Captain Kellett.

Kellett could not have asked to have a better man as his second in command. Francis possessed a self-assurance that was born of his ability to honestly assess his strengths and weaknesses. What he did not know he either learned quickly or left to others. What he did know he put to good use, and whatever tasks he completed he completed conscientiously. A simple enough formula for success, Kellett thought to himself, yet one that was not all that easily put into practice and was difficult to find in very many people.

Captain Kellett cleared his throat. 'I am sending out four travelling parties to build and provision supply depots for the spring sledging expeditions. You must begin your preparations immediately and be ready to leave by the last week of the month. You should then have enough time to complete your journeys and return to the ships before the winter sets in.'

He spread a map of Melville Island on the table pointing out the routes he intended his officers to take.

'Mr. McClintock, you will travel west and north with Dr. Scott and nine men to the head of Liddon Gulf. I also want you to take Nares with you. He has much to learn before leading his own team in the spring. Mr. Mecham, you will take our French volunteer and nine men Southwest around the coast. If you are able to reach the mouth of Liddon's Gulf, you must place your cairn there. Pim, I want you and your men to first retrieve the musk ox McClintock killed a few days ago near Bridport Inlet. After your return with the meat, you will follow the coastline west and join Lt. Mecham's party. Hamilton, you will travel along the coast to the east, around Palmer Point and into Skene

Bay, and then proceed northward as far as possible into the Sabine Peninsula before building your cairn and depositing your supplies. Are there any questions?'

Kellett looked expectantly at each of his officers. They were all experienced Arctics and they knew the dangers that lay ahead. Only one of them, Commander McClintock, looked convinced about the sanity of this notion of autumn travelling.

It was a recent innovation in Arctic exploration for sledging parties to be organised in the autumn after the securing of winter quarters. The pioneer of this technique was Commander McClintock himself. During the 1850 expedition, he had worn his commander down with a persistent belief in his idea to use the autumn for sending out travelling parties to forward depots of provisions for the following spring sledging teams. No one believed that venturing out in the twilight before winter was something a sane man would do. Undaunted, McClintock continued to lobby for making use of what he considered a wasted opportunity. While his superior officers remained unconvinced, he had used his time alone in his cabin to redesign the structure and weight of the sledges minimising the effort and time needed to travel a greater distance. Mecham had been part of the seven-day experiment to which Austin had finally agreed. To McClintock's delight, and the relief of the men, it had been a complete success.

'Mr. McClintock has carried on with his innovations for fall sledge travel. We will put into practice some of his new ideas for victualling and housing the men when you are encamped en route. The Navy has supplied us with the tents he designed, which are lighter and take up less space when packed on the sledges than the tents with which you are familiar. He assures me they will also make setting up and breaking down camp much quicker and easier.'

Lieutenant Hamilton, who usually kept his face free from emotion, looked apprehensive as he waited for his captain's dismissal. He could not even look up for fear that his captain would see he thought him demented to be ordering them out like this into the darkness. Lieutenant Mecham did not look very happy either.

'Captain Kellett, Sir, I do not intend to question your orders. However, the men, myself included, who returned successfully from autumn sledging in the 1850 expedition, only went out for seven days. The travel you are proposing could take three times as long. Are you confident the weather will hold?'

'I cannot make any guarantees to you, Mr. Mecham. You know that, but you must remember we are balancing our personal safety against the possibility that any time lost could mean the difference between life and death for Franklin and his men, as well as for the McClure and Collinson Expeditions. Your success this autumn will give the spring sledging parties that much more of a range for travelling when they set out next year. Our ships are secure, and we simply cannot waste this valuable time.'

The cabin was silent. Mate Nares looked nervously at the faces of his superior officers.

'Any other questions?'

Commander McClintock glanced at Mecham, Pim, and Hamilton. 'No questions, Sir.'

'Dismissed.'

⚓⚓⚓⚓⚓

The following days passed quickly for Fair Abe, joining in as he did with the others working to get the ships ready for winter, or assisting in the preparation of the travelling teams. He helped the men gather food and other supplies for the depots, as well as camping gear, medical supplies and twenty-five days of food. The day before the parties were to leave a heavy gale struck, creating deep snowdrifts, yet the provisioning continued. Captain Kellett did not waver in his decision to send the men.

September 22nd, the morning of the sledge parties' departure, arrived with clear skies and a light breeze. Fair Abe, the Resolutes and Intrepids gathered on the ice at half seven and Captain Kellett led the ships' companies in a short prayer, then he addressed the men.

'Your work in the next weeks will greatly further the cause of our search for the lost men and on you are riding our hopes for success.' The men cheered. 'I know you will do your best to reach your destinations. Every man here will benefit greatly in the spring from the work you do now.' The enthusiasm of the ships' companies drowned Kellett's voice and he paused while the men roared their encouragement. 'We all wish you God's speed in your travelling and await your safe return. Now, lads, a hearty farewell!'

Fair Abe shouted 'huzzah' with the others and the travellers departed amidst the enthusiastic hollers from the men they were leaving behind. The sense of optimism generated by the captain's words and the kind weather served to dispel most of the apprehension they felt about the lateness of the season and they set out with high spirits.

Lieutenant Pim had to return, however, within two days because there was no ice that could be safely travelled upon near Cape Providence. By midday on the twenty-fourth, a violent Northerly gale descended upon the ships causing a white-out of thickly falling snow. The bitterly cold winds drove the snow into deep drifts and everyone was apprehensive about the safety of the sledging parties. Kellett did not let Pim leave the ship to join Mecham as he had previously ordered him to do.

Alone in his cabin, the captain sat with bowed head, oppressed by the solitary mantle of authority that had settled as heavily onto his shoulders as the snow had settled around the ships. If he had seen any sign that the weather was going to deteriorate this quickly he would not have sent the men out, something he could confess to himself but to no one else. He alone was responsible for whatever now befell the travellers, and his concern deepened as the storm worsened. Naps nudged his master's elbow in sympathy. Kellett smiled. He didn't know how Napoleon always knew when he was feeling low or lonely, but his loyal friend constantly reminded him he was not as alone as he felt.

To relieve his mind he called Fair Abe to his cabin. Fair Abe enjoyed talking with the captain. They discussed everything from Shakespeare to abolition. He felt flattered by the attention that Kellett gave him, hoping it would not upset any of the men. Sometimes, he felt better understood by this man than his own father. It was certainly easier to disagree without getting angry. But they rarely did differ. Kellett shared the young man's view that slavery should be abolished quickly and forever. Fair Abe still contended that the South could not possibly justify war over this issue, but it was there that the older man's experience bade him speak against his guest.

'You must understand, Fair Abe, that men have fought wars over much less than this. They may disguise it, pretend the issue is something else, but if they either believe strongly in the institution, or know they will suffer serious financial ruin if it is stopped, they will fight.'

'Thou makest it sound like a financial matter, not a moral one.'

'It is a moral issue with financial repercussions. And there are men more moved by money than morals. There is always a financial side to war.'

While Captain Kellett and Fair Abe discussed these issues, Hamilton's trip was proving short and disastrous. After his return, Abe listened while he told the story of their fatal trip.

'Just before the full force of the storm's fury engulfed us, my sledge broke through the ice, an accident that cost me the life of one of my men. As the sledge plummeted into the water, it dragged Tom Mobley down with it. His heart proved incapable of coping with the shock of the freezing water and by the time the others had pulled Tom out he was dead.' Hamilton looked completely demoralised. 'I cannot tell you how upset I was that the expedition's first loss of life should have happened on my watch. I turned the team back toward the haven of *Resolute's* wooden walls.

'No one saw or heard us searching for the ship during the storm. Unable to find my bearings with zero visibility, I had my exhausted men set up camp, which in the gale force winds was no easy task. When the storm subsided, we were both dismayed and relieved to find ourselves only a hundred yards from the ship!'

The news of Mobley's death spread throughout the ship and the apprehension brought on by the storm deepened into sadness in the hearts of the Resolutes. Fair Abe had found Mobley to be an amicable and trustworthy fellow. It seemed to him that the officers and men had genuinely liked him. As he had been his messmate, McDougall requested and received the honour of delivering the eulogy at Mobley's funeral.

Fair Abe helped to dig the grave, which took many hours in the frozen ground, but finally the men gathered to bury their shipmate. McDougall spoke for twenty minutes concluding, '...Thomas was an upright man, beloved by his shipmates and respected by the officers. He died as he lived- a sincere

Christian and the noblest work of God: an honest man. He will be missed; but, God willing, his death will not have been suffered in vain.' After a moment of silence, Fair Abe and the men returned to their quarters, their sombre mood reflected in the painfully beautiful and mournful sound of Bryant's fiddle as he played Turlough O'Carrolan's Farewell to Music, the final notes lingering in the timbers of the ship and the hearts of the men long after the fiddle had been laid down.

⚓⚓⚓⚓⚓

After the two divisions split, and Kellett headed to the West, Belcher to the North, Osborn's worse fears proved to be unfounded. Sir Edward's spirits actually seemed to have lifted. He walked amongst the men with a benevolent smile touching the corners of his lips. He had asked his brother to write several prayers for him before he left England, and he bestowed these prayers upon the men at regular intervals. Sir Edward also gave the men morale boosting lectures any time he came across more than two men together. He frequently reminded the men that their well being on this voyage was dependant upon each of the men and officers contributing positively to the happiness of the ship. 'Very important,' he told them frequently, 'to stay away from the backbiting that can become so destructive.'

Lieutenant Sherard Osborn did not trust this new, kindly disposed leader. Before the ships had split into two squadrons he had experienced the darting sparks of Belcher's hot temper, sparks that left him feeling burned and raw. Nor could he forget what Belcher had done to Fair Abe. None of the men involved in the rescue had confronted Belcher and he had carried on as though he had never had any prey, nor that his prey had escaped.

Every time Belcher passed on a benevolent homily, Osborn saw Fair Abe's broken body or Belcher's face screwed up with anger the way he had seen it when the men did not get into Lively Harbour with out mishap. Yet, as the days passed without event, the memory of that anger receded and Osborn began to relax. He found this new Belcher so easy and friendly that he even began to question if the whole Abraham episode had really happened.

Ultimately, it was a matter of trust. It was simply too difficult to keep supporting his attitude of mistrust, and so much easier to let go of his apprehensions, lay down his armour, and join in the light and easy feeling engulfing the rest of the crew.

HMS *Assistance* and *Pioneer* made good progress toward their winter harbour destination. Everyone took the frustration and danger of Arctic sea travel in their stride; they worked hard and relaxed vigorously. With two fiddlers on board, there always seemed to be music and laughter rising from the lower decks.

Alone in his cabin, Belcher drank. He drank to lighten his mood, but gathered an angry gloom around him instead.

While her husband was settling into the relative safety of his winter quarters, Alice Kellett was approaching dangerous waters, not with the ship upon which she was travelling, but with her heart. Nothing had been said between them, and she could allow nothing to be said, but she knew. How she longed for Henry to be with her now! If he were here she would be surrounded by his love and affection and would be satisfied to be so. She loved her husband deeply and they were happy together, but he was so far away and her loneliness was getting the better of her. She did not know if she would be able to resist the magnetic pull of Carl's feeling for her.

Carl's feelings. She must be honest with herself; could she resist her own feelings for Carl? She could think of a myriad of reasons why this thing was wrong: she was a happily married woman, he was much younger, her daughter was attracted to him as well, he was leaving his old home behind, and she was simply visiting America and had no interest in leaving her home. To have an illicit affair was a sin and it would do little to honour the love, yes, she could name it love, which was growing between them.

In a week's time they expected to be docking in New York City. If only she could avoid seeing Carl during that time! It would be impossible at meal times, but then he would have no opportunity at table to declare his feelings. Meal times would be safe, but she would have to guard against any encounters where they would be alone together. And how could she hide her sentiments from Margaret? Her daughter was unusually perceptive regarding the emotional states of the people around her. It was, however, to Alice's advantage that the young woman was struggling with her own infatuation. Perhaps that would make it more difficult for her to be aware of her mother. On the other hand, it could well make her more sensitive to anything related to the object of her feelings. Alice's thoughts swirled around, making her dizzy with apprehension.

Alice had always been faithful to Henry through his many long commissions at sea. Clonacody kept her so busy there was no time to even contemplate having an affair. She had seen her mother handle the same difficulty with her father's absences, so she had known what she was getting into when she fell in love with her husband. Henry's presence on leave more than made up for the lonely times, because when ever they were reunited it was almost like being newlyweds. Henry was such a romantic! But there wasn't much temptation put in Alice's way at home, or if there had been she was always too busy to notice. Idle hands, the Devil's workshop, she thought. Ship board passion, that's all this is. Combine idleness and the romance of the sea and this is what will occur.

That evening, when she was leaving the dining room, Carl approached her and asked in a whisper if they could meet on deck. 'I think it best not,' Alice replied and she hurried to her cabin. I am acting like a foolish schoolgirl, she chided herself. I really can't spend the rest of the voyage being a furtive beastie; I will have to tell him I have no feelings for him and stop this from going any further.

She put on her cloak and gathered together the library books she had read, planning to stop in the library before going on deck to look for Carl. When she got to the library it was empty and she quickly re-shelved her books. The door opened behind her and she turned to see Carl standing in the doorway.

Alice strode to the door to go out past him, but he blocked her way.

'Please, Alice, let me talk to you. There is much I vant to say.'

'I know, Carl, but I think it is best that we leave what you are about to say alone. It can do no good.'

'I love you. There, it is done. I have said it. And I know you feel the same way, I have told it in your eyes. Zis is so, yah? No, do not speak, come.' Carl led Alice back into the library and closed the door. He took her face in his hands and kissed her. Against her intentions, she found herself kissing him back.

Suddenly Carl pushed himself away. 'Not. You are right and zis is very wrong. You are a married women and I cannot bear responsible for the destruction of a marriage. I am sorry I spoke. Please, forgives me.' Carl left her quickly before she could say anything. She had been so worried that he would pursue her despite any protest she would give, that the turn of events took her breath away. She had not wanted him to leave and now she felt bereft, the evanescent joy of his kisses leaving her lips dry and stained.

Alice kept to her room and they did not see each other again until the morning they docked in South Street Sea Port, New York. Only once had she sent a message to him, begging him to come to her cabin so that they could speak. But he did not come and he sent no return message. Her feelings were in such a state of upheaval that, when she didn't eat for three days Margaret sent for the ship's doctor. But Alice refused to see him.

Margaret did not suspect the feelings Carl had for her mother, nor her mother's for Carl. She was so wrapped up in her own first experience of love that she felt nothing but her own heartache when Carl gave no sign of returning her affection. They kept up their English lessons; this was the one claim she had on him. She was eager for the time spent in his company and he was eager to learn as much as possible before the voyage ended.

Everyone came up on deck, all drawn to the spectacle of their first glimpse of America. Alice and Margaret were standing together when Carl came up to Alice's side and covered her hand with his. Alice took her hand away and, turning toward her daughter, asked her to fetch her extra cloak from their cabin. When Margaret had gone, she turned to look toward the shore.

Carl took her hand again, and this time she did not pull away.

'Please come with me. I have plenty of monies to start my new life here. I can no longer bear the thought of doing it alone, without you. What I said is true, I love you. I vant you to be my wife.'

Alice couldn't answer him as she struggled to blink away her tears. Mustering her courage she replied, 'My husband is a good man and I love him, but you have come into my heart and I now feel that I love you too. It is true I suffer loneliness, and I long for a companion who could be by my side all the time and not so far away as often as Henry is. But our life is happy when we are together; until now it that has been enough to sustain me through the lonely days and nights.' She turned toward her lover. 'Don't you see how impossible you have made it for me to go back, or to go forward? I am lost.'

Carl saw Margaret working her way toward them through the crowded deck. He reached into his pocket and pressed a paper in Alice's hand. 'I understand you have a difficult choice to make, and I vould dishonour you if I insisted upon an answer given in haste. Nor vould I vant you to regret choosing me. This is the address of my dearest colleague in Wisconsin. He vill know vhere I am. Write to me here, and your letter will find me.' Carl embraced and released her, departing before her daughter could reach them.

Three days later the Kellett women arrived at the Fairfax Abraham home in New London, Connecticut. Alice and Martha shared a long embrace in greeting, and Alice introduced her daughter to her old friend. Sitting in the warm, plain parlour, Margaret noticed a family portrait on the wall. While they drank tea and the old friends reminisced, her eyes returned again and again to the face of the Abraham's oldest child.

'Thou hast noticed our family painting. My husband wanted it, but I laboured hard and long against it. I do not believe it is in keeping with our faith and desire for plain living. But Fairfax was so taken with the idea that I finally gave in, and now I like it very much. What dost thou think?'

'I think it is very nice. You have a very handsome family,' Margaret replied. 'I wonder what it is like to live with so many brothers and sisters. One could certainly never be lonely!'

'Shall I introduce thee to them?' Martha named each of her children in the portrait and Margaret's eyes rested again on the image of the oldest son. The artist had captured something in his eyes that intrigued her.

'Where are they all?' Alice asked. Martha explained that most of the children were at school, the youngest ones were napping, but that Fair Abe had sailed with one of the firm's whaling ships into the Arctic.

'Several of the crew returned recently to inform us that the ship had been crushed in the ice. We were very worried because Fair Abe was not among the men who returned. However, the bo's'n had a note from him for us wherein he explained he had decided to stay in the Arctic with an exploration squadron, led by a Sir Belcher.'

'My husband is a captain in that very expedition!' Alice exclaimed. 'Did he say which ship he was joining?'

'The bo's'n was rather circumspect. He gave us no details and acted rather reluctant to be very specific. Father Abraham was quite distressed by this turn of events. He is afraid Fair Abe has gotten himself into more than he can handle. He was meant to come home after one season, but now we don't know how long he will be gone.'

'If he is with Father he will be as safe as he can be. It is amazing to think that we are here with you and your son might be with Father.'

'If he is on *Resolute* I know Henry will take good care of him,' Alice added. 'Let's hope he didn't get into the way of Sir Edward. My husband has found him a most difficult man to serve under in the past. I haven't heard anything against him recently from Henry, though, so perhaps he has mellowed in his age. I am sure Fair Abe will be fine and come home with many an adventure to tell!'

That night Margaret's dreams were a jumble of images of her father, the Atlantic voyage, arctic ice, and the face of the young man in the family portrait whose eyes had so captivated her.

❦❦❦❦❦

When the weather began to clear, Captain Kellett called for Lieutenant Pim. 'I cannot insist, in the light of the death which occurred, that you follow my original order of joining Mecham's sledging team. However, I will ask you for the sake of the morale of the men on board, and the safety of the men travelling, to give it your thoughtful consideration and to tell me honestly if you feel you and your men can undertake the journey.'

'I can be ready tomorrow morning, Sir.'

'Thank you, Pim.'

Despite the reluctance of some of his team, he readied his men and set out to join Lieutenant Mecham. Kellett kept the remaining men busy with final winter preparations. He sent out a hunting party after 'Stoneman' Wilkie sighted several muskoxen and he had the meat hung from the mainmast to freeze, saving it for a welcoming feast when the men returned from sledging. He had a number of the men assist the clerk in charge with the completion of a thorough inventory of all supplies. With their help, the clerk reorganised and tidied the stores. All the sailors took their bedding and clothing off the ship; aired, repaired and returned them to their respective cabins and sea chests. Kellett assigned five men to Joseph Bacon, the ship's cook, to assist in a thorough cleaning of the galley.

The result of all this busy work gave new meaning to the phrase 'ship shape'. By the time the sledging parties returned, every bit of brass and copper was gleaming with a warm, welcoming glow. This time all the men returned safely from successfully completing the building and provisioning of supply cairns for the following spring.

Mecham had been gone for a precedent-setting twenty-two days. He and

Pim brought good news. Having travelled round the coast as far as Liddon's Gulf, and having established a depot of provisions at Cape Hoppner, he and Pim travelled home along the coast visiting Winter Harbour. It was there that they found the journal and record of proceedings left there by McClure. A party from *Investigator* had visited Melville Island that same spring after navigating, for the first time, the Northwest Passage from the West to as far as the Bay of Mercy. The record indicated, as of its writing, that the ship was helplessly trapped by ice in Mercy Bay.

Such excitement ensued from this information that the very men who were recently feeling discouraged suggested that a relief party be sent out at once in the hope of finding the Investigators still there. Their enthusiasm not withstanding, Kellett deemed travel now impractical and dangerous, but he resolved to send men out as early as possible in the spring.

At mid day on 2 November Fair Abe, the Resolutes and Intrepids gathered with regret on the ice to say goodbye to their old friend, the sun. The sky above them was brilliant with crimson and intense yellow, the horizon shining of gold. McDougall, never at a loss for words, spoke.

'Alas! Like many another friend whose value we do not realise until after they are gone, I believe we will find that we have not sufficiently appreciated this dear friend. You see him now departing. Look there! The last glimpse as he vanishes. Now darkness will truly fill our lives! The colour is draining away as I speak these very words! Farewell, my friend! We salute you with three cheers!'

A dispirited chorus of huzzah echoed away across the frozen land as the sun dipped below the horizon. With deep regret, the men returned to their ships, their gloomy mood unbroken until three days later, when they celebrated Guy Fawkes Day complete with effigy parade. Though he did not join in the extra ration of grog given to the men, the combined sounding of gongs and wild drumming revived Fair Abe's spirits. The celebrations seemed to revitalise the men as well. The sailors committed the Guy Fawkes effigy to the flames of a large bonfire amidst dancing and unearthly yells and a good time was had by all.

Now that all the men were safely ensconced in their ships, the Resolutes and Intrepids enjoyed several nights of feasting on fresh muskoxen and drinking stout. While the weary travellers rested the officers gathered in Kellett's cabin and gave their attention to organising events for the men during the coming months of monotony. Captain Kellett, Dr. Domville, and Mr. McDougall were elected the Theatrical Committee of Management and they began working immediately. McDougall had almost finished writing a play and volunteered to take charge of directing, costuming, and set creation.

'Mrs. Kellett and I enjoy going to the theatre whenever we have the opportunity. I will be glad to set up auditions and do the casting, but what I really want to do is act in the play. Do you think there could be a part in your play for me?'

'Sir, I am certain if there isn't I could write one. I am equally certain that you would do a fine job of acting, but I believe the men would find it difficult to rehearse along side of you, and they would really be unhappy about not having the chance to perform for you. I believe they might need you more in the audience.' McDougall seemed to hold his breath while his captain thought about what he had just said. A captain is a captain and, no matter how amiable this one was, if he insisted on acting then act he would. However, McDougall had already heard about Captain Kellett's enjoyment of opera and his attempts to honour the art form with his singing. If he was proposing to honour his interest in theatre in a similar way, the production could prove to be an absolute disaster.

'I see what you mean. Perhaps instead I should take charge of putting together after theatre refreshments to show my appreciation. Maybe next winter I could be more involved with the play itself.' McDougall released his breath. 'Mr. Domville, what shall you do?'

'It would be very helpful to me if he were to assist in the rehearsals and the staging,' McDougall said.

'Right ho, Mr. McDougall, he is all yours. But, what about also doing a lecture series?'

'I could arrange that, Captain. Would you be willing to give one of the talks? Yes? And you, George Frederick, can you spare the time from making costumes and creating sets to hazard a talk on something?'

With that, Dr. Domville was off to a roaring start having already filled the first two slots of his lecture series. One thing he enjoyed was organising. Anything. Men, his medical instruments, his books, papers. Heading up the lecture series was a perfect use of his skills, and he was eager to get on with it.

'Is there anything else we need to do right now, Captain? I have a few ideas about which men I want to approach about speaking, and I would like to get to them before they have any chance to think up good excuses for not doing it.'

'I believe we are done. Mr. McDougall, do you have anything else?'

'No, Sir.'

'Then we are finished. Dismissed.'

PART TWO

GATHERING

1854 and 1855

CHAPTER ONE
APRIL 1854

Latitude 74 degrees 41.53 minutes North
Longitude 101 degrees 11.00 minutes West
28 miles Southwest by South of Cape Cockburn

'I won't do it!' Captain Kellett stared in disbelief at Commander George Henry Richards from the flagship, *Assistance*, and Naps cowered under the table, glancing nervously toward the source of the enraged voice, 'What does he mean by *suggesting* I should abandon my ships? Despite having McClure's men on board with us, we have enough food to last another winter, if we must, and my ships are not in danger from the ice; our morale is good and all conditions are favourable for us to continue the search.'

God knows it hadn't been easy spending the past year and a half in the ice. But the men had done remarkably well. Hunting parties had been regularly sent out, the fresh meat keeping hunger and scurvy at bay. Theatre and lectures had kept minds agile and occupied throughout the two long winters. During the spring and autumn of '53 sledging parties had fanned out in all directions and covered distances unheard of before. Though they had found and rescued McClure and his men, most of their tasks were still not accomplished: they had not been able to determine what had happened to Franklin, nor had they been able to find and re-supply Collinson and his men. After all the expense and effort to get this far, he simply could not give up.

'Is this an order?'

'No, Sir. Captain Belcher did not say as such.'

'He damn well better make it an order!' Kellett pounded the table with his fist making Naps jump with a yip, then stand and shake, with his head lowered. 'I will not take it upon myself to abandon my ships at his "suggestion". I intend to continue my preparations for our sledging trips until I receive orders to abandon, <u>written</u> orders you understand? I will have no choice but to obey an unambiguous, unequivocal, written order to abandon although even then, I will do so only under protest. Make that very clear to him.'

'Yes, Sir.'

"I am sending McClintock with you so he can report back to me and you

92

will not have to make the return journey.' Kellett looked at his second in command. 'Be ready to leave in the morning.' He dismissed Richards but asked McClintock to remain.

'I do not have to tell you that I am disturbed by this "suggestion" that we abandon ship. I want you to keep your eyes and ears open when you arrive at the *Assistance*. I do not trust Belcher, as you well know. If there is something amiss I want to know about it when you return. I want a report of any information you can gather...from the men more so than from Sir Edward...and I want you to make a confidential, verbal report to me in person, no written reports. Do you understand?'

'Yes, Sir.' Kellett dismissed McClintock so he could get ready for his trip and looked down at his frightened Naps. 'Oh, ye faithful beastie, I am sorry I worried you. Come here.' Kellett stroked Naps' head to calm them both. He could not understand his commander's sudden desire to leave the Arctic. Perhaps his ships were in greater danger than *Resolute* and *Intrepid* or he was troubled with sickness amongst his men. He would have to question Commander Richards before he left on his return trip. Whatever was going on, he would be able to trust McClintock's assessment of the situation. In the meantime he would continue his preparations for the departure of the spring sledging parties. There were still vast areas they had not yet explored. With his men out sledging when the final order came, at the very least he would not be able to abandon the ships until all the men were safely back on board. The miles covered this spring could be the critical ones that would reveal Collinson's location and the fate of the Franklin expedition.

Captain Kellett had done everything in his power to keep his and now McClure's additional men happy and healthy. During the long winter months the men were required to take four hours of exercise per day: whenever possible they were out of the ship on the ice where they played rounders and other games until it became too cold, and then they continued exercising on the enclosed deck under the housing. The lecture series had been successful both winters with a wide variety of topics: Dr. Domville spoke on Chemistry, McDougall gave several lectures on the history of Arctic exploration, Nares explained the nature of wind and weather, Pim had given a humorous lecture on geology and another talk on the nature of mechanics: pulleys, levers, wedges, etc. Even Kellett himself had given a talk on Astronomy, which traced the progress of knowledge in that science from the earliest period through the various theories, explaining the train of reasoning by which astronomers reached their present degree of excellence. Many of the men had kept themselves busy with the study of navigation, reading, and arithmetic. One had even studied the full encyclopaedia from the ship's library, all ten volumes!

He had kept the men's spirits high with Christmas festivities and numerous engagements of the Arctic Theatre Royal, including performances 'King Glumpus', and 'The Taming of the Shrew' given by Resolute's men, where

Petrucio had laboured under the disadvantage of having a broad north country accent. The officers of both *Resolute* and *Intrepid* had put on a performance of 'Two Bonny Castles'. New Year's Eve of '53 had been celebrated with a musical band consisting primarily of flutes, accordion, triangle, tambourine, and drums.

In order to maintain communication between the two ships during both winters the carpenters had rigged up an electric telegraph, so even in the worst weather the men could keep in touch with each other. The only sadness had been the recent death of their shantyman, 'Stoneman' Wilkie, who had been buried on February third, the same day the sun had made its first appearance for the new year of 1854. His heart had simply given up.

Kellett asked his cox'n Brooke to request Commander Richards' presence; he needed to find out what was actually happening in the Wellington Channel, where *Assistance* and *Pioneer* had been searching for the past two years. Commander Richards returned to find Kellett deep in thought.

'Please sit,' Kellett waved the tired officer toward a chair. 'As you could see, I was taken aback by the instructions Captain Belcher sent with you. Please understand I was not angry with you, though I am sure it must have seemed that way. More than anything, I would like to understand why he is so anxious to leave when it does not appear our ships or men are in any danger. Perhaps you could share with me your perceptions, in an unofficial capacity, of course, of conditions on board *Assistance* and *Pioneer*.'

George Richards looked away. He had not seen Captain Kellett since their joint rescue of the Abraham boy. Could he trust him with an honest appraisal of the situation on board *Assistance*? Would he be putting his career in jeopardy if he told Kellett about the paranoia of his commanding officer, and the fear and depression of the men?

'I am in a difficult position, Captain Kellett. It is not my place to criticize my superior officer…'

'Do not fear speaking your peace with me. I will hold anything you share with me here in the strictest confidence and report it to no one. Do not forget we are "comrades in arms" and will be making a joint complaint to the Admiralty about Sir Edward's treatment of Fairfax Abraham.'

Richards hesitated. Then he burst out, 'We have been in hell!' His exclamation hung in the air while he gathered himself to tell his tale. He had to struggle to keep his voice under control. 'I don't know which has been worse, Captain Belcher's petty persecution of the officers, Osborn in particular, or his drunken paranoia. He is so convinced that we are all in cahoots to show him disrespect and to bring him dishonour that at one point he had all of us, all the officers, under arrest! Instead of paying attention to the real dangers around us: the Arctic winter, illness, and low morale among others, he imagines danger surrounding him in the guise of mutinous crew! In his diabolical search to rout out any lack of respect, he has destroyed any respect that may have been lingering in any of the men. Poor Osborn! He has born the brunt of it.'

Richards spoke at length about his captain's drunken tirades, the discovery of 'plots' against him at every turn, and his making decisions that could do nothing but undermine the fragile morale of the men as they struggled through the long and dark winter months. The occasional glimmers of humanity, when Belcher allowed the men to put on theatre productions and print up newsletters, were swallowed up by the enforcement of punishments grossly out of proportion to the 'crimes' committed. Richards was pacing up and down the cabin and Kellett exclaimed, 'Please sit, George!'

'Captain Kellett, can you believe a report from Osborn written on the incorrect size paper occasioned his arrest and the cessation of all communication between the two ships for weeks? Belcher even cancelled Christmas! The men on *Assistance* were afraid even to talk with each other after the festivities were called off for fear Captain Belcher would assume they were talking about him: plotting against him, of course. I do not know why he has suddenly decided we must all return to England, and I know we have not yet accomplished what we set out to do, but I don't believe any of us on board *Assistance* or *Pioneer* would regret leaving as soon as possible. I don't think we can survive another winter with him!'

Kellett thanked Commander Richards for his candid remarks. He could understand the men's reluctance to be locked in the ice for another winter with the squadron commander. Richards had said Belcher was frequently drunk. Was that making his fragile emotional state even less stable? As much as Kellett would like to relieve the men in the Wellington channel by agreeing to return to England, he certainly could not abandon his two ships without a clearly written order, and he still felt his mission was unfinished. All would ride on what news McClintock would bring on his return.

⚓⚓⚓⚓⚓

In America the news was bad. While Father Abraham did his best to keep his mind on the firm's work, he kept thinking about the reports coming from Washington. Nor could he believe the turn of events taking place out west. With Senator Douglas' proposed bill being debated in Congress, it was looking more and more likely that the new Nebraska and Kansas territories would be organised with popular sovereignty as their cornerstone. Popular sovereignty would be a disaster for those like himself who had been working so hard to contain and abolish slavery. If the bill passed and President Pierce signed it into law, there would be every possibility that slavery would come into being north of the Mason-Dixon Line. This new bill would annul the long standing Missouri Compromise of 1820!

Many of his friends and colleagues were so concerned that there was talk of forming societies that could help Free Soilers and Abolitionists settle the new territories. If the new settlers were going to be the ones to determine the status of slavery in the West, then there would need to be as many anti-slavery people staking their claims to land as possible; the more the better. But if there were suddenly a race to see who could get the most folks into the territories, then the opportunities for conflict (and violent conflict at that) would greatly increase. Certainly, as soon as a society was formed to facilitate the migration of abolitionists, an opposing society would be formed to aid the settlement of slaveholders. Such activity could only increase the probability of violence.

Once again, Father Abraham found himself face to face with contradictory values. As a Quaker he was committed to the end of slavery. But the Religious Society of Friends had a long-standing adherence to the principle of non-violence and Friends were conscientious objectors to all wars. Could he become involved with any anti-slavery actions that might precipitate violence? For Quakers there was no solace in the concept of 'the ends justify the means'.

The town clock striking two bells startled Father Abraham. Where had his morning gone? Without having his son to help him, his workload was almost brutal. He had no time for social concerns during his workday. With fifteen ships in their fleet, he had more than enough to keep him busy without the worries of the Nation down pressing his shoulders. He could not ignore the national issues, but he did have to be certain he was giving enough of his energy to his work and family so that they did not suffer. Tonight he would ask Martha to sit with him after the children were in bed. He could rely on her clear insights and guidance. With that thought, he attacked the company's books with renewed vigour.

Perkins, Smith and Abraham had four ships working the waters near Desolation Island: *Atlas* captained by Lyons, *Franklin* captained by Stroud, *Mechanic* captained by Edwards, and finally *H. Brewer* captained by Brown. In March, the *Charles Carroll*, had brought home 784 barrels of whale oil, and 12,800 pounds of whalebone from the North Pacific, and the *Corinthian* had just returned from Desolation Island with eighteen barrels of sperm oil, 2,871 barrels of whale oil, and 11,000 pounds of whalebone. The Perkins Smith fleet in the Pacific included the *Benjamin Morgan* captained this time by Chappell, *Brooklyn* captained by Newry, and *Lark* with Captain Kiblon. The two Buddingtons were both in the Arctic in Davis Strait. Captain Sidney O. Buddington was in charge of the *Georgiana*, and had left New London in the company of his uncle, James Munro, in the *Armaret*. The ships had departed on the 13th of July '53, with the intention of returning this autumn.

Of all the captains in their fleet, Father Abraham was the fondest of James Buddington. As a young boy Buddington had been building a stone wall on his father's Connecticut farm, when he just decided he had had enough of the hot sun and boring work. Sneaking away, he had joined a whaling ship as cabin boy. With some men of the sea one could say he never looked back, but not with James. He seemed to be torn between the sea and a life working the soil. Abraham mused that being a sea captain and being a farmer must feed this man's soul in different ways. Or perhaps he was just restless, always thinking that life was better on land when he was at sea; or at sea when he was on land.

Whatever the reasons, in 1846 James Buddington had left the whaling business to buy and work a farm out west in Illinois. Abraham had never discovered if the farm had been a failure or if Buddington had just missed the sailing life, but it was in '52, when Buddington joined Perkins, Smith and Abraham, that he met James for the first time. For someone who was so torn between two very different lives, James was one of the steadiest and most reliable captains in their whaling fleet. Because of this he had been chosen to lead the firm's 1851 experiment of leaving men in the Arctic, over wintering without a ship. They stayed to continue sealing after their full ship had been sent back to New London. The men were supposed to return in '52 with the ill-fated *McClellan*, the very ship his beloved son had sailed on.

Not for the first time, Father Abraham's thoughts were consumed by concern for his son's well being. Most of Buddington's men and the crew of the *McClellan* had returned on board other whalers, some had chosen to continue whaling on other ships, but Fair Abe had decided the join a British exploration squadron and was still somewhere in the frozen ice. Father Abraham and Martha shared the concern for Fair Abe's safety, but only Father carried the guilt for having sent him away in the first place. Martha did not blame him for their son's prolonged absence but he blamed himself. And he prayed daily for Fair Abe's safe return.

Martha Abraham opened the letter she had just received from Ireland.

> My Dear Friend,
> Thank you for your last letter with all your family news. While life at Clonacody seems to move peacefully from day to day, there is nothing but war in the papers. You may have already learned that Great Britain is at war with Russia. I do not know if they will be recruiting in Ireland, but the press is reporting that war fever is rampant in England and men are rushing to join up. I confess that I have not paid much heed in the past months to the tensions between Russia and Britain and am unclear about the reasons why this conflict has erupted. But because of this I feel I have an advantage: I am not caught up in the hysteria, and I feel like I am watching events unfold as though they are a theatre play and I am the audience. It is madness!
> The papers and Parliament are doing everything they can to stir up patriotic

feelings in the people. It all seems so false and self-serving. I have thought more and more in the past days about the Friends' peace testimony. I cannot say I believe all wars are alike in being immoral, because I still believe some wars are justified. However, I am seeing for the first time how manipulative the government is in getting the support of the people, and I know it will be the poor from England and Scotland and Ireland who serve as the cannon fodder.

My Margaret still appears to be taken by the image and stories of your son! The portrait in your parlour and the tales you told left quite an impression. Perhaps some day more than friendship will unite our families!

Know that I am always
Your devoted friend,
Alice

Martha smiled. She thought about her son. He was so shy around young women! What would he do if he knew about the devotion his portrait had inspired in the breast of this lively girl? She wondered what their inevitable meeting would be like when the explorers returned home to Britain. Martha was suddenly struck by how quickly her children were growing up. Somehow, it seemed easier to accept that her first-born child was old enough to be in the Arctic, than that he was old enough to go courting and getting married. But this letter drove home the realization that Fair Abe was indeed the correct age to settle down and begin his own family. Could she really be old enough to have a child ready for marriage? It didn't seem possible!

⚓⚓⚓⚓⚓

War, war and more war! War was declared on the 5th of April. All that the press could talk about was the latest war news and that Lord Raglan had left England for Paris on the 10th, en route to Gallipoli in the company of the Duke of Cambridge. He was off to command what the press referred to as the 'finest army that had ever left the shores of Britain'. Hundreds of well-wishers had gathered to see him off. To Alice, it looked as though they all considered war to be a grand game. Patriotic slogans, flag waving, marching bands. But what about the soon-to-be-dying? The public would be fed this sanitised excitement for as long as possible, but sooner or later the blood would flow. Many sons and husbands would not return, and others would return as broken shadows. It won't be all fun and games then.

What about her husband? He was safe for now amongst the ice floes, but what about after his return? He would not be so safe in the shallows of a Russian shoreline. As much as she wanted to see Henry, and as much as she had been hoping for his return from the Arctic this year, now she was afraid he would be taken from her as soon as he set foot on British soil. Although he was in the Hydrographic Department of the Royal Navy, and never in command of a war ship, Henry had been in the thick of the Chinese hostilities, and she had no doubt he could be sent into the battle zones again, piloting ships under fire as he had done at Canton.

And what of this new alliance with France? Henry had told her often enough that since 1815 the Admiralty's readiness was based on preparation for further hostilities with France. Now they were expected to work with their old enemy. Alice did not harbour any hostility toward France. To her the Napoleonic War was in the distant past. She also saw it as an historic conflict between England and France, and the longer she lived in Ireland, the more she felt that Ireland's interests and England's interests were not automatically the same thing. Granted, Henry worked for the Royal Navy and the money that supported their home came largely from his salary. But her life was the land. And the land was Ireland.

She thought more and more about her Quaker friends and their commitment to end all wars, and the causes for all wars. She felt Parliament, the press, and the government could be working to resolve the current conflict peacefully with as much energy as they were putting into the war mongering, if they would but choose to do so. She looked at the Russian war as a tremendous waste of resources and human lives. It would cost more in both than anyone would admit. Wars were so easy to start, with promises of quick and certain victory, but they never ended as cleanly and promptly as predicted by their proponents.

Alice admired the Quaker men from England who had travelled to Russia to meet with the Tsar in a last minute attempt to forestall the outbreak of hostilities. The press had vilified Joseph Sturge, Robert Charlton, and Henry Pease; they called them traitors and madmen. But the true mad men were the ones that had pushed the country into war. Hers was not simply a selfish concern; she did not want only to protect Henry, she wanted no other men to die needlessly.

Wanting to know if any other actions for peace were planned, she sat at her writing desk and penned a letter to the London Yearly Meeting of Quakers. Mrs. Kellett would never forget, nor stop feeling grateful for the help the Quakers had given the people of Ireland during the Famine. Hoping it was not too late she decided that she would do what she could to help the peace effort.

Margaret Kellett was restless. What was wrong with her? She did not enjoy working with her horses the way she always had. Riding brought her no release, and she had no appetite. Some days she felt happier than she ever had, and then on others she plunged into dark depression. No matter how tired she was she could not sleep. She studied herself in the mirror daily. She had never been all that concerned about her looks, but now no matter what she wore, or how she fixed her hair, she could only find fault with what she saw. If only her hair was not so bright, nor her face so freckled! She had never noticed before that her eyes were so far apart, and her lips so full. Today she looked pale. Sickly, she thought. Well no wonder, it had been weeks since she had had a full night's sleep.

Her thoughts returned to the voyage to America and the time she had spent with Mr. Schurz on board the *London*. They had spent many enjoyable days discussing books while she helped him to improve his English. She wondered how he was doing in his new home, and if he ever thought about her and Mother.

Perhaps she could find solace in reading. She had always enjoyed her family's library and now it became her constant retreat. She read in rapid succession the older novels: all of Jane Austen, Swift's *Gulliver's Travels*, and Shelley's *Frankenstein*. She read Samuel Johnson's *Rambler* and *Adventurer* and then turned to more recent works. She particularly loved the women: Catherine Gore, Elizabeth Gaskell, Dinah Mulock Craik, Catherine-Anne Hulback, the Bronte sisters. She didn't care much for Trollope's *The Macdermots of Ballycloran* or *The Kelleys and the O'Kelleys*. He was trying to understand Ireland with out having a clue.

For weeks she spent every day and evening curled up with books. McCaffrey took over the care of her horses while she devoured Thackeray's *Vanity Fair, Mrs. Perkin's Ball, Pendennis,* and *Henry Esmond*. Then she worked her way through Dickens, her father having a complete set from *the Pickwick Papers* through to the recently published *David Copperfield.*

Margaret's world expanded daily. Dickens' works opened her eyes to the economic conditions in England, which she had never considered. Trollope's work, though leaving her unsatisfied as a reader, made her think about the famine years. It prompted a long conversation with her mother. Margaret had never thought much about economics or politics and she had been too young, too sheltered by her mother, to remember much of the hardship many had experienced during the Famine.

'You met Martha Abraham during the Famine, didn't you?'

'Yes. In fact, it is very curious that you should mention her. I have been thinking quite a bit lately about that time, and the help the Quakers gave Ireland. Perhaps it is remembering our visit to America, or all the talk about the Russian war, but I find myself wanting to know more about the Religious Society of Friends. They don't preach about Christ, but they seem to be more Christ-like than many other Christians I know. Their emphasis is not on doctrine as much as on doing good works. I struggle, however, with their belief that all wars are wrong. I know we are commanded "Thou shalt not kill". But sometimes it seems evil can only be eradicated by force. The Quakers do state that they are striving to eradicate the causes of war, so perhaps even they recognise that not all wars can be prevented. At least not in our time.'

'I know you are concerned about this new war, Momma; do you think Father will be involved when he comes home?'

'I don't know, but I fear so. You know how much I miss him when he is away, yet even so I find myself hoping they spend at least one more year in the Arctic. As dangerous as it is, it is comforting to know that no one is actually shooting at Father!'

'I wonder how Fair Abe is coping. Isn't it funny that he and Father have been together for the past two years? He looked so young and serious in the family portrait, I would think at the very least he will be aged by the experience.'

'According to his mother, he is very comfortable in the out-of-doors. He has always sailed around the harbour in small skiffs and was known to take wilderness hikes that lasted for weeks. But the Arctic is like no other place, so you may be right in that it will age him: he will be older in experience and physique when they return. I certainly hope Father is taking good care of him! Martha would be forgiving, but I know your father would take it very hard if any thing untoward were to happen to the boy on his watch! But, come, I don't believe you came to discuss Fair Abe: at least not this time!'

'This time? Do you mean I talk about him frequently? Just to make conversation, really. But I came to ask you about the books I should read if I want to understand economics and politics a bit better. What do you suggest?'

'There is one woman who I admire. Her name is Harriet Martineau. I have both of her books, *The Hour and the Man* and *A History of England During Thirty Years of Peace.* She has been involved with the Anti-slavery Movement, and speaks eloquently about the rights of women, or the lack of them. I think you will find her interesting, but she is not necessarily easy to read. I also have John Stuart Mill's work, *Principles of Political Economy.* I would enjoy talking with you about their different theories after you have read them.'

'I always felt so stupid when Mr. Schurz would talk about economic conditions in Germany. He tied many things together: politics and economics seemed interwoven with issues of justice and liberty. I didn't understand everything that he talked about, but I wanted to. He made me want to be a better, a more thoughtful person.'

'Again, you have brought up someone I have been thinking about lately. I know what you mean about wanting to be a better person, but I was almost a very bad woman.'

Margaret blurted, 'What do you mean?' Could Mother have known how close she had been to an indiscretion? Was she trying to get her to speak about it through some sort of ruse?

'I know how you felt about Carl.' Margaret blushed as her mother spoke. 'It was so obvious that you harboured feelings for him. But you were so wrapped up in your own world that I wasn't sure if you noticed the attentions he began to pay me.'

Margaret frowned as she tried to remember.

'Don't upset your self about it now.'

'I am not upset! I am just struggling to remember the times we were all together. Do you mean to say he was courting you?'

'Yes, he was; and I was attracted to him, too. I am ashamed to own up to the strength of the feelings he awoke in me.'

'But what about Father? How could you think of...'

'I know, Margaret. I know. I wasn't thinking. I was feeling alone and lonely. Carl made me feel young again, and wanted. You have no idea how difficult it is for me having your father away so much of the time! I know you miss him, but I miss him, too. A wife longs for the love only her husband can give her. Your father loves me, but he isn't here to show it! And Carl was there, next to me, touching me.'

Alice watched her daughter struggle with this new knowledge. Should she tell the whole story, or had she been wrong to mention what she had already said. She had gone this far; she might as well be complete in her honesty.

'He asked me to leave your father and stay in America with him.' Margaret looked shocked. 'I thought about it, and I was truly torn. But in the end, it was Martha Abraham who helped me to see that my family meant more to me than the feelings I had for Carl. You and your father mean the world to me. I could never do anything to hurt either of you!'

'You told her? She knows? Weren't you ashamed?'

'I was confused and she is one of my dearest friends. I knew what the right thing was to do; I just needed to hear it from someone else. I needed her strength because I felt weak. So you see, I am no saint! Do you hate me now?'

'Oh, Momma, I don't know what I feel. Confused. Scared.'

'Very much how I felt. Both your father and Carl Schurz are good men. Before he began courting me I even thought Carl would be a good husband for you, despite your age difference. He treated you with such respect, but it became clear to me that he didn't have romantic feelings for you. I was very afraid you were going to get hurt, so I was relieved when you started asking about Fair Abe and stopped thinking about Carl.'

'Why do you speak of those two in the same way? I was in love with Carl! I don't even know Fair Abe. I don't know why you keep saying I talk about him all the time. It is true, though. I don't think about Carl any more. At least not the same way I did. Now I think about the ideas he shared and I find myself wanting to understand them. He held a mirror up to me, and I didn't like the person I saw. I am shallow and selfish and...'

'Don't say such things about yourself! You have many qualities that I admire.'

'I do?'

'Yes. You are strong and talented. The way you work with your horses is magical. It is true that, until now, you haven't expressed much interest in the world beyond our home, but I always felt that was only a matter of time and maturity. You have too agile a mind not to become curious. And, see? Now you are.'

'You are trying to change the subject, Mother! How could you think of leaving Father? How could you even dream that I would want to leave him, too! I can't bear the thought that you let Carl touch you, or turn your head.'

'Margaret, please…', Alice reached her hand out to her daughter.

'No! Don't touch me!' Margaret threw her book against the wall and stormed out of the room. With a confusion of emotions and ideas, Margaret returned with her mother's recommendations to her favourite chair in the library and opened the *Principles of Political Economy.* But she could not settle down, or read. Grabbing her cloak, she strode out of the house and headed for the nearby woods, hoping that a long walk would help to calm her anger.

⚓⚓⚓⚓⚓

Fair Abe volunteered to go with the sledge trip to Beechey Island. It was a fine, but very cold, morning when they set off to the cheers of the remaining men. For the first twelve miles or so they had smooth ice floes to travel over and they made good time. But then their luck changed drastically. They came upon an area full of hummocks and in order to proceed they had to struggle with the sledge. Fair Abe and Roche worked together, hauling one minute and pushing the next. Their labours only ceased when, descending a particularly steep hummock, a runner snapped.

'What a day!' Roche and Fair Abe looked down on their sledge. 'And we don't have any way of repairing it! We will have to make camp and return to *Resolute* tomorrow. This has been a complete waste of time and energy!'

Fair Abe nodded in agreement. 'Thou hast done all that could be expected. Captain Kellett will understand we did our best.'

'That doesn't make me feel any better about not accomplishing what we set out to do. At least one thing is in our favour: we haven't covered all that much ground. I would be surprised if we are more than fifteen miles from the ship. Let's set up camp.'

The men unpacked their tents and ate their evening meal before retiring. Sleep came quickly to the exhausted men, not one of them remembering their dreams.

Upon returning to the ships, Fair Abe learned that Commanders Richards and McClintock had set off for HMS *Assistance* that morning. Every one seemed anxious about the future: would the ships' companies be staying for another winter? It was rumoured that McClintock might return with written orders from Sir Edward telling them they must abandon ship. The following day Captain McClure and twenty men left for Beechey Island. Then Captain Kellett ordered Roche and Nares to organise clearing the snow from *Intrepid's* upper deck. It seemed the captain wanted to keep the men busy, continuing with daily tasks in anticipation of staying through until next spring. Perhaps the rumours were false!

Kellett sent out several hunting parties to re-supply the larder with fresh meat; Fair Abe went with them. He had mixed feelings about the possibility of leaving. He had discovered during his two winters in the Arctic that he loved being here. Yet he looked forward to returning to his family. He missed them very much and thought about how much his baby brother William must have grown in his absence. But even if they left the ships now, he realised it would be quite some time before he would see home again. The ships would sail directly for England. He would have to wait there until the courts martial, and he gave his testimony against Sir Edward.

Whenever Fair Abe became uneasy, anticipating having to testify against the squadron commander, his mind turned to lighter matters. He would think of the captain's daughter, and the ugliness of his earlier experiences became strangely juxtaposed against her beauty. Reflecting on the portrait he had seen in Captain Kellett's cabin, he wondered if he would have the chance to meet Miss Kellett while he waited in England to testify. Ever since he first saw Margaret's miniature he had speculated about who the young woman might be behind such a captivating face. Even though Captain Kellett enjoyed talking about his family, all Fair Abe had been able to gather about Margaret was that she loved her horses. If that was all there was, she would be very shallow, he thought. But something more might be there! It must be! He wished he could get a better look at the miniature, but the times he had been called into the Captain's cabin for conversation he felt it would be rude to be so obviously interested and he always found himself looking away.

On the 28th McClintock returned from the *Assistance*. Every one was anxious to know what orders he carried, but they were kept in suspense for two days. Finally on the 30th, after divisions, Captain Kellett assembled the men.

'With the deepest regret I must inform you that we have been ordered to abandon our ships.' A gasp escaped the men. 'The orders from our squadron commander are now clear and unambiguous.' Kellett could not meet the men's eyes so he read the order to his men instead, and then continued. 'We will be leaving for Beechey Island as soon as the vessels are in a fit state.' He looked out upon his loyal officers and men. He saw dismay, anger, and apprehension there. But also trust. They trusted him: to lead them, to make the right decisions, to preserve their lives. This was one of the most difficult moments in any man's command: to disagree so profoundly with an order, and yet to lead one's men, men who trusted their commanding officer to do the right thing, down a path which that officer believed with all his heart to be wrong. When is disobeying an order a sign of courage and not folly? Should he disobey this order? Was he certain he would not be putting his men's lives at risk if he ordered them to stay instead? If the order was one that would cause needless loss of life, he would be more inclined to disobey. But this order merely put their honour at risk. Merely. The officers and men waited for their captain to continue.

'I will allow each of the officers to take forty-five pounds weight of gear and clothing to take with them, and the men thirty. Please mark all your packs with your names. There is still the possibility that Captain Belcher will rescind his order and we will be able to re-occupy the ships. It will be easier for you to locate your personal effects if they are labelled.'

Fair Abe saw that Captain Kellett had tried to keep the sadness from his face when he gave the orders to ready the ship for abandonment, but, he had been unsuccessful and the sadness was contagious. All went quietly about their business, almost as if some one had died. Somehow it didn't seem right for seamen to abandon their good and steady ships to such a fate: one that would most likely be brutal and deadly at the hands of the crushing ice.

In this subdued mood the men readied their ships. They hoisted boats inboard, and secured them; coiled cables; stowed the booms and hoisted in the rudder; every moveable thing they either took below or lashed securely to the deck. They laboured for five days.

Because Kellett had been ordered to abandon *Resolute* without even waiting for his returning men, Roche and Nares and seventeen other men, took two sledges and left for Cape Cockburn with caches of provisions for Lieutenant Mecham and his men, who had been sent to Princess Royal Islands to look for any signs of HMS *Enterprise*. Lieutenant Hamilton also took a sledge and five dogs to Dealy Island in order to leave a message for Mecham's party to proceed directly to Beechey Island without returning to the ships.

On Saturday, the 13th of May, the first men, with a fair wind, but heavily laden sledges, left *Resolute* for the rendezvous with the squadron commander on Beechey Island.

'I have so many things I want to take with me,' Master McDougall lamented to Fair Abe. 'Forty-five pounds simply doesn't allow for anything but the necessities. I don't know how the men will manage with only thirty pounds each. It's impossible!' He shook his head in despair and asked Fair Abe to help him pack the navigational instruments and then clear the wardroom.

The sun rose on a clear day, very much like the morning when they had left England so long ago. The day for abandonment had arrived. The sadness deepened as the men made their last minute preparations. Fair Abe joined the party of men on deck to watch the signal books being burned as the ensign rose to the foretopmast head.

'If our gallant ship must be crushed and sink in the Arctic Ocean, then she will go down with her colours flying.' Captain Kellett ordered the men to stop their work and he bowed his head. 'May the Good Lord look after her better than we have; I cannot help feeling as though I am abandoning a close friend. We would be doing right by her if we had been so allowed. After all, she has done right by us. Always.'

Murmurs ran through the deck. A raised voice shouted, 'It should never 'ave 'appened!'

'Belay that! Silence! We have our orders!'

By midday, the sledges were loaded; even Napoleon had packs of food to carry. All hatches and skylights but one were closed and caulked. The men and officers gathered in the darkened gunroom for their last meal. McDougall attempted a few light-hearted jokes, but they sank like stones beneath the waves of despair felt by the men. The mood was no better in the captain's cabin when the officers raised their glasses.

'To RESOLUTE! Three cheers!' They joined in 'huzzah!' between sips, then gulps, of wine. Setting their glasses on the table, they departed for the last time, taking up their sledges with Roche, the junior officer, in the lead, and Captain Kellett bringing up the rear. About a quarter mile away from *Resolute* and *Intrepid,* they stopped, turned and simultaneously gave three more heart-felt cheers for the ship. As they struggled across the snow and ice with their heavy burdens, some men hoped their fellow crewmen did not see their eyes watering in the icy cold, while others burned inside with the resentment of trained seamen abandoning perfectly sound ships.

CHAPTER TWO
OCTOBER - DECEMBER 1854

O n board HMS *Waterloo* in Sheerness Harbour Captain Kellett was restless in anticipation of his court martial. Commander Richards' court martial was still in session, though he had expected it to be finished long before now. What could be making it take so long? If there was any difficulty in Richards' acquittal, which should have been a mere formality, that would not bode well for his own trial. Every officer was automatically subjected to a court martial if they were unfortunate enough to lose a ship. Even Nelson had undergone the ordeal. It was in the expectation of just this event that Kellett had insisted on Sir Edward giving him the orders to abandon *Resolute* in clear, unambiguous and written form. He did not foresee any difficulty in being exonerated; after all, he had just been following orders. But with Belcher, somehow, one could never be certain that the just and correct outcome would be the one to take place. Kellett did not know how Belcher always slithered through difficulties, no mud ever sticking to him. Not this time, he vowed. Not this time.

Kellett stood as Commander Richards walked away from the captain's cabin. A slight nod and Kellett saw he was carrying his sword again. Thank God! Richards had not been blamed for the loss of the *Assistance*! That the Admiralty had given him his sword again meant that he had been acquitted of any wrong doing.

'Captain, will you come this way?' Kellett rose, smoothed his coat and entered the cabin.

The Honourable William Gordon, Vice Admiral of the Blue and Commander in Chief of Her Majesty's Ships and Vessels in the River Medway and at the Bay of the Nore, sat opposite the doorway. He would be presiding over the court martial. The Captains Sir Thomas Pasley of HMS *Royal Albert*, Christopher Nevill of the *Wellesley*, John Jervis Tucker of *Formidable*, Keith Stewart of *Nankin*, Edward Henshaw of *Cossack*, and George Seymour of the *Cumberland*, sitting on either side of him, were the judges. Henry Kellett lowered his eyes and saw his sword lying across the captain's table. When this was all over, would he walk away with it once more at his side?

'Captain Kellett, do you have any statement to make to the Court?'

'Sirs, I acted under orders of Sir Edward Belcher, the senior officer of the squadron, in abandoning HMS *Resolute*, and I produce those orders.'

Kellett handed the president the letters he had received from Belcher. He was asked to sit down and the clerk in charge of HMS *Assistance*, James Clark, was sworn in. He examined the letters, dated 1st February, 2nd and 21st of April 1854, and identified them as having been written in the hand of Sir Edward.

Captain Kellett continued his testimony by producing additional letters and asked that he be allowed to read them into the court record. The first two were the long and rambling, convoluted letters he received from Belcher before the clear orders to abandon ship had been written. In the five pages of largely incoherent musings that were read into the record, it was difficult to ascertain a direct order. Kellett noticed confusion on the judges' faces. Very well, he thought to himself, now at least I know that those letters would confuse almost anyone.

'Sirs, I conferred with my junior officer, Commander McClintock, and neither of us felt a clear order to abandon ship had been contained in the communications received thus far from Sir Edward. Therefore, on the 12th of April I wrote as follows:

> 'I have come to the conclusion that nothing contained in any of the said orders would justify me in abandoning Her Majesty's Ships under my command...I now send to you Commander McClintock, who is entirely in my confidence, and is in full possession of all my views, with authority, indeed enjoined, to give you every information relative to it. You, Sir, are in possession of their Lordships' views and instructions and fully authorized to act on them.
>
> 'I have therefore to request that you will give me final, most decided, and unmistakable orders for my guidance, and whatever orders you give shall be carried out to the letter.'

'Did you send this letter to Sir Edward?'

'Before the opportunity arose, Lieutenant Hamilton arrived with a private letter from Sir Edward. In it his orders to abandon *Resolute* and *Intrepid* were much more direct. However, I must say again that this was a private letter. Because I whole heartedly disagreed with the necessity to abandon ship, I wanted the orders be given to me in the clearest way possible; I wanted the decision to be made officially and unequivocally by Sir Edward Belcher.

Therefore I penned another letter, which I planned to send with Mr. McClintock, and I now request that I be allowed to read that letter into the record.'

He read the letter. 'You seem to be, Sir, on the very edge of being insubordinate in this letter,' Sir Pasley said. 'In these passages: "I certainly hoped before you took so decided a step as the abandonment of these vessels you would have conferred with me on the subject…I have to request you will do me the justice to give me plain and distinct orders on the subject." No senior officer has ever had to confer with his subordinates when giving orders! Did you suppose that by asking him to repeat his orders that you would get him to change his mind? That is not your business, Sir!'

'I do not believe Captain Kellett meant to be insubordinate,' Captain Neville cast his gaze upon his fellow judges. Turning to their examinee, 'is it not so, that you merely wanted clarification? Also, perhaps, you were making sure no future blame could be attached to you if the Admiralty were to find fault with Sir Edward's decision?'

'I strongly disagreed with Sir Edward's order, but it was never my intention to disobey him. It is true: I did want to give him every opportunity to change his mind and avert what I saw as a very expensive mistake. Not only would we be losing four valuable ships, but we had not yet determined the fate of the Franklin Expedition. Nor had we found and re-provisioned Captain Collinson and his crew. Sir Edward's decision put all those lives at risk. Even though I had Captain McClure and the crew of *Investigator* onboard my ships, thereby increasing the number of men that needed feeding and clothing, we had more than enough provisions to insure the safety of all of the men. The ships were not in danger, and the men's morale was high. In short, all the circumstances were favourable for successful Arctic survival and exploration.'

'Do you have any further statement to make?'

'*Resolute* and *Intrepid* were 28 miles Southwest by South of Cape Cockburn. We were caught in the ice on the 10th of September, and drifted about in the pack until the 12th of November in young ice. In consequence of the orders I received from Sir Edward Belcher, I abandoned the ships on the 15th May 1854. I left the ship in perfect condition, battened down: top gallant yards and masts upon deck, and sails bent. I left provisions enough for 50 men to survive for over a year.'

'Have you any complaint to make of any of the officers or the ships' company of the *Resolute* or the *Intrepid* on the occasion of their abandonment, or any instance of disobedience or neglect to your orders upon that occasion in any of the officers or ships' company to notice?'

'No, Sir,'

The evidence was closed and the court cleared while the judges proceeded to deliberate upon the form of sentence. None of the Resolutes spoke to or made eye contact with each other. They had all thought Kellett's Court Martial would be a mere formality, but the judges did not appear unanimous in seeing

Kellett as faultless. Sir Thomas Pasley in particular seemed antagonistic. For Captain Kellett it was a tense interlude. He knew he had done no wrong, but the questions asked by Sir Thomas regarding insubordination made him feel wrong-footed. How much weight would the other judges give to his perception? Belcher certainly never seemed to suffer for his actions, only others, and it was not unheard of for a scapegoat to take the fall for Belcher's mistakes.

The deliberations were brief, and in less than half an hour Kellett and his officers and men were called back into the captain's quarters. Captain Kellett saw that his sword was facing away from him, the hilt ready for him to take it in hand. He had been acquitted! He was asked to stand and the Deputy Judge Advocate read the sentence.

'Having enquired into the cause and circumstances attending the loss of the said ship, *Resolute,* and her tender, *Intrepid,* as afore said, and having heard the statements of the said Captain Henry Kellett, and the Evidence produced by him, and having maturely weighed and considered the premises the Court is of the opinion that no blame whatever is imputable to the said Captain Kellett, his officers, or his crew; but that the said Captain Kellett acted under the orders of Sir Edward Belcher, his superior Officer, in abandoning the said ship HMS *Resolute,* and her steam tender, HMS *Intrepid*, and that no other course was open to him. And the Court doth in consequence thereof adjudge the said Captain Henry Kellett, Companion of the Most Honourable Military Order of the Bath, his officers, and crew to be fully acquitted.'

A sigh of relief escaped several of the crewmen. The presiding judge, the Honourable William Gordon, asked Captain Kellett to step forward. He took the captain's sword from the table, offered his congratulations, and handed it to Kellett. 'You acted in the only way an honourable man could, under the circumstances. Wear your sword with pride, Mr. Kellett. The Admiralty owe their unreserved gratitude to you, and others like you, who bring such integrity and dignity to our service.'

Kellett thanked him as he slid his sword into its scabbard, his eyes momentarily blurring. He could not wait to get word to Alice and Margaret, who had come over to London from Ireland to be with him during this ordeal, and he knew they were anxious to learn of his fate. No doubt, the Resolutes would be relieved as well, and they would enjoy celebrating together tonight. His thoughts turned to young Fairfax Abraham. This trial had been the easy one. In a few days time it would be Belcher's turn to be examined. We have much work to do: Richards, Fair Abe, Osborn and I, Kellett thought as the bo's'n piped him into the waiting tender. He could only hope justice might prevail again.

⚓⚓⚓⚓⚓

The New England Indian summer lingered while the brilliant orange, red and gold autumn leaves stubbornly refused to give up their lives, clinging tenaciously to maple, birch, and hickory, rejecting for as long as possible their future as brown and broken bits on the forest floor. The beauty all around belied the ugly brutality of the political storm that was brewing in the country. Father Abraham's spirit was deeply troubled. The burden of running the whaling firm without Fair Abe just added to the chaos. On the one hand, he could not wait for his eldest son to return from England. Yet, on the other, he hoped the boy would stay away until some of the heat of the slavery issue dissipated. The temperature of the debate, and the conflict brewing in the Kansas Territory, were creating an explosive situation he knew Fair Abe would find difficult, if not impossible, to ignore. His firebrand son would probably be in the thick of it, he admitted.

Immediately after the Kansas-Nebraska Act was signed into law, anti-slavery groups in the New England States got busy creating emigration societies, helping as many abolitionists to move to the Kansas Territory as possible. If Kansas was to decide by popular vote whether to enter the Union as a free or slave state, then the more abolitionists that lived there the more likely it was that it would become a free state. Already, 1,200 New Englanders had been sent to live in the towns and to lay claim to homesteads. The newspapers reported, on a daily basis, that the pro-slavery people in the South were forming similar organizations. Hundreds were already pouring across the border from Missouri; what had begun as a trickle of slave holders was rapidly becoming a flood. Once the opposing factions faced each other in the Territory, all hell could break loose.

In the evenings, Father Abraham and his wife, Martha, discussed the news from Kansas and the nation's capitol. They struggled mightily to discern what actions would be the best manifestation of their faith. While they felt very strongly that they had to continue their support for the abolition of slavery, they were increasingly concerned that this cause was rapidly moving toward open and violent conflict. As Quakers, they shared an equally strong commitment to their peace testimony. But every day they felt a non-violence solution to the slavery problem was receding farther and farther from their grasp. Would carrying on with such vocal support for abolition push them closer to violating their peace testimony?

Father Abraham knew that American Quakers had peacefully given up their slaves before there was a ratified Constitution. It had not been easy. Monthly and Yearly meetings had laboured long and hard for years before the Society had been able to reach a consensus. That was the way the Society of Friends worked. Decisions were not made by a majority vote. The Meetings had to reach unity, all members agreeing to any new policy before it was adopted. Some people thought that was an unreasonable and impossible way to get anything done. But once a Meeting made a decision, there was no minority left feeling resentful and un-heard. No anger fomenting to create disturbance later. Laborious? Time consuming? Yes, but American Quakers had managed to be ahead of England by several decades in banishing slavery from their midst, and ahead of the American government's debate of the issue by more than a half century.

Watching this issue tearing their beloved country asunder caused the Abraham's much anxiety and grief. Night after night, they prayed and sat in silence, searching for a way to open; a way that would resolve the conflict between their two strongly held beliefs: abolition and non-violence. And while they prayed, the darkness deepened around them.

On this beautiful autumn day, Father Abraham had to close his mind to both the beauty and ugliness around him in order to concentrate on the work at hand. He had to continue monitoring, unloading, and refitting the Perkins, Smith and Abraham fleet. Amongst the fifteen ships Captain Brown, on *H. Brewer,* had returned in July from Desolation Island in the South Indian Ocean with 137 barrels of sea elephant oil, 1,748 barrels of whale oil, and 6,499 pounds of whalebone. After doing routine repairs, the barque had been sent back out again on the 19th of August to Desolation Island, this time with Smith as her captain. In June, Parsons took the *Charles Carroll* west around the Cape and was now in the North Pacific, hopefully having a successful voyage. Captain James Munro Buddington on *Amaret* had returned from the Davis Strait on 29 August with 369 barrels of whale oil and 8,000 pounds of whalebone, and *Amaret* had just been sent back to the same hunting ground on 7th of September with a different captain.

The most recent return was the *Georgiana.* James' nephew, Captain Sidney Buddington, and his crew had brought the firm 890 barrels of whale oil and 16,000 pounds of whalebone. Thus far, it had been a very successful year. Father Abraham was in the process of building the fleet back up again, continuing the negotiations on the purchase of more ships. He had the goal of doubling the fleet by the end of 1855. By hunting farther away in the Pacific, and in the Indian Ocean, they were increasing their harvest again. Nothing to equal the heyday of the mid 40's, when they had 41 ships in the fleet, and hauls as big as 30,000 pounds of whalebone from just one trip, but Father Abraham saw the firm's profits increasing, and by diversifying to seal hunting and collecting guano while still hunting whales, he believed they had many productive years ahead.

In the mid 1840's, New London had had the second largest whaling fleet in the world. Father Abraham could only guess at the percentage of the local citizens who were still involved in the trade. The industry supported not only ship owners like himself, but the captains, crew, shipwrights, carpenters, riggers, caulkers, coopers, blacksmiths, rope and sail makers, painters, and the boat builders who thronged the streets and businesses. Along the quay the whaling firms employed countless draymen, stevedores, and warehouse workers. The local farmers and merchants depended on whaling as well, for they provisioned the ships that went out on the seas. And then there were the men who transformed the raw materials of seal and whale oil and the whale bone into the many products used by all: candles, oil lamps, cosmetics, corset stays, buggy whips, parasols, and canes. Most of the industrial lubricants came from whaling as well. But then the returns began to decline. Opening new hunting grounds and expanding their business beyond whale oil and bone, to include guano and seals, was now helping the business to revive.

With all the ships away now, Father Abraham spent most of October concentrating on the purchase of the first two ships he wanted to add to the fleet. The *George Henry* was a barque with a tonnage of 303 and he planned to use this ship in the Davis Strait for arctic whaling. The other ship, *Laurens,* he wanted to use for the South Indian Ocean and the Heard Island sea elephant hunting. He hoped to have the *George Henry* in time to send her north in the spring. Father Abraham already knew who he wanted to captain this new ship, James Munro Buddington. The son would sail in the *George Henry* on her maiden voyage as his father's cabin boy. Buddington's son, James Waterman Buddington had just joined the firm last week, when old man Buddington had come to him asking if his son could join the whalers. Young James had worked on colliers in the Long Island Sound for several years; he was fifteen, strong and eager, and Abraham has hired him on the spot.

'Will ye be coming home now, Father?' Fairfax looked up from his desk to see his wife, Martha, standing in the doorway. 'It's been dark for an hour now, I thought I could light thy way home.'

'Yes, I have just completed all I needed today, and I will be glad of thy company. I must prepare my desk for the morning, and then I will be ready to walk with thee.'

Father Abraham and Martha walked quietly towards their home in the crisp evening air. 'I feel the winter coming in tonight, though the day has been bright and warm.' Martha sighed. 'How did thy work progress today, Father?'

'Very slowly in the morning, I must confess. I find it very difficult to concentrate, and must force myself to do so. But once I did centre down, I made some good progress toward the purchase of two new ships: one for the Arctic whaling and one for the Southern Indian Ocean trade. The first three quarters of this year went better than I had expected, and we are now in a position to expand the firm again. But even as I do the work to make this happen, I feel a cold fear in my heart. What if the political turmoil around us should break out into violent conflict? God forbid, what if there was a civil war? We have heard rumours coming from the South about the possibility of secession if the issue of abolition is forced. It seems the more pressure they are under, the more stubbornly and steadfastly they cling to that dying institution. Maybe we have been wrong to press so hard for the manumission of the slaves. Maybe we should have been more patient and allowed the market forces to bring it to a natural death. What have we done, Martha, by being so headstrong? Have we brought our land to the brink of bloodshed?'

'We have acted the way we have been led: by the Light Within, by God's Word. Thy work over the years for gradual understanding, working directly with slave holders, helping them to see alternatives to the system they felt locked into, has gained the freedom for their slaves without causing resentment that could lead to violence. That there are others who would push without regard for the possibility of war does not mean our work has been wrong, or in vain!'

'Ah, but my Dear, I fear we may have played into the hands of those that may even welcome conflict, possibly civil war. I don't know how or why I fear this. I know the cause of abolition is worthy, but I question the motivation of some who have been drawn to it. I just feel this is the calm before the storm: the air is filled with electricity: one spark and all will go up in flames!'

'I must believe that goodness is stronger than evil, the Light stronger than any darkness. I must believe this.'

'Yes, Thy faith lifts me up every day. Even so, my concern continues to grow. War would be devastating. It would go against everything we work for, but it would also be debilitating for our business. I do not worry only for us. Many men, and their families, depend on us for their livelihood. If we struggle, others will suffer. I have thought of this all day, while doing the work to expand our fleet, I can't help wondering if that is the correct thing to do, if perhaps I should be battening down the hatches for the coming storm. For coming I believe it is. I can see the clouds on the horizon, and the wind and rain will soon sweep all before it. It will not be a life giving, welcomed rain; rather it will cause devastation on such a scale we have never known. I feel it, Martha; it is as if I have been given sight, where others are yet blind. And I do not know what the correct action is for me to take, either with the firm or with my faith.'

Martha gave her husband's hand a squeeze. Uniquely, she did not know what to say to alleviate the heavy burden under which her beloved Fairfax laboured. She could not even say all shall be well again; for she, too, felt the storm clouds gathering.

⚓⚓⚓⚓⚓

In London, Alice and Margaret Kellett received the messenger in the reception room of the inn where they had been staying for the past three weeks. There was no way to hide the tension and concern in their faces, but Mrs. Kellett was as gracious as she could be under the circumstances. With a sigh of relief she took Henry's letter from him and read it. 'Thank God! He has been acquitted! Your father will be joining us for a few days before he has to go back again to Sheerness for the Court Martial of that beastly Belcher. He says he will be bringing Fair Abe with him, and they will be arriving tonight. How happy I will be to see Henry, and to finally meet my friend Martha's oldest son. Isn't this the best news?'

Margaret didn't know which emotion was stronger, the happiness she felt for her father having received the justice he deserved, or excitement about meeting Fair Abe. Two years had passed since she first saw his likeness in the painting on the Abraham's drawing room wall in New London, Connecticut; it was a handsome face by any standard, and she had been taken by the strength and kindness she saw in it. Though she had certainly thought about many things since she had been in America, the memory of that painting had never been far from her mind. She looked forward to every letter her mother received from Martha Abraham, hoping to hear something about the young man behind the likeness.

Margaret had known that Fair Abe had been in the Arctic on her father's ship, and that he needed to be in Sheerness for the Court Martial of Sir Edward, but she did not know why his testimony was important. She didn't know much about Admiralty law, but she couldn't imagine what value there could be in the viewpoint of some one who was not even a British subject, let alone a sailor in the Royal Navy. So far, her father's letters had been rather cryptic about something that had happened on the *Assistance,* but neither she nor her mother knew much about it. Maybe Fair Abe had witnessed something, and by the very nature of his being an American, an outsider, his testimony might be given more weight.

Margaret knew, through snippets of overheard conversations between Father and Mother, that her father had not been happy in the past when he had come home from serving under Sir Edward, and she could imagine he had not been glad to serve under him again. But her father never really spoke about these things with Mother, and certainly not with her. For most of this year, 1854, she and her mother had been more focused on the conflict in the Crimea, and not what problems Father may have been facing in the Arctic. Their main thoughts about his service were ones of relief that he was out of harm's way where this new war was concerned. Their anxiety for him had only grown since the Arctic exploration expedition had returned to England. Margaret hoped her father would be able to come home for a while before being called back to duty. She had missed him more than she cared to admit.

'When did he think they will arrive?'

'He says they will be here in the late afternoon, certainly before tea.'

'Mother, that only gives us three hours! What shall I wear?'

'We have more than enough time to choose our dresses, Margaret. Calm down! Don't forget, haste makes waste!'

'Oh, Mother!' Margaret exclaimed as she flounced out of the room. Alice followed her, smiling at her daughter's sudden nervousness. She couldn't possibly be worried about greeting her father, so, despite all past assertions about her lack of interest in Martha's boy, she must be anxious about meeting young Fair Abe.

Margaret saw him walking into the inn with Father before either of the men caught sight of her, a moment's advantage, which she took to steady herself. He looked older than the image captured forever in the painting back in America. In her nervousness she babbled away instead of giving the calm welcome she had planned. 'Father!' she cried out and ran into his outstretched arms. 'Mother will be joining us in a moment. How was your journey? Are you tired? Hungry? We were so worried for you! You must tell us everything about the Court Martial. I am so glad to see that you have your sword back, and you have been absolved from any wrong doing.' Margaret paused to take a much needed breath. 'Hello, you must be Fair Abe, I am Margaret Kellett. Mother and I have been looking forward to meeting you for ages. We are so glad you can be with us for these few days. Will you tell us all about your adventures with Papa? How do you like England? What have you seen of it?'

Fair Abe didn't know which question to answer first, and, as if her beauty wasn't enough to tie his tongue, he was too tired to know what to do with this wall of enthusiasm which engulfed him. Henry Kellett came to his rescue before he appeared to dumb to speak, 'Now, Margaret, the poor boy has just had a long and arduous journey in the foulest weather. Let him dry himself off and get his bearings before he has to account for himself to you.'

'Oh, Papa, of course, I am sorry, Fair Abe, We will meet you later for tea. Oh look, here is Mother!' Alice swept down the stairs and into the arms of her husband.

'You are soaking wet!' Alice pulled away before her new velvet dress could get ruined. 'You must go up directly and get into warm and dry clothes. I have asked for a full dinner to be prepared for us, and it should be ready by the time you have dressed. We will wait for you in the reception room.'

Alice and Margaret rose together when Henry and Fair Abe rejoined them. Throughout the dinner Margaret kept up a nervous chatter, which had the opposite effect than the one she wanted to have. She allowed Fair Abe almost no chance to join in the conversation, yet more than anything she wanted to learn more about him. Henry and Alice thought it was amusing, watching their daughter, who usually had no time for young men, struggle to keep her composure.

Fair Abe seemed content to simply see the miniature portrait he had admired for so long come to life in the shape of this full sized, full-bodied woman sitting here before his eyes.

After dinner, Henry and Alice excused themselves and retreated to their room. 'I have missed you, my love, tell me about the Court Martial. Was it as grim as you thought it might be?'

'It went as smoothly as one could expect. There was one captain I thought might be able to sway the court against me, perhaps an old friend of Belcher's, but I had made doubly sure no blame could land on my shoulders before we left *Resolute.* They really had no choice but to acquit me. To be honest, it is Sir Edward's Court Martial I am most concerned about, and Fair Abe's testimony.'

'Why? You never did explain what happened, and how Martha's boy is mixed up in it.'

Henry told the tale of the abuse Fair Abe had suffered at Belcher's hands, Martha becoming more anxious, even fearful, as the story progressed. 'You see, he has always been able to get away with his sadistic behaviour before this,' Henry continued, 'Even when he was court martialed for abusing his men on board HMS *Aetna*, all he got was a hand slap after having tortured one man until that unfortunate sailor lost his sanity. But now we feel certain there is no way he will be able to squirm out of the allegations. I hate to say it was a good thing, but it is assuredly in our favour that Fair Abe is an impartial outsider. I wish I understood how Belcher has been able to escape the consequences of his actions for so long. Why did he even get such an important commission in the first place?'

'He must have friends in the high places.'

'Friends; or someone very afraid of him: some one in a position of great power. Never mind that now, we have loving to be catching up on. Come here, wife!'

Alice obeyed Henry with a slight smile playing on her lips, lips he covered with his own: a deep, demanding kiss that she responded to with her whole body. Henry took the pins from her thick, blonde hair, letting it cascade over her shoulders and down her back. The lamp light caught the highlights, making her face seem as though it was framed by a glowing halo. 'My own redeeming angel,' he whispered, 'Take off your dress for me, and let me see you before we blow out the lamp. All those months in the cold, so far away from you, I had to imagine the way you look. I want to see every curve: your heavy breasts, your rounded stomach, your beautiful thighs.'

'Oh, Henry, I age every time you are away. I am afraid I will disappoint you. I am not as young as I once was. Gravity has become my enemy.' She removed her dress.

'You are always beautiful to me. You are softer now, look!' Henry pulled aside her camisole to reveal her ample breasts. Taking them in his hand, he bent down and suckled one of her nipples. She shuddered. He quickly helped her to remove the rest of her clothing and made her stand away from him while he soaked up the sight of her body. She tried to come to him, but he wouldn't let her.

'Henry, stop. You are embarrassing me!' He held his arms out to her and he pressed her down onto the bed. His fingers and his mouth explored every inch of her, while she became wetter and more swollen in anticipation of his taking her. He made her beg for him to enter her, enjoying the power her desire created. He talked to her as he made love to her, telling her how it felt to be inside her warm and yielding body. Afterward, they slept without dreams in each others arms.

In the deserted dining room, Fair Abe had gently waited for Margaret to wind down, and she finally ran out of things to talk about. Her talkativeness had been a good mask for his shyness, and had given him the time to get comfortable with the young woman who had been the unknowing recipient of his longing.

'You must think me awful, nattering on like this all evening,' Margaret smiled in embarrassment.

'I think thou art the most beautiful woman I have even seen!' Fair Abe blushed, but not as deeply as Margaret. They both looked down at their hands, unsure about what to do next. Then Margaret reached across the table and took Fair Abe's hand. He pulled her towards him, and touched her cheek, running his hand gently down the softness of its curve. The electric shock of contact ran through their bodies, and their breath quickened.

'Sorry, me lovelies, it's time I were closing th' room. You'll have to do yer courtin' sommers else.' They smiled, and in that shared moment they both acknowledged that yes, indeed, they were courting. The miles that had separated them, the years that had passed between the first moments when they had become aware of each other, and this moment when they first touched melted away. Fair Abe and Margaret went to their respective rooms, happy in the thought that this was the beginning of a new story that was yet to be told.

⚓⚓⚓⚓⚓

There were only three days until Captain Kellett and Fair Abe had to leave London again for Sheerness and the Court Martial of Sir Edward Belcher. The former squadron commander had not been present for the Kellett Court Martial, and no one had seen him anywhere. Fair Abe felt more nervous everyday. However, the time he spent with Margaret helped to calm his fears. Captain and Mrs Kellett, Margaret and he spent the first two days visiting museums and seeing the London sights. In the evening, the young couple found themselves frequently deserted by the adults, giving them long hours to deepen their knowledge of and affection for each other. Fair Abe had almost forgotten the upcoming Court Martial, so immersed was he in his new found love.

This was why he was so shocked on the third day when they returned from their sight-seeing and he found Belcher waiting for him in the inn's reception room. Fair Abe stopped abruptly in the doorway upon seeing him. He felt his heart pounding with adrenaline as Belcher walked toward him, smiling.

'I had hoped to see you today; could we please sit and talk?'

Fair Abe said nothing. He didn't know what to say. Without his minions or his ship, Belcher was not as frightening; he sounded almost vulnerable and kind.

'Please? I want you to know how sorry I am for what happened to you onboard the *Assistance*. You must understand; I was under a great deal of strain. Can you appreciate the difficult position I was in? Can you forgive me?'

Fair Abe's beliefs dictated that he should be able to forgive this man, but his very soul rebelled at the thought. Would it even be right? Would forgiving him mean dropping his testimony? For that could be the only reason Belcher was coming to him on the eve of his Court Martial: to get him to withdraw his statement. How many others had Belcher wronged in the past? If I don't testify, how many more men will he harm in the future if I don't stop him, Fair Abe wondered to himself. Never before had Fair Abe felt such a conflict between the call to forgive and the call to do the right thing. His silence irritated the commander.

'Listen,' Belcher's face was turning red, 'you don't seem to understand, I am an important man in the Royal Navy; I come from a family steeped in position and rank. My forefathers were privileged members of the Royal Court, governors of vast lands in America; even though my family had to run to Canada during your war of rebellion in 1776 we still have power and influence beyond anything you could imagine. You bloody Americans think everybody should do your bidding; as far as I'm concerned, you are just another Yankee upstart. Do you know what you will be doing if you cross me? You can't hurt me; nothing you say or do will ever have any effect on my standing. But I can promise you this,' Belcher grabbed Fair Abe by the collar, 'I will do everything in my power to ruin you if you dare...'

'What is going on here?' Captain Kellett entered the room. 'Get your hands off the lad! You are in enough trouble already, without adding intimidation of witnesses to your wrong-doings. Get out!' Kellett pulled his former commander away from Fair Abe. Belcher turned on him.

'You! I'll see to you, too. I have friends, important friends. You can't do anything to me, but I can put an end to your naval career, so watch your step.' Belcher's voice was almost a shriek, and his hands shook in rage. 'You had better think very carefully about what you plan to say. How much do you value your position in the Navy? Because I can guarantee you, you will no longer have one if you persist...'

'Enough! Leave us now or I will call the Bobbies and have you thrown out!' Belcher and Kellett glared at one another, while Fair Abe began to move slowly toward the door in order to seek help should the confrontation turn violent. How much easier it was to be non-violent at home among other Quakers! Right now, he wanted to strike the man who had tortured him!

Belcher suddenly turned round and stormed out of the inn; both Kellett and Fair Abe collapsed into chairs with relief.

'Can he really ruin you, Captain?'

'Honestly, I don't know. But I am determined to see this through. He has done enough damage to too many young men. It is time someone stops him, and I mean to do it.' Kellett smiled at Fair Abe. 'Maybe I'll have to start looking for a new position, but I will not be moved from giving my testimony, no matter what he threatens!'

Later that night, when Fair Abe told Margaret about the confrontation they had had with Belcher, his concern for her father's and even his own safety, Margaret put her arms around his shoulders and said,

'Will you tell me what happened on *Assistance*? Fair Abe looked away and was silent for a few minutes; then he told Margaret his story. They sat in silence until Margaret quietly said 'You are doing the right thing. What that man did to you was horrible, and I suspect you were not the first. Nor will you be the last if you do not stand up to him. He mustn't be allowed to carry on.'

Fair Abe went to bed, but was unable to sleep. It felt good to tell Margaret what had happened; it was no longer a secret he was keeping from her. But recounting the experience stirred up many unbidden feelings, and he was still sorting through them and thinking about the upcoming trial when the morning light began to filter through the window to his room. He got dressed and walked down along the Thames, seeking clarity and strength. It was during that walk that he realised no matter how difficult it can be to 'speak truth to power', as so many Quakers before him had done, his faith and Margaret's belief in him would give him the courage he needed to see this difficult task through to the end.

When Fair Abe did not attend breakfast and could not be found in his rooms, Margaret raised the alarm. Captains Kellett and Richards found him three hours later, beaten, bruised and unconscious down an alleyway near the river. He remained unconscious into the evening, and when he awoke he did not recognise his companions.

'This is Belcher's doing, I know it!' Kellett swore. 'Richards, can we bring the testimony he was going to give to the Court Martial without him?'

'How do you know it was Belcher? It could have been a robbery gone wrong.'

'Do you really think this is a coincidence? I caught Belcher here yesterday, trying to intimidate the boy. He was getting quite angry when he couldn't extract a promise from Fair Abe to not testify. I had to threaten him with the authorities before he would leave. He acted like he knows he has some sort of immunity, but he still wanted to hedge his bets by making Fair Abe stay away. Do you have any idea why he is so sure he can't be touched or brought down?'

A messenger interrupted the two men, and Kellett read the note with a deepening frown. 'It seems Fair Abe, you and I are to report first thing tomorrow at the Admiralty. Do you suppose they know about the attack?'

The following morning, the day they were meant to leave again for Sheerness, Fair Abe still did not recognise anyone, not even Margaret, who stayed by his bedside continuously. So Kellett and Richards had to go without him to the Admiralty. When they returned to the inn, Fair Abe was conscious and sitting up in bed.

'Do you remember anything at all? Can you tell us what happened?'

'I am afraid I never saw my assailants. Two men grabbed me from behind and hustled me into an alley, but I never saw them. They struck me about the head and I do not remember anything else.'

'Do you know your name?'

'I am sorry, Sir, no. I don't know what I am doing here and I cannot recognise any of your faces.'

Kellett saw that Fair Abe was becoming agitated. 'Don't worry yourself. I have seen this before with head injuries. It is usually just a matter of time, rest and healing.'

Margaret and the men withdrew. 'He won't be able to testify, Father. What are you going to do without him?'

Don't worry on that score, we will not be testifying after all.'

'What!' Margaret rose with anger in her eyes. 'Father, you must! You cannot let him get away with what he has done!'

'It has been taken out of my hands, child. We have been ordered, and this order has come from the very highest places, to withdraw our testimony concerning Belcher's treatment of fair Abe. When I protested, we were assured that if we agree to do this, Sir Edward will never again get another commission. He will have to retire.'

'But that is not just! He should be punished by more than that!'

'I know Fair Abe will not receive justice. Other than being forced to retire Belcher will go unpunished. But the most important thing we wanted we will get: he will never have the chance to harm any more young men.'

'Why has this happened, Father?'

'I cannot tell you, for I do not know myself. But Mr. Richards has his own theory, which he conveyed to me in the carriage on our way back here.' He turned to Fair Abe. 'Mr. Richards made a journal while we were in the Arctic, you see, when Belcher's behaviour began to alarm him. The captain was frequently drunk, and when he was in his cups he would call Richards in to him. His inebriated mind took all manner of delusional twists and turns: his paranoia coming to the fore most prominently. But he also dwelt upon the multi-generational relationship his family has had with the Royal family since the mid seventeenth century. Belcher believes, somehow, that his family is the keeper of some secret about the legitimacy of the Hanover succession, and this is why he feels so protected. What truth there could possibly be in this is impossible to tell, but he is most certainly protected, and that protection comes from the very highest level of authority.

'All I know is that these are our orders, and they must be obeyed. The good in this is that Fair Abe will not have to travel, and can recover here while Richards and I go back to Sheerness.' Captain Kellett bade his family goodbye, and the two men left within the hour to witness the end of Sir Edward Belcher's naval career.

While the prior courts martial had been fairly straightforward and quick, Belcher's court martial dragged on for days. It began with the examination of witnesses by the court. Although Belcher had approached all the witnesses, just as he had Fair Abe, in an attempt to intimidate them into supporting his order for the abandonment of the four ships, not all of his witnesses toed the line. When the court questioned the *Assistance's* master about the extensive damage that the *Assistance* had supposedly suffered when a gale had blown her ashore during the winter of '53, Loney said he considered the damage of a 'trifling nature'. Asked if it would have been safe for the *Assistance* and *Pioneer* to remain where they were, Loney replied, 'Certainly'.

The Surgeon, Mr. Lyall, testified that, though the health of the master and himself would have been affected if Belcher had left them aboard the *Assistance,* he would have had little fear for their lives. More damning still, the surgeon of the *North Star* claimed that all the officers under Belcher's command, with the exception of Belcher and three others, would have been perfectly fit to stay and wait for new crew and supplies. Furthermore, the clerk in charge testified that there were adequate provisions of every kind, except tinned beef, to keep the crew for another full year.

The court then called Osborn, captain of the *Pioneer.* 'She was pressed on the shore in the autumn of 1853, but received no damage and was as safe as she could be, given the usual harm that Arctic service generally inflicts.'

'Can you not say what state the *Assistance* was in?'

'She appeared to me to be in a very similar position.'

'Was there an unusual quantity of ice in the Wellington Channel in June 1854?'

'No. It was merely frozen over.'

'Could you, at that time, form any opinion as to the probability of the vessel's getting through the ice that summer?'

'I was led to believe they would escape early by the numerous cracks I crossed on my way down to Beechey Island.'

'Are you aware what quantity of provisions there were at Beechey Island and in the *North Star*?'

'I know unofficially that twelve months additional provisions were forwarded by the Admiralty in 1853 to Beechey Island. 180 tons of coal, to the best of my knowledge, were originally landed there at the same time.'

'Were the *Assistance* and her tender, in your opinion, fit to encounter another winter in the Arctic Seas?'

'Perfectly so – so far as the ships were concerned.'

'Are you aware of any other reason why they should not have remained?'

'It would have required some arrangement relative to the crews, those originally sailing in them having become much worn and debilitated.'

'Are you aware whether an arrangement could have been made so as to have allowed those ships to remain safely?'

'I do not know if the crews of the *Phoenix* and *Talbot* were available. If they were, I should have employed them to remain in the ships. Also, provisions could have been transferred from the *North Star.* She was, after all, our depot ship and this was why she had been stationed on Beechey Island while the other four ships searched farther into the Arctic.'

McClintock's testimony was just as damning for Belcher. Drawing on his prior service, he claimed that the *Assistance* and *Pioneer* were actually in a less hazardous position than the ships had been when he served under Ross! But through all of this, and the testimony of Kellett and others, Belcher showed no signs of being worried.

Belcher then began his defence. The court listened with barely disguised disgust and impatience to Belcher's rambling, obsequious speech wherein he recounted every detail of the two years he had spent in the Arctic. Belcher called witness after witness to testify to each bit of minutia, but he skirted around any incident that could possibly put him in a bad light. Belcher read his instructions from the Admiralty into the court record, making certain that the court knew he had been given quite a bit of latitude regarding any decision to abandon the ships under his care. Belcher carefully avoided any reference to his drunkenness, calling his problem one of failing health. He even had the audacity to claim that he had given full consideration to the safety and welfare of Collinson, whom he had abandoned to his own devices.

Finally, after hours of attempting to discredit all the rest of the witnesses who had testified before he began his defence, Belcher virtually called McClintock a liar.

'I regret to find the evidence of Commander McClintock today varies so completely from the opinions he expressed earlier to me. Not only had he changed his opinion of the danger my ships were in, he also has clearly stated to this court that, as an officer, he would act in defiance of the orders he knew I held, and of which he had an authorised copy, and would have remained by his vessel. I am happy to find that the more officer-like testimony of Captain Kellett agrees with my sense of naval discipline.'

At this, the court became restless. Several officers cleared their throats and looked uncomfortable. Sir Thomas Pasley could not keep his eyes on Belcher, and looked away in embarrassment.

Sir Edward summed up in his usual rambling, self-aggrandising way. 'I have now been nearly 43 years in the Naval service of my country, 36 years a commissioned officer and for periods of nearly 20 years, I have been entrusted with more important commands and exercised greater powers than, I believe, few of my rank have ever held.

'I have met with the approbation of my Lords Commissioners of the Admiralty, that of the Foreign Office, and I trust of many distinguished officers in my profession. I have met the enemies of my country during the years of 1812 through 1816, and 1843; and, as a neutral, repeatedly under fire in the Douro in 1833, was ranked by the higher powers for the same judgement and decision, which this day, for the first time in my life, has ever been questioned, not by my Lords Commissioners of the Admiralty, but by the customary of the Service, of which, I trust, I shall not be found by this honourable Court to be an unworthy member.

'Next to the approbation of my Sovereign, and of my Lords Commissioners of the Admiralty, I value the honourable approval of my professional brethren. Jealous of my honour, and sensitively alive to the remotest shadow of blame, I confidently repose in your hands that character which during a long and trying service in every clime, and in the remotest regions of the Earth, has, I trust, not now been tarnished by obedience to the wishes, as well as the commands of my Lords Commissioners of the Admiralty.'

The Lords Commissioners of the Admiralty breathed a collective sigh of relief when they no longer had to follow the convoluted speech of their defendant; they quickly recessed the court after Belcher handed over a bundle of documents to support his defence.

The court reopened to an expectant silence as Belcher, the witnesses and audience filed in. The Deputy Judge Advocate, William Hayward, read out the court's decision without emotion, and avoided meeting Sir Edward's eyes.

Acquitted.

Belcher stepped forward to the table which held his sword, hilt facing him, expecting the same sort of commendation that Kellett had received. In this he was sorely disappointed. His sword was handed back to him in deafening silence: the worst rebuke a court could offer when it found itself in the disagreeable position of having to acquit a man they desperately wanted to convict.

Belcher walked out fuming.

CHAPTER THREE
MAY 1855

County Tipperary, near Clonacody, is a place of gently rolling open fields, which quietly rise up to meet the hills in the south. In the spring the pasture land is covered in a new bright green, and the horse farms are busy with foaling. Captain Kellett enjoyed walking the lands on his estate with Naps at his heels. He liked to stop and watch Margaret training the horses and listen to McCaffrey's praise for their horses, this year's successful breeding, and Margaret's way with the beasts. Alice spent much of her time in her walled kitchen garden, and Henry loved to sneak up on her and hug her from behind. He was never sure how much of a surprise it was, if she really didn't hear him, or could tell he was there long before she pretended to be startled. It didn't matter much, either way they were able to share an embrace. Sometimes he brought her water or tea, and sat and read from books or the newspapers to her as she worked.

And it was the news from the Crimea that started it. Henry was sitting next to Alice reading from *The Times* about the war. For the first time in history, a newspaper had a correspondent on the front, reporting the war on a daily basis. William Howard Russell's vivid, sometimes too vivid, accounts brought the war home to the civilians in a way that they had never experienced before. The war, with all its horror, was in the British home, served up with tea at breakfast, and it was more than some could take. It wasn't just the military action that was causing an outcry from the public, but the ineptitude of the War Department: the lack of medical and other essential supplies that were causing unnecessary suffering to the brave soldiers, the bungled logistics that left the men dying from hunger, exposure, disease and wounds that should not have been fatal.

Henry was unaware of the extent of Alice's feelings about the war until he began to read Russell's latest report and he was startled by his wife's strident voice. 'Having women like Florence Nightingale and Mary Seacole tending the wounded is like putting a bandage on a deep and festering wound! The whole business is rotten! I am certain what they are doing is very commendable, but what we really need is an immediate end to the war.'

'Now, Alice, there were valid reasons for this war, and the best thing we can do to end it quickly is to give the government, and our poor soldiers, our complete support. It doesn't do any good to undermine Downing Street at a time like this.'

'I am sorry, Henry, but I disagree. I have spent the last six months working very closely with the Quakers, and I feel it is my patriotic duty to act as my conscience dictates. A true patriot does not turn a blind eye when her government is doing wrong. She speaks up, challenges the powers that be. The Quakers call it 'speaking truth to power.''

'Alice! What have you been doing?'

'I have been writing letters to the papers, which I have every right to do.'

'What else have you been up to? It is people like you, who meddle in things they don't understand, that make the government's and military's jobs significantly more difficult!' When she didn't answer, he continued, 'Is it as bad as all that, then? Good God, woman, what have you done? You might be considered a traitor! If the Admiralty gets to know about any suspicious activity on your part, it could jeopardise my career.'

'Your career, is that all that matters to you? Does everything have to revolve around you?'

'You know I am not like that. My career is an important part of our financial and social standing. And I rely on you, on your clear-headedness, your even temper and your wisdom in all aspects of our life: in our marriage, in the running of our estate, and in the raising of Margaret. What kind of an example can you be for her if you are running around with anarchists?'

'The very best I can be, following the leadings of my heart to speak up about wrong doing. And, please don't exaggerate. I am not running around with anarchists. The Quakers I work with are very sincere and devote Christians with an abiding interest in social justice and peace.'

'I am sorry, Alice. I did not mean to denigrate the Quakers. But you are naive if you think all of the people unhappy about the war are all such honourable people. There are some who would use the growing anti-war feelings to tear down the government and even the monarchy.'

'Don't be silly, Henry. No one wants to...'

'Yes, they do. And using the war issue as a blind for fomenting unrest is exactly the sort of thing these unscrupulous people do. I cannot demand that you stop...'

'You most certainly cannot demand, command, or in any other way tell me what to do or believe! I am not one of your crew!'

'I did not mean to hurt...' Henry reached out to touch Alice's shoulder.

'Get away from me! Get off!' Alice threw down her trowel and stormed out of the garden. Henry watched her leave, feeling somewhat stunned. Naps, who had been getting more and more concerned as the voices rose in volume and intensity, now cowered under Henry's chair. Henry reached down and scratched Naps' head, comforting himself as well as the dog. What had happened to the Alice he knew?

In the past, even after years of absence, they had always been able to quickly re-establish and affirm the deep and abiding love they shared. Such closeness could only be described as two halves making a whole. They were one, in body, mind and spirit. Now they were strangers, their passionate lovemaking becoming a distant memory.

Try as he might, Henry could not see any way to resolve the discord which was driving them apart. He was a respected captain in the Royal Navy. Though he had always been in the Hydrographic Department, and never commanded a warship, his surveying formed an essential support for his country in times of conflict. While the navy was a tool often used for exploration, in the final analysis it was Britain's largest weapon of war. Now his life's work was at variance with Alice's passionate cause.

Henry was not a warmonger. He did not even feel Britain's decision to go to war in this case was correct. But he was an officer in Her Majesty's Royal Navy, and if called to serve, he would do whatever he was ordered to do. Pray God, he wouldn't be called to go to the Crimea, because if he was sent there, the battle to preserve his marriage could be lost forever.

⚓⚓⚓⚓⚓

It had taken six months for Fair Abe to regain his strength and return to his family. They had all missed him terribly, but now that he was back the peace of the household was being disrupted by his increasing anger. He could not believe the way that the events in the Kansas Territory were unfolding. Less than two months ago an election had been held to choose members of the territorial legislature. Border Ruffians, armed southerners from Missouri, had swelled the ranks of the pro-slavers by close to four thousand men, defeating any chance that Kansas might have to be a free state. Their new state legislature had been busy enacting bogus laws, including making it a crime to speak or write against slavery! All this in the 'land of the free' where freedom of speech, thought and press were supposed to be the bedrock upon which the country had been built. Freedom of conscience: the very thing that the Abraham's Quaker ancestors, and most of the other pilgrims, had come to America for in the first place.

Now the northern settlers were setting up their own legislature in Topeka. This would mean that the Kansas Territory would have two opposing governments. Which one would President Pierce recognise? Of course, since he was such a southern sympathiser, Fair Abe was afraid the president would most probably acknowledge the pro-slavers.

Dinner in the Abraham household was becoming a tense affair. Fair Abe's approach to abolition was becoming much too radical for Father and Martha. The boy was beginning to accept that violent conflict was going to be the only way to settle the issue, and had said last night that if it came to war he would be likely to fight for the cause of freedom. He would not hide behind his faith.

'We do not hide behind our faith, Fair Abe. Our faith is the Light by which

127

we work for justice. Thy commitment to abolition is commendable, but thou canst not forget our equally strong commitment to non-violence. Thou shalt not kill, the Lord saith. Thou shalt not kill. Dost thou truly believe thee can pick up a gun and kill with it? Even for so noble a cause?'

'Mother, I am sorry, truly sorry, but I do see a time coming when talk will no longer be enough. I am not afraid to die!'

'Oh my son, we Quakers have never been afraid to die for our beliefs. Our history teaches us this. But there is a very wide river one must cross to go from being willing to die to being willing to kill. It is not a matter of courage. Or perhaps it is. In the midst of war fever it may take much more courage to stand up and say war is wrong than to succumb to the mood of the mob.'

Fair Abe tried to listen with an open heart to the words of his father and mother, but he could not shake his belief that the time for talk would soon be over, and the sharp sickle of war would separate the wheat from the chaff.

Martha Abraham was worried over other news that was just hitting the presses. Great Britain had begun recruiting soldiers for their Crimean War in several American cities. At the beginning of the war, she had been part of a letter-writing campaign to President Pierce, urging him to remain neutral in Britain's Russian war. She knew that the official position of the federal government was that of neutrality. Martha was not naive enough to think her letters were the only reason for this. For complex reasons she did not completely understand, the United States were more empathetic to Russia anyway. Trade issues played a large part in this. Even so, she was happy that the neutrality was real and demonstrable. However, this news about the recruiting, if it was true, could jeopardise all that.

Martha wondered if Alice had heard anything about it over in Ireland. She spent part of her morning writing her friend a newsy letter about the family and the bright love that seemed to glow in her oldest son, Fair Abe. Did Margaret exhibit the same? It was more difficult to write about Fair Abe's increasingly belligerent attitudes about abolition and the tension he was causing in the family. Would mentioning it only serve to create tension in her relationship with Alice Kellett? Fair Abe had told her about the conversations he had had with Henry Kellett when he was onboard *Resolute*. Martha knew her friends strongly supported the abolition of slavery, and that they did not approve of the length of time the United States was taking to follow Britain's lead. More diplomatically, she wrote about the slavery issue by relaying the latest news from Kansas, 'Bleeding Kansas' she had heard it called.

But at the end she asked the questions that was troubling her most. Did Alice know anything about this recruiting? How was the Crimean War being portrayed in the presses in Great Britain? And lastly, did she know anything about what the British Quakers were doing to bear witness to their peace testimony?

She ended her letter with love, and sent it with Father to post the following morning.

Breathing hard, Alice stopped outside the scullery door to quiet herself before entering Clonacody. After yet again another argument with Henry, it wouldn't do to have the cook see her like this. The cook! Alice didn't like to see herself like this! After all the time she had been spending with the Friends, she had hoped some inner serenity would keep her from being so fiery about these issues. She couldn't believe such a quiet, understanding, and loving husband could have made her feel so angry! They had never had so much tension between them as they did every time they discussed the war. Was the issue worth ruining her marriage? Could anything mean more to her than the love she felt for Henry, and the peaceful home they shared with their daughter? How could she be campaigning for peace, yet bring such violent emotions into their lives?

She fell so short of her ideal for herself. It was difficult to keep from inappropriately releasing the disappointment and anger she felt with herself on her husband and daughter. The angrier she became with herself for being angry the worse the anger became! How would Martha handle such a situation? She should write to her friend and ask her for advice: how do Quakers handle family conflict? She would have to make amends with Henry, apologise for losing her temper, but not for her beliefs, nor her actions for peace. After all, this was the only political voice she had; she could not vote, but she could let the powers that be know how she felt. And in this, she would continue.

Sitting at her desk, Alice opened the file of newspaper articles she was collecting. First, there was the article that castigated the Quaker delegation, Sturge, Charlton and Pease, which had visited the tsar in 1854, just before war was declared. Then she pulled out the article dated the 12th of October, 1854, written by Russell from the front for *The Times*. It was this article that solidified her opposition to the war. In it, Russell described the inadequate medical preparation for the treatment of the wounded: insufficient surgeons and nurses weren't the worst of it. There wasn't even linen to make bandages! Men had been left up to a week without any medical attention, and were dying because of it. Such a level of incompetence was difficult to fathom. Did Great Britain hold the lives of her young men so cheaply that she could not even supply old rags to bind their wounds?

She wept when she reread Russell's eye witness account of the Charge of the Light Brigade. 'Desperate valour' he had called it. Begun just after eleven on the morning of October 25th and lasting only 20 minutes, the casualties had been horrific: out of nearly 700 horsemen only 195 survived; the 17th Lancers had only 37 men left; and the 13th Light Dragoons could muster a mere 2 officers and 8 men. The Russians had killed many of the wounded as they lay on the field.

Lastly, she read the report of the speech made on the twenty third of February this year by the Quaker MP from Manchester, John Bright. Bright and Richard Cobden were the two most outspoken politicians against the war. They had worked together to repeal the Corn Laws in the 1840's, and now found themselves again on the same side of a divisive issue. In his impassioned speech he recalled the biblical imagery of the first Passover:

> 'The angel of death has been abroad throughout the land; you may almost hear the beating of his wings. There is no one, as when the first born were slain of old, to sprinkle with blood the lintel and the two side posts of our doors, that he may spare and pass on; he takes his victims from the castle of the noble, the mansions of the wealthy, and the cottage of the poor and lowly.'

The angel of death...winging his way through the villages and cities, through farm and country, taking away the best hopes for the future of Britain by the thousands. The thing that made her most angry was that only a small percentage of the deaths were from actual battle, it was their own bungling government and military that were killing most of the young men.

It was in this fatal absurdity that Alice was able to see the futility of war, and in that spirit she decided to write to Martha Abraham.

Margaret found her mother sitting at her desk, gazing out of the window to the distant hills. She wasn't certain if she should disturb her, and had just resolved to turn away when Alice faced her and smiled.

'Did you need me?'

'Yes, Mother, I want your advice. I am writing a letter to Fair Abe, mostly telling him about the latest news about the war, and then a few stories about the horse I have been working with lately. But I don't know how much I should say about my feelings for him. I want to tell him how much I love him! Would that be wrong?'

Alice felt so pleased to be involved in such a bright and happy concern that she almost laughed out loud. She stopped herself with a smile just in time. It would not do to have her daughter believe she did not take her seriously. Any time her almost grown daughter came to her to talk or ask her advice she felt it was a gift, a valuable gift not to be squandered but honoured.

'So, that is what you are seeking my advice for?'

'Yes. You see, when we were together it was obvious to both of us that we felt passionately for each other.' Margaret blushed when Alice raised her eye brows. 'Not that we did anything passionate! Well, we did kiss. A few times. But he is a true gentleman, Mother; you have nothing to fear...'

'I never thought I did! I trust you and I also trust the upbringing he has had. In fact, I meant to tell you, when I saw your attachment to each other growing, that I am very happy for you.'

'Are you? Sometimes I worry about how far apart we are. We are in two different countries divided by a huge ocean. In fact, I don't know where this can possibly lead. I would never want to leave Clonacody!'

'You must take it one day at a time, my love. Do not worry about the future. I believe if two people are meant to be together, they will not only find each other, as you and Fair Abe have, but a way will open for your love to grow. So, for now, let's see about your letter. What do you think you should do?'

'On the one hand, I want to tell him how deeply I love him. But on the other, I am afraid to be so open. What if he doesn't feel the same way? What if I scare him with my honesty?'

'You should never be afraid of being honest with someone you love. If you have to be afraid, then there is something wrong, and the man is not the one for you. But, there is a considerable difference between being honest and being a bit mysterious.'

'What do you mean?'

'It does no good to lie. So, you wouldn't be wise to write that you don't care for him at all. That would not be true. However, being a bit mysterious can make a man want to get to know you better. Instead of exposing your heart so completely, just show small glimpses. Take small steps toward each other, rather than enormous leaps. Do you understand?'

I think so. Rather than waxing lyrical about how much I love him, maybe I could just say that his tenderness has touched my heart.'

'Yes! That is it exactly! A truthful, yet small step, and, if I am any judge of the young man, it will leave him wanting to touch your heart again, in new and different ways.'

'Thank you, Mama!'

Alice smiled at her daughter's retreating back, and then returned to her own letter. She told her friend, Martha, about domestic news, and included her recent conversation with Margaret. Both mothers were hoping that the young ones would be able to find a way to build a life together, and were doing all they could, without appearing to interfere, to encourage the match. She asked a generic question about how Quakers resolve family conflict. Then she wrote about her recent peace work, knowing her friend would encourage her to continue, but she did not tell her that this work was destroying the very fabric of her life.

⚓⚓⚓⚓⚓

The pro-slavery vote of March 30th in the Kansas territory had sparked heated debates in New England, and Fair Abe's ability for listening to moderates seemed to be slipping farther and farther from his grasp.

Now there was the added matter of trouble with Great Britain. Hotheaded articles began appearing in the press. During the past two months, recruiters for the British army had been arrested in New York, Boston, and Philadelphia. While abolition and recruitment had nothing to do with each other, the Quakers were involved in both issues, particularly in the recruiting concern as they took on the role of mediation between those who were already taking sides.

The temper of the times seemed explosive, as though the emotions of the people were afire. Each new controversy added fuel to the flames, building and building...and Fair Abe was susceptible to the temper of the times. He held his Quaker values in high regard, yet he was a sensitive lad and he felt things deeply. He could feel himself being swept into the maelstrom, but didn't have the strength to pull away.

'Fair Abe, I would like to talk with thee in the library tonight after dinner.'

Fair Abe nodded his head, 'Alright, Father.' What was it going to be this time? He loved his father, but he was growing tired of being counselled almost every time he turned around. They shared the same beliefs and convictions, so why did they go head-to-head so often? Fair Abe recalled the relationship he had had with Captain Kellett onboard *Resolute.* It was so easy to talk with him; he would even feel comfortable asking for his advice.

Despite the danger and hardship, Fair Abe remembered fondly the time he had spent in the Arctic. He felt at peace there. He had worked hard every day, surrounded by the Glory of the Lord, everywhere displayed in icy splendour. Life there was reduced to the most elemental level: the fight for survival. And particularly after his escape from Belcher's clutches, he had experienced a degree of brotherhood with the men on HMS *Resolute* that he had never yet felt outside his family.

Thinking about that time, he realised he had forgiven Belcher for the violent harm the man had done to his person. Odd, that. He had struggled for a long time to find forgiveness, but it had eluded him. His physical wounds had healed long before his return from the Arctic, but inside his spirit had still bled. Mother had told him to focus his prayers on the spiritual strength to heal. She had said that God was not interested in forgiveness that was given before the spirit was restored. To try to forgive while still deeply wounded was like putting a dressing on the skin when the injury was causing internal haemorrhaging, which would cause that haemorrhaging to become infectious, poisoning your whole being. 'Thou must heal from the inside out, and then forgiveness will come to thee. Then thou canst lay down what has been forgiven at the Lord's feet, and it will feel like relieving thyself of a burden that has become too heavy to carry.'

And it had happened just as she had said it would! He did not know the exact moment in which the act of forgiveness had happened, but he felt as though a tremendous weight had been lifted from his shoulders. He no longer thought of Belcher with anger, but almost with compassion.

After dinner, he met Father Abraham in the library. Father closed the door and asked him to sit by the fire. 'Thou knowest we have one of our new ships, the *George Henry*, leaving for Baffin Bay at the end of the month. Captain James Buddington will be in command. Whouldst thou go with him? Thou hast learned a great deal about being in the Arctic after thy experience on *Resolute,* yet very little of thy time was actually spent whaling and getting to know the company's work. I would like thee to go as the second mate.'

Fair Abe did not know what to say. That Father would ask this of him on the same day he had been reminiscing about the two years he has spent in the ice seemed providential. Perhaps God did work in mysterious ways! Yet he felt conflicting emotions about the opportunity that his father was presenting to him. He would have to leave his anti-slavery work. Yes, he would have to leave...

'Dost thou want me to go just to get me away? If so, I cannot...'

'No, my son, thy mother and I share concern over the intensity of thy abolitionist feelings, but we both admire thy conviction. But, we must always find a reasonable balance between our works for justice and the work we must do for our family, and for the men who rely on us for work. Thou dost remember, when I sent thee in '52, it was to learn the trade. However, that opportunity was lost to you when the ice crushed our ship. Now, I see another chance to broaden thy understanding of our livelihood, before thou must settle down and take my place in the office. Sailing with the *George Henry* will be an invaluable experience that will help you in the years ahead to run this company in a responsible manner. My partners, our employees, and our family will be depending on thee.'

'Yes, Father, I see. I feared for a moment you wanted me to leave because we disagree so often about the way the Abolition Movement must progress. I almost feel cowardly in admitting this, as though I am running away from the issues here, but I do feel drawn to the Arctic. I know it was dangerous, and the work was hard, but my spirit soared when I looked out upon the mountains of ice, and travelled with the men, exploring and searching. I was just reflecting on it; and thy request seems almost as though thou didst hear my heart speaking to thee.'

'This work will be different, of course. Thy time will be spent onboard, at sea, hunting and processing the whale.'

'Yes, I know. But it is being on the sea that draws me as much as travelling on the ice.'

'Does this mean that thou shalt go with the *George Henry*?'

'Yes, Father, I will go.'

The 29th came more quickly than Fair Abe expected. Once again, his mother prepared his sea trunk with the necessities, including putting his Bible in between the layers of warm clothing. Once again, he stood on the dock, facing his whole family, his brothers and sisters, now three years older than the last time he bid them farewell. Last time, he had had no idea of what lay ahead, he only felt excitement. This time, his elation was tempered by knowing how much could happen between now and when he would see his family again. Father looked old, not worn, just old, and maybe a little tired. And grey hair was beginning to frame Mother's face. Would he see them again? Would they all be here to welcome him home? And what about Margaret Kellett? He had sent her a letter this morning, possibly the last one for a long time. Would she wait for him? She said in her most recent note that his kindness had warmed her heart. Well, he had risked all in his response. He told her he loved her; that he planned to make it his mission for the rest of his life to find new and better ways to warm that heart, and to fan the flames of her affection into a full-blown love.

CHAPTER FOUR
SEPTEMBER 1855

K ellett, now with the new rank of Commodore, looked up at the sails, the oppressive air making them limp and heavy. He had just arrived at the Jamaican Station in the West Indies onboard HMS *Medea,* and it was going to take a while to adjust to the heat and humidity. It was good to have many of the old Resolutes on board, including Pim and McDougall. He smiled to think that they couldn't be in a more different environment, from the arctic ice to lush tropics, yet the camaraderie between them was the same, and the Resolutes took their new appointment, and the harsh conditions, all in stride.

Fair Abe would appreciate these orders, Kellett thought, to monitor the slave trade and intercept slave ships between Jamaica and Cuba. Even though slavery was still legal in the United States, both America and Great Britain had outlawed the slave trade almost fifty years ago. No new slaves were supposed to be being taken from Africa and brought to the States. However, the slavers didn't want to stop such a lucrative business, so they circumvented the law by bringing slaves to Cuba, where the trade was still legal. Slaves were then smuggled into the southern states and auctioned off.

When it became obvious that abolishing the trade had done nothing to stop it, the United States passed a law in 1820 making participation in the slave trade an act of piracy, punishable by death. The States, however, lacked the political will to uphold either the 1808 law that criminalized the slave trade or the 1820 piracy law. Great Britain saw that outlawing the trade while keeping the slavery itself legal was only half the job done and Parliament abolished slavery throughout the Commonwealth in 1833. But slavery was still legal in the United States, so Britain's effect on the slave trade was negligible. Britain had been trying since the 1820's to get the States to cooperate in stamping out the trade by creating a mutual agreement to allow the search and seizure of slave ships at sea. Americans wouldn't agree, basing their opposition on issues of national pride and the freedom of the seas.

America's schizophrenic approach to slavery, passing laws and then ignoring them, was indicative of the divisive nature of the issue. Most American politicians scrambled over each other in their haste to distance themselves from making any stand for or against it, with the exception of those few on either side willing to be branded extremists. Not only did they prefer ignoring their own laws, they wouldn't cooperate with Britain when she attempted to put her teeth into their mutual anti-slave trade legislation.

Commodore Kellett, therefore, was in a diplomatically delicate situation. He had the legal and moral right to stop and seize all slave ships; yet he had to be very careful when stopping or searching American ships, because this was the same issue that had sparked the war between Britain and America in 1812. This was something American captains were quick to point out.

But, even when Kellett spotted a non-American slave ship, he could not just give chase. The unfortunate side effect of an illegal trade in combination with legal slavery was that the profits on the cargo were extremely high and the men who owned slave ships were amassing huge fortunes. Therefore, the loss of a ship, which had to be replaced and paid for, far outweighed the loss of the cargo, comparatively free for the taking. In an effort to minimise loss and maximise their vast profits, the ship owners gave the slaver captains orders to dump the cargo over board if they were in danger of being stopped or seized.

The cargo. This was the way the slavers talked, as if the dumping of the human beings in their holds was as simple as pitching barrels of rum into the deep. What the slave crews did was throw hundreds of living human beings into the ocean. They did not have time, or did not take the time, to un-manacle the men, women, and children. Chained together, they had no way to save their lives once in the water. They were expected to die, and die they did: clawing and kicking their husbands and wives, brothers and sisters, in one last effort to get to the surface to gulp the precious air before, lungs exploding, they could no longer resist breathing in the salt water. Then their chains dragged them down to their unmarked graves on the ocean floor.

Commodore Kellett felt that these deaths, if they happened as a result of his chasing a ship, would be just as much on his shoulders as on those of the slaver captains and crews, so he played a game of cat and mouse. He had his men spying on the operations: what bays did they use to unload slaves? What was their schedule? The Medeas, as well as men from the other four ships he commanded, recorded the slavers comings and goings for weeks before Kellett was ready to make a move.

It was easy to tell which ships were slavers: you could smell them five miles away if you were down wind of them. How the crews onboard could stand it, he didn't know. It was a unique and putrid stink: a combination of sweat, fear, vomit, human excrement, and decaying flesh. Even so, Kellett had learned that the chase on the high sea was worthless. He had to catch the slavers in harbour, but before they finished unloading their cargo.

The slavers knew, of course, that this was their most vulnerable time. They posted guards, paid their own spies to dispense misinformation, and got away as soon as they could in order to minimise their risk. The American slavers even sailed under false colours; using any ruse to keep the trade going and the money pouring in.

By the 9th of October, Kellett was able to complete a detailed report for the Admiralty, which included the names and nationalities of numerous slave ships, and the harbours and routes used by them. In his report he asked for more ships. It was clear to him that the level of trade was going to be impossible to stop with anything less than eight ships: two ships to cruise between Cuba and Jamaica, one off Cape Cruz, one in the eastern channel, and one each at Boca Grando and Boca de Cabellanores. He asked that the two last ships, which he wanted to place between Boca de Cabellanores and Cape Antonia, have a shallow draft so they could get into the small coves and bays used by the slavers. If the Admiralty granted his request, it would mean that each ship would then have just a little over 80 miles of coast to watch. He could almost affect a blockade, and get results.

As challenging as this posting was proving to be, Kellett was glad he had not been sent to the Crimea, not because he was afraid to fight for his country, but because he was afraid it would bring his marriage to the breaking point. He had not realised the extent of Alice's peace commitment. She had never been so against war in the past. Was this the influence of her Quaker friends? Through his long conversations with Fair Abe, he had begun to admire the ideals they strove to incorporate in their daily lives. But was it their influence that was destroying his marriage? How could a naval officer have a pacifist wife? What if the Admiralty learned of her political activities? Would it effect his career?

Yet, he loved her! The years did not diminish her beauty in his eyes. He had seen her grow in stature and confidence over the years of their marriage. She was now a very independent woman: she had to be to run Clonacody during his long absences at sea. He had come to rely on her quiet strength like a house relies on bedrock for a solid foundation. Where would his fortitude come from if their marriage failed? Henry did not believe divorce was the answer to marital problems, but if she could no longer love him, if her love completely died, would he be able to force her to stay? Would he want to?

Alice had been right to tell him he could not demand that she stop her work. He had no business trying to treat her like one of his crew, requiring her unquestioning obedience. He could only hope that his letters about the work he was doing in the West Indies would help him to recover her good graces. This was the sort of work that she could admire, and which would not be in conflict with the beliefs she held about the Crimean War. The Admiralty may have just saved his marriage!

⚓⚓⚓⚓⚓

'Mother, hast thou seen the news about the trials?' Father Abraham sat next to his wife in the drawing room where she was darning the children's stockings. 'Doest thou remember last spring and summer when some British recruiters were arrested in New York, Boston and Philadelphia? There was a trial in Boston last July, and now this week the trial for the fellow Hertz, who was recruiting in Philadelphia, is beginning.'

'They were signing men up for Britain's war with Russia, weren't they? In her last letter Alice Kellett mentioned something about it and sent me an editorial column from a London broadsheet. The editor said some very unpleasant things about America: all about how we want Britain to lose the war because we won't allow willing men to join up for the good fight. He even denied that the recruiters had done any thing wrong, and he castigated the United States for aiding and abetting the enemy! Not a word was said about the fact that they had broken our laws by recruiting on our soil without approval from Washington. Nor about how their actions could affect our neutrality. Doest thou think there is a danger that Russia will see the United States as a belligerent country and declare war against us?'

'That is not the danger I fear most, I am afraid. Here is a similar editorial in today's paper, but from an American point of view. Shall I read it?' Martha nodded her head.

"When will we stand up to Old England? She is trying to treat us as though we were still one of her colonies. She has no respect for our Sovereignty, for our domestic laws, or the international laws of the nations. With complete disregard for our rights, she has trampled our independence beneath her feet and is besmirching our honour. And for this we will not stand.

"She calls us cowardly, but we are not cowards because we do not want to fight a war with Russia. Russia is our friend and trading partner, we have no argument with her. Do not slander the bravery of our men!

"Does England want to see the mettle of our fighting men again? We showed her what we are made of in 1776 and again in 1812. Trample our rights once more; push us into a corner and pick a fight with us and we will show you just how brave and ready we are to fight!

"Yet, bravery is not the issue here. The real problem is the insult Britain has proffered to us by not honouring our status as an independent and equal nation.

"England! It is not too late to rectify the situation. All you need to do is admit you were wrong, and apologise. We are of the same family, and, like members of one family, we may squabble and disagree. But we don't disown our sister because she has done us wrong. We stand ready to forgive, once amends have been made. You must admit you were wrong when you entered and recruited in our sovereign territory without permission. Admit that you were wrong to violate our neutrality and put our relationship with Russia in jeopardy. And admit you were wrong to question the bravery of our young men.

"Ask our forgiveness and we will give it! We stand ready to extend our hand in friendship once you have given yours to us. This is the natural and correct path to take. But make no mistake, if no apology is forthcoming, we will not hesitate to defend our honour and our sovereignty. We can whip you again if that is what you insist you want!'

Father Abraham put the paper down and looked across at Martha. She had stopped her darning and was looking out the window. She turned to him and smiled sadly. 'I know that this editorial is the voice of just one man, but it saddens me to think that someone has thought to rattle the sabres so quickly. Certainly this situation does not merit talk of war! The courts will do their job. If wrong was done, I have faith in our legal system to find a punishment to fit the crime.'

'This is just one hot head. But I must confess that I have a greater fear. I do not believe the truest danger of this recruiting business is conflict with Russia. When I look at the state of our country...no, I am being silly.'

'What doest thou fear, Fairfax? Tell me.'

'I fear that soon, possibly within this decade, our country is going to be torn apart, violently, over the issue of slavery. The issue is escaping our grasp, and extremists on both sides of the issue are moving us closer and closer to a civil war.' He put his hand up when Martha started to speak. 'No. Hear me, Martha. Perhaps I see this so strongly because I fear it so deeply, but the emotions on all sides are spiralling out of control. It must tear at the president's heart, to see this happening to the country he loves and serves. If I was in his position I would do almost anything to divert us from this course. Even...'

'Scare up a war with our old nemesis, England?'

'Yes. Thou hast voiced my fear exactly. Unite the country in hatred for our old enemy. History is full of examples from the past when this has been done, and I am certain history will record other occurrences in the future. If a government is facing a conflict it feels no one can win or conflict where the cost of winning will be unimaginable, it can avoid the abyss by distracting the people and uniting them in a fight that can be won at a lower cost. And maybe, just maybe, the first conflict will resolve in the meantime. Also, for politicians who put their own career's interest before the interests of the country, this tactic can make a hero out of a man who was too weak to fix the real problem facing his administration.'

'But thou believest this could happen with the recruiting issue? Perhaps this one editorial voice will be lost, and no one will pay it any heed? Couldn't it all just blow over?'

'Thou knowest not how fervently I pray to God that I am wrong and my fears are unfounded. Perhaps I am becoming a reactionary myself!'

'Ah, Fairfax, thou art the farthest from being a reactionary that thou couldst possibly be. I simply hope, and will pray with thee, that thou art wrong. There is enough turmoil in the world without this issue getting blown all out of proportion.' Martha set her mending down. 'Shall we gather the children and go for a walk? No matter how worried I am, I can always find comfort and joy when I am with them. And a good walk clears my thoughts and feeling like nothing else.'

The children came to their father's call; Martha, Father and Samuel helped the youngest into their jackets and hats. They spent the afternoon down by the water front, watching the ships and the people working. The ordinariness of the scene before them: the happiness of the children running along the pier; the same woman, who was there everyday, selling cakes and coffee; the same men unloading vessels...all these things helped to dispel Father and Mother Abraham's concerns for the future. For how could the storm clouds of war be gathering when life quietly carried on in its usual way?

That night Fairfax and Martha made passionate love and fell into deep and dreamless sleep in each others' arms.

⚓⚓⚓⚓⚓

In order to more effectively campaign for peace, Alice and Margaret Kellett had spent most of August in London, where they accepted hospitality from a Quaker family in the Westminster Monthly Friend's Meeting. Every Russell report in *The Times* that came back from the front made more people uneasy about the war. His vivid descriptions of the suffering men, the disease and lack of supplies made Alice's heartache, but it made many men and women angry.

Most of the everyday people didn't understand the government's reasons for going to war in the first place, so the images of such suffering weren't juxtaposed against a justifying ideology. All that the people saw was young men dying by the score for lack of adequate logistics. It wasn't that they did not believe in sacrifice for the sake of the country, or even empire, but sacrifice because of incompetence was too much to bear.

The reports that Sebastopol fell on the ninth brought joy to many, but did not diminish the dedication of the Friends to find a way to a peaceful resolution to the conflict. They did not solely work to find an honourable peace, but worked just as diligently for the relief of suffering. Three Quaker doctors went to the front. There were some men who were conscientious objectors to the killing but who still wanted to support their government and the men who were dying, and they formed an ambulance corps. Four of the women Alice knew went in support of the medical personnel as nurses and nurses' aides.

Most evenings, Alice and Margaret met with other women to make and roll bandages, to knit stockings, and to create care packages for the wounded and sick. After a month of reluctant involvement, Margaret caught her mother's fever for the work. From being a rather uncooperative hanger-on, Margaret became one of the most productive workers.

But it still took Alice by surprise when her daughter first voiced her desire to go to the Crimea.

'I applaud your newfound dedication, and your heartfelt concern for the suffering of the soldiers, but can't you find some way to fulfil your desire to help here in London? Your work here can be just as valuable.'

'You have always said you admire Florence Nightingale and Mary Seacole, and that they are not only a good example to all of the Queen's subjects, but also particularly to women. I thought you would be pleased that I have taken those words to heart.'

'An example, yes, but I never meant for you to go out and do exactly as they have. I wanted you to be inspired by them, as I am inspired, not to be bound by the norm of what is expected of us as women, but to work up to, and yet within, our capability.'

'Well, I am inspired. And it is within my capability to be a nurse's assistant.'

'But you could be hurt! You could become ill, or worse. Mary and Florence both work very near the front, and stray enemy fire is an ever present danger. As much as I want you to be inspired, I want you to be safe even more! Darling, don't turn away from me when I am speaking to you. You are young; you don't fully realise...'

'Yes I do, Mother! I know it is dangerous, but it is something I want to do more than anything else. But even more important than my desire, it is the right thing to do. Besides, all I have ever done my whole life is play around with horses. I know I could be injured if I go to the war, but as far as getting ill you have always bragged about my robust constitution. Let me use it to some good purpose. I have never been ill in my life. I am young and strong and I can't just sit here rolling bandages. There are plenty of old ladies who can do that.'

'Many young women are here every night, knitting stockings and rolling your scorned bandages, so don't tell me it is an old woman's job. I admire what you are saying, but I cannot put aside my concern for your safety as easily as you can. What about young Fairfax Abraham? I know how much you care for him; it is obvious in the number of letters you write. And he must also care very much for you to judge by the number you receive. What do you think he would say?'

'What, indeed! He is a man of deep faith and like all of your Quaker friends he believes in actions speaking louder than words. I'd like to think he would approve. But even if he didn't, I think I can make this sort of decision for myself!'

Alice looked at the determination that was evident in her daughter's face and knew further argument would be to no avail. If she had any chance of changing Margaret's mind, it would not be through a frontal assault. If only Henry were here. But, as so often in the past when making decisions about the running of Clonacody, or in raising Margaret she knew she was going to have to handle this crisis on her own.

When Margaret saw her mother's face soften, she mistook it for acceptance, and she moderated her own temper.

'Besides, Mother, I want you to be proud of me.'

'I am proud of you; you don't have to prove yourself to me. You must understand it is my God-given responsibility to keep you safe from harm. It is a responsibility that does not go away, even when one's charge is an adult. You will be, God willing, twenty in four month's time. I can no longer tell you what you can and cannot do. Even though your father might disagree with me on this you are no longer a child; you are a young woman, and a strong willed one at that. But I can see that all you are really leaving for me to do is to accept that you are going to do this, whether I agree with your decision or not. A very difficult thing for any parent to do under any circumstance.'

Margaret lay awake that night thinking about Fair Abe. Despite what she had said to her mother, she wondered what he would really think about her being so close to war. In the early hours of the morning she fell asleep, and in her dreams he came to her. They were standing side by side, looking out over the sea. He turned to her and pulled the pins out of her hair, and let it fall over her breasts. He kissed and held her, and the warmth and sanctuary she felt while encircled in his arms made her wish to be held by him forever and to never be parted from him again.

But she tore herself away, and when he let go, she floated away over the green waves. She watched as he disappeared into a small speck; she watched the shore until it disappeared below the horizon. When her feet touched down, she was surrounded by a scene from hell: the spectacle of war. Broken bodies lay all around her, the cries of the wounded drowning out the din of the cannon. To her surprise she felt no fear; in her heart Fair Abe's arms were still holding her securely, and as long as they did she was safe.

⚓⚓⚓⚓⚓

Cruising in Baffin Bay, the *George Henry* hadn't had an easy time since leaving New London in May. Unusually, by the middle of June, she had encountered large floes of ice through which it was impossible to navigate. The ice seemed to be entirely blocking the Davis Strait and Buddington had decided to follow the edge of the pack in order to minimise the damage to his ship. All of this indicated that an exceptionally difficult winter lay ahead.

On August 20th, the floes opened and *George Henry* was able to enter the Arctic Circle, forcing her way through the ice for almost 150 miles. After collecting and processing 184 barrels of whale oil, a fierce storm, which lasted three days, descended upon the ship. All Captain Buddington could do was to allow the *George Henry* to drift southwest with the ice.

Locked in the ice and with such a small reward for their months at sea the spirit of the crew began to sink. The older, more experienced men shook their heads and stared gloomily at the ice. Their stories full of foreboding didn't help, nor their repeating of the fact that they had never seen the ice this thick so early in the year in all their years of whaling. The young men grew impatient with them.

With the old ones, things were always either much better or much worse in the olden days. The world always seemed to be going to hell, yet in their stories the youngsters today had it easy compared to the harsh conditions they had had to face when growing up. Whichever way the stories went, today invariably suffered by comparison. While the younger members of the crew shrugged their shoulders and did their best to disregard the omens the old men saw in the ice, they couldn't keep their spirits from sinking into the collective depression.

Then, on the 10th of September, when they were drifting just northwest of Cape Mercy, and still beset in the ice, the lookout saw what he thought might be a ship in the distance. He called down to the deck where his captain was standing. Buddington decided to take a look himself and climbed the rigging to the crow's nest. Bringing the image into focus in his telescope, the distant object did indeed appear to be a ship drifting under bare poles.

'Curious,' he said and the lookout nodded his head in agreement. The ship was listing to port, and did not have her top masts set. 'By the look of her size I am certain she is no whaler; and I am afraid, from the state of her rigging, that she is either in dire straits or no one is aboard.' Buddington returned to his cabin where he had the charts for Baffin Bay spread out on his table. He judged the ship to be about fifteen miles away to the northeast, which put it in the lower Davis Strait near the entrance to Cumberland Sound. Ascending to the deck again he set his ensign, but received no answering signal from the ship. 'So, she is indeed empty,' he muttered to no one in particular.

The ship stayed in sight for several days, but the condition of the floating ice made it impossible for anyone to go and investigate. In the meantime excitement spread throughout the *George Henry* dispelling the former malaise. The crew began vying for the opportunity to go, when conditions permitted, to explore what they began calling The Ghost. At almost anytime of the day at least one crewman stood by the rail, gazing at The Ghost through his telescope. Fair Abe did the same, and when the ships were no more than six miles apart he began to think the ship looked familiar. At least the shape of her was similar to the arctic exploration ships he had grown accustomed to when he was with the Belcher Expedition.

More than just curiosity seemed to draw him to the poor ship, and he decided to use his position as the company owner's son, something he never did, to secure a place with the men who were going to investigate her. On the sixth day after the first sighting, Buddington sent four men to The Ghost: Fair Abe, the First Mate John T. Quayle, Second Mate Norris Havens, and one of his boat steerers. Fair Abe's excitement was not at all dampened by the difficulties they encountered trying to reach The Ghost. It took them almost a whole day of struggling over ice hummocks and through half-frozen water to finally arrive at her side. No sooner had they climbed aboard, but the wind intensified and heavy snow began to fall and swirl so thickly that the search party completely lost sight of the *George Henry*.

'How long is this going to last?' Quayle groaned.

'It looks like we will have to stay here until the weather clears,' the steerer replied. 'Who knows?'

Fair Abe didn't even hear the others grumbling. A smile spread across his face as he realised he was in his old home, for The Ghost was none other than his old *Resolute!* But how could this be possible? The last time he had seen *Resolute* was more than a year ago, and twelve hundred nautical miles to the northwest, on that horrible day of abandonment. He ran his gloved hand along her rail affectionately, spying the rudder he and Roche had stowed neatly on deck. What sort of miracle had taken place to keep *Resolute* from breaking up and sinking in an icy grave? What magic brought to her this very spot where Fair Abe could salvage her? And how could she possibly have come such a long way without getting nipped between floes and crushed, or at least damaged? The only thing that appeared wrong with her was that she was sitting low in the water, probably with water in her hold from not having been pumped for the last seventeen months; and she had a serious list to port, caused by the heavy layers of ice on her north-facing side, which the sun had not been able to reach while she had drifted in the pack to the southeast.

'She's HMS *Resolute!* And I know this ship!' Fair Abe shouted to the others. 'I spent two years on her with Captain Kellett, before the squadron commander forced us to abandon her. She was one of the five ships in the Belcher Expedition. Look! See how we caulked and locked her, and prepared her before we left? I helped to stow the rudder and the masts. Mr. Quayle, will you break the lock, please, so we can go below?'

Fair Abe could not keep the eagerness out of his voice, and his enthusiasm was contagious. But as soon as the men descended to the captain's cabin an eerie stillness surrounded them. They stopped jostling each other and gazed around the room. The wine goblets with which the officers had toasted the ship just before leaving her still stood on the captain's table. Captain Kellett's epaulets lay next to them and many of the captain's other personal items were still where Kellett left them. Silently the men spread out to search the ship.

Fair Abe went down into the hold where he found almost seven feet of water. He made a mental note of the things that needed doing, the first of which was getting her pumped out to free her of this water. The men would also have to chop the ice away from her port side, so she could regain an even keel.

Walking through the officers' cabins Fair Abe noticed the discarded items that the Resolutes had not been able to take with them: costumes from their pantomime plays lay moulding on the deck, and photographs of loved ones gazed at him from behind their glass. Briant's fiddle was in the crew's quarters, books and other personal gear were scattered all around. He gathered up the photos and the fiddle, and he gently wrapped Captain Kellett's epaulets in a cloth he found that was not mouldy.

The men each lay claim to an officer's cabin, none bold enough to take the captain's quarters, and they foraged for dry blankets. There were still matches and candles, and oil for the lamps; once the lamps were filled and the candles lit the ship began to feel less gloomy. Fair Abe took coal from the abundant supply and lit the stove, while Norris Havens raided the galley and found ample food to keep them fed until the storm passed. In fact, there was enough food to feed a complete crew for months!

Fair Abe kept the men entertained with stories about the expedition: the plays they staged, the sledging and hunting trips they took, and the antics of Kellett's dog, Napoleon. He did not recount his brutal experience at Belcher's hands.

The storm lasted for two days, and the men kept boredom away by drinking the wine that had been left behind; and dressing up in the uniforms and costumes; putting on impromptu plays; and generally carousing. But, finally, the men were able to travel across the ice to the *George Henry,* which had drifted a couple of miles closer. Buddington sent them back to *Resolute* with a newfangled pump. None of them could work it, so Fair Abe had to go back to collect the captain. It took three full days of continuous, around the clock pumping to rid *Resolute* of the water in her hold, and it took until the 23rd to chip away the ice. But finally she proudly sat higher in the water and on an even keel.

Buddington gathered all his officers and men the following morning.

'I have decided to abandon our whaling trip in order to salvage the *Resolute.*' A couple of the men groaned. He raised his hand. 'Hear me out. I thought you might be worried about your share of whale oil profits, but I believe the ship will be worth quite a bit more than any oil we may gather. The value we receive for her salvage will be split between us in the same percentage of shares as always, so do not be concerned. The main difficulty we face is the division of the crew. A ship this size usually needs a crew of at least eighty to work her. There are only twenty-six of us, and we have to get two ships back to New London. I will take Fair Abe and nine others to crew the *Resolute.* I am leaving Mr. Quayle in charge of the *George Henry*, and the remaining fourteen men will help him sail her home.'

'Huzzah!' the men shouted now that their fears of losing out on a season's whaling profit were allayed. Fair Abe followed Captain Buddington to his cabin, as the captain had ordered, and they bent their heads over the charts.

'Now, Fair Abe, we have quite a challenge ahead of us!' Buddington clapped the young man on the shoulder. '*Resolute* has none of her charts, and you say Master McDougall took all the navigational instruments with him when you all abandoned ship. I am very familiar with these waters, and have drawn an outline of the American Coast from my charts, which I believe will be sufficient for our purposes. I have my watch, my compass, which seems to be acting up, and my chronometer (which is not, thank God) and this will have to do, I am afraid.'

'Sir, I believe that we will be able to handle her more readily if we use only the lower masts, and don't bother with the tops'ls or t'gallants. Much of the sail cloth is rotten, but we can patch together enough to make three sails, one for each mast. She will sail more slowly, but the ship will be more manageable. In this way we can compensate for being so short handed.'

'Yes, Fair Abe, good thought, I appreciate that. And I will be relying on your knowledge of *Resolute.* Ah, before you say anything, I know you do not have much sailing experience, but you know this ship. And that counts for much. Anything you can tell me about her, whenever it comes to you, will be helpful. I will not ask you to advise me about things you do not know.'

'Yes, Sir, I will be happy to assist thee.'

The men spent the next two days repairing sails, setting the rudder, checking the food supply for spoilage, hauling fresh water, and bringing the sailor's gear from the *George Henry:* doing everything they could to make *Resolute* seaworthy and ready for the voyage to New London. Additionally, Fair Abe and the crew familiarised themselves with the ship.

Buddington planned to keep the two ships within sight of each other, although he gave Quayle orders to make his own way home if the ships got separated. It took until the 16th of October for *Resolute* to finally break out of the ice, and by then the *George Henry* was long gone. The two ships never saw each other again.

HMS *Resolute* set sail for New London with eleven intrepid American whaling men on board equipped only with a faulty compass, a watch, a chronometer, and a piece of foolscap roughly outlining the American coast. And she headed straight into the worst autumn storms in recorded history.

CHAPTER FIVE
DECEMBER 1855

On the night of the December new moon, US brig *Laong* quietly dropped anchor in English Harbour, Jamaica. Her captain hoped to do their business quickly and be gone before the next sunset, heading to Charleston, South Carolina. She was on a return trip from Great Britain, carrying cloth woven in Manchester, made from the cotton she had taken to England from America months earlier. The final section of her hold needed to be filled with rum, and then she would be on her way. She had already stopped in San Juan, Puerto Rico, where she had picked up the cargo her captain hoped would not be found while they were in Jamaica.

But aboard HMS *Medea*, Commodore Kellett was fully aware of the US brig *Laongo's* illicit cargo, and he was waiting. He had already lowered one of his boats, and now that *Laongo* had dropped anchor, he ordered Pim and three seamen to row over to the American ship and request permission to board. Although he was acting in an official capacity and had the powers of search and seizure, he wanted to present as non-threatening a presence as possible, and therefore he sent Pim and the others without firearms. He watched the boat approach *Laongo* through his telescope, occasionally shaking the tension from his shoulders.

He saw Pim being received onboard and taking part in an animated conversation with the captain. Suddenly, *Laongo's* men began to muster, taking their stations with their arms loaded. 'Get out of there, Pim!' he muttered to himself. Out loud he ordered his men to muster and to haul out the starboard guns, training them on the American ship. He watched the other captain bring his telescope to his eye and look directly at *Medea*.

'So much for the softly, softly approach, Mr. Pim,' Kellett said as he led his returning officer and men to his cabin. 'What happened?'

'They seem to have taken offence to my request to search the ship, Sir.'

'Yes, I could see that. Why did the captain muster his men?'

'I would say our intelligence is correct and he has something to hide. He clearly had no intention of letting us check their cargo.'

'And now they have also run their guns out. Check, I would say! A stalemate! We certainly cannot begin a war with the United States over one fugitive slave, but we must not be seen as being weak, nor can we have an

146

American captain telling us what we can and cannot do in one of our own harbours. The international law is on our side, even American law supports us. We are here, after all, to enforce American as well as British anti-slave trade laws. But I must consider carefully what my next steps will be. You are dismissed for now, but stand by for orders.'

Kellett sat heavily at his desk. 'Brooke! Get me a glass of wine.'

'Yes, Commodore.' His faithful cox'n poured a liberal glass and placed it before him. Kellett stroked Napoleon's head while he drank the wine. He paced in his cabin, and then on the quarter deck. Occasionally he raised his telescope to see *Laongo's* captain either pacing or watching him. So, he is just as worried as I am about what we should do now, Kellett thought. He called Pim to him. 'I am going to go to the *Laongo* at first light, and I want you to accompany me. This time, we will fly a flag of truce, but take our swords!'

'Yes, Sir!'

'Welcome aboard, Commodore Kellett!' Captain Jenkins extended his hand. 'We have ourselves a situation here.'

Kellett nodded, 'Yes, may we speak in confidence?' Jenkins held his hand out in the direction of his cabin, 'After you.' Below deck the two men silently sized each other up, and then they both tried to speak at the same time.

'I beg your pardon, you are my guest.'

'You do understand we have the right to search your ship, do you not?'

'With all due respect, you have the right to search slave ships, not any old American vessel with which you desire to interfere.'

'I have been commissioned to do all in my power to stop any illegal transport of slaves through these islands, and I believe, Sir, that you are involved in just that!'

'Here is my cargo manifest; you can see for yourself that there are no slaves aboard this ship.'

'Oh, I don't expect to find slaves listed on your manifest, Captain, but you are transporting a slave none the less.'

'What are you saying? Do you believe I have falsified my records? Why would I risk all of my cargo, not to mention my ship, for the sake of, what did you say, <u>one</u> slave?'

'Why, indeed!' Kellett looked at the man who was quickly becoming his adversary. After a considerable silence he merely said, ' Jon Ross.'

Captain Jenkins's face coloured as he looked away. *Check mate*, Kellett thought to himself. 'Shall we stand down?' Jenkins did not meet Kellett's eyes for several minutes. 'I will stand down,' Jenkins said, bringing his eyes back to meet Kellett's. 'But I will not allow you to search or seize my ship. I will have the fugitive brought to the deck.'

Kellett struggled to keep a smile of satisfaction from his face, and a sigh of relief from his lips. 'Remove his manacles, first, Captain; bring him up from the hold as the free man he is, and I will consider how I write up this incident.

And I caution you to think carefully about your own report; after all, the men I sent to you were unarmed. Perhaps we were both a little hasty in mustering our men, and training our guns on each other. We don't want to give anyone in either of our countries the opportunity to make more of this than there is.'

'I understand, thank you, Commodore. I apologise if I acted hastily.'

Kellett breathed his long held sigh of relief after Jon Ross was safely brought aboard HMS *Medea,* but that feeling of having successfully escaped a difficult situation was short lived. On December 13th, the USS *Cyane* refused to show the customary courtesy to him by entering English Harbour without any gun salute: an insult he could not ignore. This time, he sent for the ship's captain to come to him. 'I am getting annoyed with these pernickety Americans, Pim. I know I must be careful and diplomatic, but there is a limit!' The two men stood at attention while the *Cyane's* captain was piped aboard.

'Captain Fairfax at your service.'

'Commodore Kellett at yours. Will you join me in my cabin, please?' The three men retired to Kellett's cabin while Brooke and Kellett's servant set a decanter of wine and glasses on his table.

'To what, Sir, do I owe this discourtesy?'

'Commodore Kellett, I have been sent by the American consul at Saint Thomas to investigate the *Laongo* affair. Our government is very displeased with the altercation that took place ten days ago, and I am here to demand an official apology for your inexcusable behaviour.'

You pompous little upstart, Kellett thought to himself. *Be careful, Henry*, he could almost hear Alice saying. *Control your anger, don't let it control you.* Solid advice he usually didn't need, because he rarely had his hackles raised to this extent; but he was not about to be told he had to apologise for doing what he was obligated, by both law and morality, to do. He took a sip of his wine and let it slip slowly down his throat, while he composed he feelings and his response.

'Captain Fairfax, my men had every legal right to board USS *Laongo,* and they were unarmed when they did so. I sent them without arms intentionally to avoid any sort of blustering response. They did not even carry their swords. When they were still onboard your ship, the American captain mustered his men, rifles at the ready. While I was happy to be doing my duty in the most peaceful way I could, I was not about to stand by and have my men, or my ship, threatened in this manner without showing my teeth. 'You, Captain, are acting as though an injury had been done by me to your country, but I beg to differ. Your captain confronted unarmed men of her Majesty's Royal Navy with an armed and mustered crew! Even so, at the time of this 'incident', *Laongo's* captain and I reached an amicable resolution to the problem. Yet now you have insulted Her Majesty's flag with your discourteous refusal to give us the honour due to us upon your entrance to our harbour! You cannot seriously believe I am going to apologise to you, can you?'

Kellett waited for the American to respond, but seeing him struggle he carried on in a milder tone, 'Surely you must see that it is my duty to stop the transporting of slaves through these islands, and by doing so I am also upholding the laws of your own country?'

'Yes, Commodore, I know that the local authorities have the right to board if there is a slave on board a ship, even an American one. But my countrymen also must obey the law, and the law of the land is that we must do what we can to return any fugitive slave that crosses our path.'

'The law of your land, yes. Within your country's boundaries I have heard there is such a law. But we are dealing with International Maritime Law in this instance, as well as laws which both of our countries have created that make the transporting of slaves in the high seas illegal.'

'True. But the sovereignty of one nation should not be transgressed. It was this precise issue of unjustified search and seizure which started the last war between our countries!'

'Exactly why I sent unarmed men onboard the *Laongo*!'

'Well, I was given to understand by the Saint Thomas Consul that this was not the case.'

'I am beginning to understand why we are at such an impasse, and I suggest that you meet with the American consul here. He accepted the joint report we gave him before the *Laongo* set sail, and he will be able to confirm what I am saying. Perhaps you would care to dine with me tonight after you have had the opportunity to read that report.'

'Thank you, Commodore; I will accept your invitation.' Captain Fairfax bowed stiffly and the *Medea's* bo's'n piped him back over the side. Kellett watched him go. 'He can't admit he was wrong, Mr. Pim. We will have to find some way for him to save face. I believe we have a man here who does not like to find himself in error, and he might do something stupid to avoid having to acknowledge it.'

That afternoon, Kellett received orders from the Admiralty, which came with his newly arrived ships, requested by him in his last dispatch. Due to rising tensions between Great Britain and the United States, he was to move his squadron immediately to a position just off the American coast, near the mouth of the Chesapeake Bay. Once there, he was ordered to commence practising naval manoeuvres, and to keep his eye on any ships departing from, or approaching, the American capital.

He sent his regrets to the *Cyane's* captain, but had to leave the situation unresolved because he had to follow his new orders to depart immediately. What in God's name is this, now? Surely his little contretemps amongst these Caribbean Islands could not be causing this sort of naval escalation. Whatever the cause, the animosity between America and Britain must have been what had caused such an over-reaction to his rescue of the fugitive slave, Jon Ross, from the *Laongo*. Had he, by doing his job, unwittingly played into the hands of the powers that be? The powers, which for their unknowable reasons, wanted to pit the ancient naval might of Great Britain against the new, but formidable, maritime might of the United States? Exactly what game was afoot now?

⚓⚓⚓⚓⚓

Father Abraham was on his company's New London quay when the *George Henry* arrived. He was surprised to see her because he did not expect her home so soon, and he waited anxiously for the dock hands to finish securing her so he could go aboard to see what was wrong. When Captain Buddington did not appear on deck, his concern heightened. Pray God Fair Abe is alright, he thought, as he stood on the deck surveying a much reduced crew.

Mr. Quayle hurried from the quarter deck, extending his hand to his employer. 'Mr. Abraham, I am so...'

'Sir, please, what has happened? Where is Captain Buddington? Is my son alright? What sort of disaster didst thou encounter to bring thee home so soon with so many of thy men missing?'

'Do not worry, Sir. The captain and young Mr. Abraham, as well as the rest of the crew are all safe, at least as far as we know.'

'As far as thou doest know? Thy words bring me no comfort! I am sorry; please accept my apology for interrupting. Thou hast clearly much to tell me and the more I interrupt the longer thy story will be in the telling.'

'Shall we go below to the captain's cabin, Sir, so I can explain our sudden arrival?' Father Abraham followed Quayle and accepted a glass of wine as he took the seat behind Buddington's desk.

'We have had the greatest good fortune, Mr. Abraham. We found the abandoned Arctic exploration ship HMS *Resolute!* The very ship your son was on in the Polar Regions. Imagine his surprise, Sir, when he boarded her, being as he last saw her 1200 nautical miles from the spot where we found her. Why, he must have never thought he would see her again! But we have her, Sir. Captain Buddington, young Mr. Abraham, and some of our crew are sailing her home to New London. In fact, we thought they might have arrived before us, but as soon as I saw your worried face I knew we were the ones to bring the news. We stopped our whaling, you see, because the profit from the salvage should be much more than we could ever get filling the holds, and after we come home, see, we figured we could go back out. Captain thought we could end up with twice the monies in the same amount of time as if we had just left the ship and gone about our business. He was hoping, Mr. Abraham, that you would see he done the right thing. He did, didn't he, Sir?'

'Take a breath, my good man, and have a sip of thy wine! Yes, if she is in good enough repair to be sailed home, she should be worth a good penny in salvage, and I believe Captain Buddington has made a very sound decision. Didst thou leave the ice at the same time?'

'Well, sir, we was supposed to, but we lost them in weather so I am not sure if they broke free as soon as us. We never did see them again, but the ship is sound, Sir. There ain't no reason to think she won't be coming in right behind us, so there ain't.'

Father Abraham took his leave and headed for home. He wanted to be the first to let Martha know what was happening. She would be more upset than he had been if anyone told her the *George Henry* had arrived without Fair Abe, and there was no point in making her worry needlessly.

The next day, Father Abraham was pleased to see that the *George Henry* had not come home dry; at least she had 184 barrels of whale oil in her hold. All in all, if the British ship made it home safely, the profits wouldn't be too bad from this trip.

It was a long, anxious week for the Perkins, Smith and the Abraham families, one made more difficult by the fact that it was the week before Christmas. Although Quakers did not make a fuss over the special days in the church calendar, Martha always made a few small gifts and baked special cookies for the children so they would not feel left out by the elaborate celebrations their non-Quaker friends all enjoyed. In the Abraham household, and in the homes of the Buddingtons and the other crews' families, what should have been a time of high and happy spirits was one of worriment and unease. Everyone was gripped by the fishermen's weather reports, and concern deepened when the men brought news of the off-shore storm, which had reached almost hurricane levels of wind speed and wave height.

It wasn't until Christmas Eve that the news spread throughout New London: the *Resolute* was on her way into port. At first only a handful of Perkins, Smith, and Abraham employees gathered on the pier. The entire Abraham family soon joined them. As the light began to fade, more citizens appeared carrying torches. A gentle snow began to fall.

Father Abraham turned to speak to Quayle and was surprised to see the dock crowded with people, all waiting in expectant silence, an occasional cough the only sound. 'Mother, look!' He took her by her shoulders and turned her 'round. She put her hand to her mouth in surprise. 'All these people here for one old ship, canst thou believe it, Fairfax?' He took her in his arms as they turned again to see old *Resolute* finally rounding the point, being towed in by the harbour tugs so she could come to rest at the dockside instead of having to anchor out.

A loud cheer broke out from the waiting crowd. 'Huzzah! Huzzah! Huzzah for *Resolute*!' The Abraham family saw Buddington, Fair Abe and the rest of the crew lined up along *Resolute's* rail, waving and shouting back to their cheering friends and families. Not one of them could be having a more exciting Christmas Eve, or better Christmas present, than the triumphant return of the Perkins, Smith, and Abraham men and boys, nor, after all she had been through, could *Resolute* have been made more welcome to her new American home.

ℰℰℰℰℰ

Alice read the first letter that Margaret had sent from the front over and over again. She had never expected to miss her daughter so much, and the letter did little to alleviate the empty place in her heart. But it did help to ease her concern for Margaret's safety. At the time of her writing, Margaret was far behind the front lines, and in no danger from enemy fire. Her first duties had been light; she was writing letters for the men who were too injured to sit up, and she was helping to feed those who could not feed themselves. She was also tending the wounded horses.

With her thoughts about her daughter at ease for the moment, she turned her attention to the Appeal, which the Westminster Friends had written. Much deliberation had gone into how to get the Quaker Peace Testimony into general circulation. The London Friends had already reminded all the members in the Yearly Meeting of the need to remain committed to the testimony. The Meeting for Sufferings, the committee that addressed social justice issues, had also sent a letter to all the local meetings encouraging all Friends to examine their business dealings so that they not only lived up to the peace testimony in the very overt way of being conscientious objectors to the war, but also to make certain they were in no way profiting from the conflict. Any contact with companies that were supplying the army in anyway had to be severed.

Several Quakers had written a general appeal, and Alice had helped. Even though she was not a member of the Religious Society of Friends, Alice had begun attending Friends Meeting six months ago and was now worshipping every week. As an attender, she could help with committee work if she wanted, but she would not have been able to be a part of decision making in the monthly business meetings. It had taken only a fortnight to complete the Appeal, which articulated the Friends belief that all war is utterly incompatible with Christian belief and the teachings of Christ. Alice helped with the posting of 40,000 copies of the Appeal to Londoners, which included sending it to all the men in the government and all the major daily and weekly newspapers. Now she was collating the responses.

There were many encouraging letters in which the writers expressed their agreement with the Quakers, and articulated their belief that the publication of the Appeal would most certainly help channel the popular feelings against the war and toward support for peace. A few letters called the Quakers traitors to the Crown, but these were a small minority and overall Alice felt cheered by the responses.

She could not take the accusations of being a traitor lightly, however. There were a growing number of dissatisfied men and women who had begun using the genuine and principled anti-war sentiments held by so many as the fertile ground for an anarchistic movement. She did not want to be associated with the people who had begun gathering in public houses calling for the overthrow of the government, and even the end of the monarchy. She wanted the government to be pressured into looking for an honourable peace as soon as possible, not to feel under threat for its very existence. She did not want her deeply felt beliefs about the war to be co-opted by men advocating a violent revolution. Talk of revolution reminded Alice of Carl Schurz, and the political revolution he had championed in Germany. Carl had been working for democratic change, but these disgruntled folk already enjoyed the freedoms that he had struggled for.

Recently the newspapers turned more and more to the news about recruitment in America and the arrest and prosecution of the recruiters. The United States were neutral in the Crimean War, and, even though Great Britain had violated the international laws that govern neutrality, the British press was raising a hue and cry denouncing the United States for arresting the recruitment officers. The editorials in the London newspapers had turned their attention from the Crimean War to this new and explosive issue.

Alice now read, in the papers, the same words about America that had so recently been used against Russia: words meant to stir up the public opinion against 'our old nemesis' and our 'traditional enemy'. Alice shook her head in despair as she sat down at her desk to write letters to Henry, Margaret, and Martha. She was particularly anxious to find out what the American Press was saying about the recruiting and the recent arrests, and to learn what her friends thought of it all.

Why is it always so easy to get people riled and angry, and so difficult to get them to look calmly for a peaceful resolution to a complex issue? This was the first question she posed to Martha in what became a very long letter.

&&&&&

It was amazing to see the pier awash with people and lit by the torches they carried! Fair Abe searched for his family amongst the crowd. Everybody was waving and cheering, and he couldn't help responding in kind. By the time he saw his father and mother, and the happy faces of his siblings, he was almost hoarse from shouting.

They had had a difficult time on the voyage home. Just north of the Newfoundland Banks, they came across an iceberg fifty feet high with detached ice at its very top, which threatened to come crashing down on the ship. Buddington ordered all the boats made ready, anticipating the worst, but after much hard work, the men cleared *Resolute* from the danger. It was bad enough that they had been short handed and without adequate nautical charts and instruments in a ship that needed a thorough refit. But no sooner had they broken out of the ice they had been hit by a severe storm. 'We knowed the signs,' the older crew muttered. 'We seen it in how the ice was so damned thick when we was heading north. This ain't no common winter.'

With no ballast, *Resolute* was very light and rolled heavily in each swell, making the passage exceptionally uncomfortable for the men. Fair Abe had done what he could to help Captain Buddington understand the *Resolute,* but despite the best work of the crew and the navigational skills of the captain, nothing could keep the violent weather from sweeping the ship all the way down to Bermuda. For days the storm had forced *Resolute's* timbers to leak faster than the men could pump out the water, and the rising water had made the ship slow to respond to the helm. There had been times when Fair Abe had seriously wondered if he was ever going to see his home again.

But the skies did clear, and, after a passage of sixty four days, Captain Buddington was able to set the course for the New London Harbour. Now Fair Abe felt like he had gone from a nightmare to a pleasant dream and the best part of the miracle was coming home right on Christmas Eve to such a fine reception. His face lit up with joy when he finally saw Father and Mother surrounded by all his brothers and sisters, waving to him from the pier.

He could hardly wait to get off the ship, and he was one of the first to clamber down. He swept Mother off her feet and twirled her around and around until she giggled like a little girl. He shook Father's hand and then pulled him into a hug, too. Both Samuel and Timothy held out their hands for their brother to shake, hoping to avoid the embarrassment of getting hugged in public, but the twin girls and the little ones all hugged and clung to Fair Abe at once. He took little William, now a chubby three year old toddler, and set him upon his shoulders, and the family slowly made their way towards home.

Many men slapped Father and Fair Abe on their backs as they passed by in congratulations, some stopped them to ask Fair Abe about the voyage. It took the Abraham family a long time to extract themselves from the crowds, but finally they reached their home. The children collapsed into chairs in the front parlour, and regaled Fair Abe with questions.

'Children! Children! Thy impatience to know all of thy brother's adventures is very understandable, but he is very tired, and I believe thy questions can wait until the morrow.'

'Oh, Father, I am so excited about being safely home that I couldn't sleep a wink if I tried. I would love to tell thee everything that happened, or as much of it as I can remember right now. I did keep a journal, Mother, at thy suggestion, so I will be able to give a more detailed account after I unpack, but for now...ask away!'

The twins, Isabel and Anna, competed with each other to get their questions out first, while Timothy, being an awkward teenager in awe of his oldest brother, sat quietly listening to all that Fair Abe said. The littlest ones fell asleep before Sally, the scullery maid, brought out a cold supper. Father carried them to bed while the rest of the family reassembled in the dining room.

Upon his return, Father raised his voice in a prayer of thanksgiving before the family began passing the platters of food, and Fair Abe could not keep the tears from his eyes as he bowed his head.

Two days later, on the 26th, the first letter came from the British Government to the Perkins, Smith and Abraham offices. It was from Mr. Crampton, the British Minister in Washington DC. In crisp terms he lay out Queen Victoria's claim to HMS *Resolute.*

'Does Great Britain have its own rules for salvage on the high seas? How can they still think they have any legal rights to a ship they abandoned a year and a half ago? We are the ones who took the risks to bring her back to civilization, so we have the right of salvage. Is this not so?' Fair Abe passed the letter to his father, and studied his face while he read it. 'Perhaps what they are saying is that they will be the ones to pay us the salvage price.'

No,' Father Abraham replied, 'I believe they are saying that they want the ship given back to them. I shall have to bring this to the attention of my partners before we make any response.'

'We will have to be very careful, Father. With the recent kafuffle about this recruiting business, and the news about some naval altercation in the West Indies, tensions are getting high between us and England. We may want to be certain that we claim our rights, but we will have to do it in the nicest way. We don't want to do anything that will make matters worse; though when the time to draft a responding letter comes, I believe thou art the best man for the job.'

Father Abraham accepted his son's compliment with a slight smile, and then both men returned to their day's work.

For days, newspapers ran articles about the *Resolute.* Praise was heaped upon Buddington, and the crew that sailed her, for their courage and skill; one paper guessed that she was worth $50,000.00 and showed how the monies would be split, according to custom, between all the men who had sailed in the *George Henry* and the firm who owned her. Hundreds of people came down to see *Resolute* and to walk on her decks. The people of New London did not feel any of the animosity that was building in the rest of the country. They were expressing a warm and brotherly feeling toward the country that had sent men into the Arctic, like New England's own Mr. Grinnell, to look for Franklin and the other lost explorers. Whaling men sat in the pubs, smoking pipes and discoursing on the conditions the Resolutes would have faced before abandoning their ship; the George Henries told and retold their narratives of the trip, how they spotted *Resolute* and called her The Ghost until young Abraham recognised her. Buddington and Fair Abe were the toast of the town, men bought Captain Buddington a drink whenever they could; they shook Fair Abe's hand and congratulated him on his part in the whole adventure when they passed in the street.

On New Year's Eve Perkins, Smith and Abraham sponsored a seafront display of fireworks, and *Resolute,* still tied up along the Perkins pier, looked serene, and almost happy, beneath the coloured lights. Fair Abe went on board her the next morning and revelled in his memories: the Arctic Theatre Royale, the friendships he enjoyed, the conversations he had in the great cabin with Captain Kellett. And he realised the Kellett's might not yet know of the rescue.

He spent his New Year's Day writing to Margaret and her mother at Clonacody, and he enclosed a separate letter to Captain Kellett for them to forward on if he was stationed away from home. Later, it was with a great deal of sadness that he read President Pierce's annual address in the newspaper. The president made much of the insult given to the 'Honour of all Americans' by Great Britain when they ignored and violated our neutrality.

He also referred to a recent confrontation in Jamaica, where an American merchant vessel had been wrongly stopped by the British Royal Navy. President Pierce reminded the country that this very issue caused the War of 1812. He left the possibility of sending American war ships to Jamaica hanging between the lines of his words, 'We have to protect our rights on the high seas no matter what the cost.'

Rather than looking for a way to resolve these conflicts, President Pierce seemed to be going out of his way to fan the flames of resentment. Did he realise his words sounded like warmongering? Just where did he want his speech to lead us, and would the country follow? Within days, the HMS *Resolute* story joined the recruiting issue and the Jamaican incident in centre stage, and the war of words did nothing but escalate as the New Year unfolded.

PART THREE

WAR AND PEACE

1856

CHAPTER ONE
JANUARY 1856

Commodore Kellett had only two days of clear weather on the passage to his new station near the Chesapeake Bay. Although this was usually the time of quiet and predictable weather patterns, with the hurricane season long since over, the Caribbean was experiencing a very unsettled winter. While none of the storms that hit Kellett's ships came close to hurricane force they had, none the less, caused extensive damage. They had even made Napoleon sick. Kellett had planned a quick stop at Nassau for provisions, but had ended up spending three weeks there doing necessary repairs, much to Naps' delight. Kellett and Naps were able to take long walks along the shore while the works were being completed. However, the ships did not arrive off the Chesapeake until the last week in January.

Kellett's orders were to practice manoeuvres, to use his ships for gunnery work and the sail handling that would be needed if a chase or battle ensued. While he had no intention of disobeying his orders, he felt the sound of cannon fire would be too much for the American Navy to ignore. He was in International Waters, but only just. The orders had been clear that he was not to violate American waters. But he was certain his cannon fire would be heard by the Americans. He did not want to provoke a fight, though he was in no doubt that somebody in the government or Royal Navy (or both!) would not be disappointed if conflict ensued.

Had he unwittingly played a role in this increasing tension? During the trip from Jamaica he had reviewed over and over again the steps he had taken to obey his orders while he had been stationed there. He could find no other way he could have handled the situations. Kellett wondered what sort of report Captain Fairfax of the USS *Cyane* might have sent to his superiors. Would the Americans believe Kellett had shown disrespect to Fairfax, or had antagonised him in any way? Would they even know anything about what had happened in the Caribbean? He truly did not believe that his actions could be the reason why the Royal Navy was now one step closer to finding itself in conflict with the American Navy, but he could not prevent the sinking feeling that he had contributed to the current hostility.

The ships that now formed part of his squadron had brought post from England when they had joined him in Jamaica. In his letter from Alice he had received the distressing news that his only child was now in the Crimea, in harm's way for all he knew. Alice had also written about the rising public anger against the United States regarding the recruitment issue. Neither his actions in Jamaica, nor this recruiting business seemed like issues worth going to war for, yet here he was, on the doorstep of the American capital. He vowed to do as little as he could to provoke the Americans while still following the letter of his orders. His presence off the American waters was antagonism enough. He would put his men and ships through their paces with sail handling and manoeuvres, leaving the gunpowder out of the 'dummy' gun practice.

The loneliness of command meant that Kellett could not, under any circumstances, discuss his thoughts about his orders with Pim and McDougall, but he could brighten his mood by inviting them to his cabin for dinner. He revelled in their company and good cheer, as did Napoleon, who ran with delight from friend to friend, getting his head and stomach rubbed by all. Kellett slept the better that night for having spent the evening laughing and enjoying McDougall's story-telling.

⚓⚓⚓⚓⚓

On the 7th of January Perkins, Smith, and Abraham received a second letter from Mr. Crampton, the British Consul in Washington D. C. In it Mr. Crampton had enclosed a copy of *The Union* newspaper from the 2nd of January, which reprinted the notice contained in the November 10th 1854 edition of the *London Gazette*, wherein Her Majesty's Government asserted a continuing right to *Resolute*, and the other abandoned ships, on behalf of the Queen. The partners called an emergency meeting to discuss the firm's response. They read and reread the letter and article; the morning was gone before they had formulated a reply. Could such a claim really override the age old customs of the seas? Simply putting a statement in the newspapers did not change the fact that the Royal Navy had left *Resolute* to her fate, with no reasonable expectation of the ship ever re-appearing: after all the most likely outcome for a ship left in the Arctic was for the ice to crush it to bits. *Resolute* should have long since become scrap wood and it was a miracle that she had escaped an icy grave.

The partners asked Father Abraham to draft the responding letter, and he finally completed it on the tenth. It laid out for Mr. Crampton the firm's legal claim to HMS *Resolute*. Their position was clear: their men had salvaged a ship that had been abandoned; the firm and its employees had the salvage rights to her. Father Abraham knew, given the rising tensions between the two countries, that his reply might only fan the flames, but he could not in good conscience take any other course. On this point the partners were in complete agreement, their men had risked their lives to bring this ship home, not as a goodwill gesture, but with the rightful expectation of receiving a share of her value. The partners had to do justice first for those who relied upon them for their livelihood. If it had just been a matter of the profits he would receive, Abraham felt he could have made a different decision, albeit with the approval of his partners. No, he had searched his conscience: he must lay claim to the ship and stand firm, speaking truth to power.

Martha replied to her most recent letter from Alice, answering her questions about the temper of the American press. She did not have good news to relate. Editorials in two of the leading papers were urging the president to take firm actions to preserve and defend the American honour and way of life. *The New York Herald*, on January 15th, referred to the country as being on the brink of war. It also reported the build up of the Royal Navy in Jamaica, and its redeployment to somewhere off the American coast, urging the American government to match the Royal Navy ship for ship. Martha wondered if Henry Kellett was a part of the British fleet, but knew she could not ask Alice. And Alice, even if she knew, could not divulge such sensitive information to someone who might, in a very short while, be considered an enemy.

An enemy...Martha would never consider the Kellett family her enemies!

ℐℐℐℐℐ

Margaret had hoped after the fall of Sebastopol that conditions amongst the men might improve. She had even hoped the war would be over. Even though there had been no major battles since the successful attack on Sebastopol, the men continued to need all the medical care they could get. The joint problem of inadequate supply lines and insufficient medical provisions continued through the winter. Margaret had steeled herself for what she would see before she had set sail from England, but she had still been unprepared for the degree of suffering she saw. Men still came back from the front sick because of malnutrition and exposure, rather than from wounds received in battle. She worked alongside the other nurses and aids, stretching food, blankets, and bandages as far as they could. Florence Nightingale trained her nurses to follow modern methods of hygiene, and she insisted on opening the windows to clear the fetid air in the hospital wards. Still the men died, and sometimes all she could do was offer comfort, kindness, and a hand to hold at the end.

She stopped crying over the letters the men dictated to her. She stopped feeling so overwhelmed by the death all around her. Her heart became numb, and this took the sharp edges off of her experience. While this protected her from feeling so much pain, it also dulled her ability to feel any great happiness. The memory of Fair Abe, which had sustained her in the first months, faded day by day, and now she failed miserably each time she tried to recall his face or the joy she had felt. She could no longer remember her life before the Crimea, and she lost entirely her ability to envision life after.

Margaret tried to write her thoughts in letters home to her mother, but the words on the page were so inadequate that she finally stopped writing. Now all she did was write the soldiers' letters home. Loved ones didn't want the truth, or at least Margaret couldn't bring herself to write it, so when a soldier died of malnutrition she wrote he had died quickly of wounds gallantly received in battle. The days bled into each other, the letters blurred into one long denial of the horrible deaths taking place all around her.

⚓⚓⚓⚓⚓

Fair Abe lost no time after his return with *Resolute* to resume his involvement in anti-slavery work. Tensions were rising in the Kansas Territory over the fate of its statehood: would it join the Union as a free state or a slave state? Over the past year and a half anti-slavery settlers and 'Free-Soilers' had moved into the territory, many aided by the New England Emigrant Aid Company, in the hopes of creating a majority of residents so that when the time came they could vote themselves into the union as a free state. The pro-slavery 'border ruffians' from the southern states, primarily Missouri, did the same. During 1855, just before he had left for the Arctic on the *George Henry,* Fair Abe had been appalled to learn that the pro-slavery faction had far outnumbered the abolitionists, and had voted in a territorial legislation that favoured their cause. They incorporated the Missouri slave code, which provided severe penalties for anyone who even spoke or wrote against slavery, and this in the land that was founded on freedom of expression and thought. Additionally, anyone convicted of helping a fugitive slave faced the death penalty.

The anti-slavery settlers were so outraged that they had set up their own Free State legislature, making Topeka their territorial capital. Each territorial government outlawed the other. The war of words escalated throughout 1855, with the Missouri Senator David Atchinson urging the southerners to defend slavery with 'bayonet and blood…to kill every God-damned abolitionist in the district.' Violent actions followed violent words throughout the territory. Now, in a speech given on the 24th of January, President Pierce weighed in on the issue by recognising only the pro-slavery government and declaring the Free State government a government 'in rebellion'.

When Fair Abe had begun believing that he would fight for the freedom of the slaves if it came to a war, his vision had been that of a righteous crusade, banners unfurled, honour and glory for the brave, fallen heroes. Not this squalid barroom brawl it was becoming in Kansas!

Despite his reservations about the events taking place, he spent his evenings after work helping the local branch of the New England Emigrant Aid Society to organise the next group of Kansas settlers due to leave for the territory at the end of the month. Everyone there was angry with the president for so blatantly siding with the south. It was through a co-worker there that he obtained a copy of Harriet Beecher Stowe's _Uncle Tom's Cabin_, and he heard that the author's brother, Henry Ward Beecher, a Congregational minister in Brooklyn, was sending rifles to Kansas in boxes labelled 'Bibles'.

'Beecher's Bibles they're calling them,' Fair Abe sat with Father in the parlour.

'Doest thou believe this is a good thing Reverend Beecher is doing? Isn't it like taking the Lord's name in vain? Surely, it can't be right to be so dishonest, even for a good cause?'

'I don't know, Father. Sometimes I begin to believe that anything we can do to defeat slavery is righteous, because the cause is righteous.'

'The ends justify the means?'

'Yes…well no, that can't be correct. I don't know anymore.'

'I believe thou doest know, Abe, and that is why thou art so upset of late. The means as well as the ends must be righteous in the eyes of the Lord. I know people of other faiths may believe otherwise, but our Quaker faith teaches us this…'

'Father! Talk, talk, talk. It's all just talk! Actions speak louder than words, and the time is coming when our actions will have to match our words. If we truly believe in freedom for slaves, we will have to support that belief with our actions.'

'I have always done just that, my son, as have at least two generations of Friends. But thou must realise that to commit violent actions in support of our beliefs is to cross a line…'

'I know! I know! In my heart I know that the violence erupting in the Kansas Territory is wrong. It's becoming an ugly and sordid affair, but I believe that to march in an army to free the slaves would be marching in the Lord's army. And I would be honoured to be on its muster list.'

'And throw away the moral compass by which thy life has been led?'

Fair Abe threw up his hands in despair and walked out into the street. How could Father not see the coming storm when words would no longer be enough? Snow was falling gently and, as he raised his face to the sky, the melting flakes mingled with the tears on his flushed and burning cheek.

CHAPTER TWO
FEBRUARY 1856

Commodore Kellett continued his war games off the American coast, exercising his ships in all respects except the firing of his cannon. He did, however, have the men do mock firing exercises, pretending to load the guns, running them out, 'firing' them, and 'reloading'. If he were anywhere else, he would have liked to do actual target practice. But, though he could not see the halls and meeting rooms of Washington DC, he knew the sound of his cannon would reverberate through them.

In late February more ships arrived, this time from the Crimean field of operation. With the war there beginning to wind down, the Admiralty freed up five ships to augment Kellett's command. Another packet of letters arrived from England, including several from Alice. Though she had not received any letters from Margaret for several weeks, Alice did send Henry the last letter from their daughter. With relief he read that her work was far behind the front lines, but felt some concern over the lack of emotion in her words when she wrote about the actual work she was doing. He hoped the realities of war were not crushing the exuberant spirit of his daughter.

Alice also sent along two months' worth of the *London Illustrated News*. Kellett called Pim and McDougall into his cabin and invited them to share in the feast of news from home. Naps settled down in their midst after an enthusiastic greeting for his friends, and the men arranged the newspapers by date, beginning with the news from December. These carried the stories about the fall of Sebastopol and speculation about the war ending soon. No sooner did one editorial rejoice at the possibility of the end to that war, than another began rattling sabres and condemning the United States over their response to British representatives recruiting soldiers in several American cities.

In addition to its own articles and editorials, the *Illustrated London News* reprinted articles from various American newspapers, which made it possible for Henry to see the war of words from both sides of the Atlantic. An American article in December claimed the sentiment in the United States toward Britain was peaceful, yet the tone of the English press was very warlike. All that the United States wanted was an apology for the insult to her sovereignty, yet the transcript from President Pierce's State of the Union Address in late December showed a diatribe against Britain that went on for pages.

'I don't think we owe them an apology!' Pim exclaimed. 'I don't think we did anything wrong by making it possible for men who were willing to fight to join the army. It's the Americans that are making a big issue of all of this.'

'I don't know,' replied McDougall. 'They are neutral in this war. We wouldn't like it if they did the same to us for some war the States might be fighting. We should have at least asked for permission first.'

'If we had asked they would have denied us. This article in the *News* says the recruiters just gave the men money for transport so they could get to Canada to join up. They didn't sign them up on American soil.'

'I think you are splitting hairs there, Pim.' McDougall read out an English letter to the *News* editor in January which refuted President Pierce's complaints against Great Britain regarding her abuse of American sovereignty and neutrality: 'The article says "...We have hitherto exercised a wise and statesmanlike forbearance in not inciting or in any way exacerbating the ill feeling already too prevalent against England in the United States...which shows the United States that England preferred patiently to endure almost any insult rather than commit the sin of embarking in a fratricidal war..." Judging from the number of ships we have with us, I think it a bit disingenuous to say England is patiently enduring anything. We are the ones with the warships at the other nation's doorstep!'

Kellett nodded his head in agreement. 'Not to mention there wouldn't be any reason for forbearance with America if Britain hadn't violated her neutrality in the first place by foolishly recruiting on her soil in five major cities! And without permission!'

An article in the 23rd edition of the *Times* made Kellett smile. 'Listen to this, Messrs Pim and McDougall! Our old *Resolute* has been salvaged! Do you remember that young Fairfax Abraham? He was part of the whaling crew that found her more than a thousand miles from where we left her! He was serving on the whaling ship from his father's New London firm that found her.'

'I can't believe it, how could she ever survive the Arctic ice?'

'I always said she was resolute!' McDougall exclaimed. 'Do you remember, Sir, one of the first conversations we had had been about how she would always take care of us? Looks like she took better care of herself than we took of her, with us leaving her like we did.'

The men listened while Kellett read the account of the rescue from the ice, the long, stormy voyage, and the reception his ship had received in New London when she sailed in on Christmas Eve. 'That's all the good news, I'm afraid. The next article here is about our ships being part of a naval build-up, first in Jamaica, and now off the American coast. It sounds as though the Americans will shortly match us, ship for ship.'

'Do you think we could be close to war? I don't see how that recruitment issue could be justification for an all-out war with the United States, can you, Commodore?'

164

'Mr. McDougall, I have never understood half the reasons why countries go to war. If the United States really feels we have violated her sovereignty, and that by doing so without apology we have also insulted her, then I can easily see why her hackles are raised. Add to that our own confrontations with USS *Laongo* and *Cyane*, and the way folks in America might perceive that, well…I have seen wars scared up over less. But it takes two countries to start a fight: both countries have to be itching for war. Unfortunately, it appears to me that there are warmongers in both countries right now. The only bright spot seems to be the rescue of our old *Resolute.*'

The men continued their reading. The next paper Kellett looked at was The *Illustrated News* from the first of February. Again, numerous articles from American papers were reprinted in it, along with its own own articles and editorials. Kellett's heart sank as he read on.

The New York Herald reported a series of ominous telegraphic dispatches. Kellett read the dispatches aloud. One of them stated that President Pierce and his Cabinet had been discussing the subject of formally withdrawing the American Ambassador, Mr. Buchanan, from England, due to what they perceived as a complete refusal on the part of Lord Palmerston to settle the differences between the two governments. This placed the question of peace, or its opposite, onto the American Government. The editorial speculated that if this happened the recall of Mr. Buchanan would hasten events and Congress would support the president. It could even cause the downfall of the British Prime Minister, Palmerston.

The second telegraph reported, dated 16 January, referred to the United States as being on 'the eve of war'. The British response to the demand for an apology had been to ridicule the Americans for their pretensions, and a refusal to recognise that the enlistment of recruits for the British service was a violation of international law. This dispatch also confirmed the build up of the Royal Navy off the American coast and described it as an unprovoked act of aggression.

The January 17th telegraph reported leaked intelligence that, in a secret meeting with the Senate, President Pierce planned to submit the issue of going to war with England.

Kellett quoted '…It is said that the President has prepared a special message appraising Congress that he has given orders for the suspension of diplomatic intercourse with England…and a member of the Cabinet alleges we are in the midst of a crisis and that war will take place with Great Britain within sixty days.'

The next dispatch reported, dated the 18[th,] confirmed that the President would be sending to the Senate his reasons for withdrawing from diplomatic relations with England. *The New York Courier and Inquirer* also reported the latest rumour that the American Ambassador would soon depart from Britain, and that he would deliver to the British Government the American Government's request for the British Ambassador to be recalled.

'Surely, things could not have gone this far so quickly as the cessation of diplomatic relations between Britain and America! That is always the very last step before war!' Kellett shook his head.

'My paper says one of the reasons for a recall of British Ambassador was that he had been directly implicated in the recruitment issue. Perhaps all they want to do is replace him?' McDougall looked at his companions. 'It is difficult to tell what is really happening when newspapers report rumours with the same emphasis as fact.'

'I am not afraid of going to war with America,' Pim declared. 'If they want to send the diplomats home, let them. We can practice gun-boat diplomacy!'

'I disagree with all this warmongering,' McDougall responded. 'I don't really see anything here worth fighting over! If you ask me, both countries are acting like petulant children.'

Kellett read on. *'The Washington Globe* seemed a voice of reason stating it would be "wild knight-errantry for our young, vigorous, growing Republic…to hunt up a pretext to involve itself in such a quarrel." And the *New York Journal of Commerce* took a dim view of war talk as well, characterising the danger of war as: "…appalling to the interests of both nations…we fear there has already been a blameable superciliousness on both sides, and would counsel moderation and forbearance as the best solution of the present difficulties."

'So it looks like the *Globe* agrees with you, McDougall. Another war between America and Great Britain would be disastrous for the economy in both countries. Fair Abe's family would certainly be hit hard. You only have to look at what the War of 1812 did to the New England whaling industry, and then consider what our cotton mills would do without American cotton to see what a mistake war would be.'

'Well, it looks to me like there will have to be an apology, a concession or a fight,' McDougall added sadly.

'I am encouraged by the last few articles I've read,' Kellett pointed out 'At the very least they show us the American public is divided over the issue of war. There may be people in both countries always willing to fight their old nemesis, but I hope they will not be able to convert others to their views. Pim, I suppose we will have to agree to disagree about all of this. I only hope our presence in these waters is not going to be the thing that tips the balance of the scales towards war.'

The men were just getting ready to leave Kellett's cabin when there was a knock on the door. 'Come in,' Kellett looked up as Brooke entered the cabin.

'There is a boat approaching, Sir!' Moments later, to the surprise of all, the bo's'n piped Ambassador Crampton on board.

⚓⚓⚓⚓⚓

Sitting in their parlour, Father and Martha Abraham were engaged in the same activity of reading the papers. Father read out articles while Martha darned stockings. 'Martha! Listen to this! *The New York Herald* editorial has put its finger on the crux of the matter! They say that President Pierce, due to a lack of popularity, is using the recruitment issue, and fomenting war fever, to get re-nominated for the Presidency in 1856! What doest thou think of that?'

'Truly, thou hast had thy suspicions of the political machinations behind the scenes of late. Doest thou believe this is real reason for the turmoil?'

'It pains me to say it, but I believe it is possible that our president is playing with the lives of our young men purely for political gain. He is certainly not doing anything to defuse the emotions which are running so high right now in Washington. We can only hope wiser heads will prevail.'

…Wiser heads will prevail…Father Abe listened to his own words echo in his heart. Wiser heads. He was in need of following his own advice. Emotions were running high in his family, yet he had not done what a father must do, namely whatever possible in order to keep his family together. It was his responsibility to use his age and wisdom to resolve the conflict between himself and his son.

In truth, he could not begrudge his son the strength of his commitment to the abolition of slavery. Fair Abe had learned well the faith-based lessons Father and Martha had given all their children concerning social justice issues. Father felt a similar degree of dedication to the freeing of the slaves. This was the common ground he must emphasise the next time he and Fair Abe spoke. He really needed help to find a way forward without losing his son. He needed Martha.

He looked up from his newspaper and gazed fondly at his wife. The sun shone on her hair as she sat by the window quilting. Age had done nothing to diminish her beauty. *Wisdom and beauty in equal measure*, he mused.

'Martha, I need thy good counsel. Wilt thou pray with me on finding a way to resolve the ill feeling between Fair Abe and me?'

'Thou need not ask, my love.'

Mother and Father sat in silent prayer, opening their hearts to receive a leading from Christ, which they believed they would discern when they stilled their hearts. The silence deepened as the sunlight shifted across the floor. Their hearts beat more slowly, and without even forming the words in their minds, they lifted their concern up to the Lord.

Father Abraham began to see a way forward, and he broke the silence with a quiet 'Thank you, Lord.' Martha opened her eyes and smiled at him.

'Doest thou know…?'

'Yes, Martha. I remembered very clearly the words of Carolyn Fox: "Live up the Light thou hast, and more will be granted thee". Fair Abe is following the Light as he experiences it, just as we are. We believe in the same thing: the equality of the slaves and their God-given right to freedom. The Light leads all of us to do the work in our own particular way. If young Fair Abe can see no other way to follow His leading than by being willing to fight for freedom, then that is the measure of Light he has at this moment. I must accept this. I cannot force him to see the peace testimony in the same way we do, to see that it offers us the most correct way to abolish slavery.

'I believe we must accept his calling, if the time comes. I will not condone the sort of violence erupting in the Kansas Territory, nor do I think Fair Abe ever will. But should it come to war, should there be an army going forth to free the slaves, we must not disown him: we must accept that he may march with them, and we must support him with all our love.'

⚓⚓⚓⚓⚓

Margaret's fatigue permeated every cell of her body, but there was no rest for her. Malnutrition weakened the men when they needed their strength the most and their wounds continued to go septic. Men she thought were beyond danger suddenly faced the amputation of limbs that she had worked hard to save. Care packets arrived with blankets and clothing, making it possible for the nurses to keep the men warm at least. But men still died. And death was ugly when seen up close.

Day by day, night after night, Margaret dressed the soldiers' putrid wounds, fed and bathed the men, read to them, wrote their letters. The rumours that a peace conference was meant to take place in Paris did nothing to touch her exhausted spirit, but it did raise the morale of the soldiers. Their eyes began to shine with something other than fever: Hope. Could it be possible that their unceasing prayers for an end to the war might be answered?

That was the one thing Margaret could not share with the men, or the other nurses and aids. She could not bring herself to pray, because she had lost her ability to believe. The God she had believed in from her very earliest days was certainly nowhere to be seen in the battlefields and hospitals of the Crimea. If there was no one there to hear the thousands of prayers offered up every day, then there was no point in praying in the first place.

What God could allow such suffering? If God did exist, then He wasn't anything like the companion she had always felt Him to be. If this was how He worked, then thank you, but no thank you very much! The rest of them could hold onto their empty, archaic beliefs if they found comfort in them, they had little enough with which to console themselves. But for Margaret, the thought of a God that allowed such misery was too painful to contemplate. It was easier to say there was no God.

On the 25th, the very day the Peace Conference began in Paris, Margaret received a letter from Fair Abe, sent on Christmas Day. He was filled with the joy and wonder of having arrived home on Christmas Eve in his old ship *Resolute,* and of being within the loving circle of his family after his harrowing voyage from the Arctic. How could it be that Fair Abe's experience of suffering at the hands of her father's old commander, Belcher, had strengthened his faith, while her experience of the suffering of the men around her had killed hers? She wanted to feel the joy she always felt when she thought of Fair Abe, but instead she felt nothing.

She looked like someone who was alive: she ate, breathed, and did her work, but nothing broke through her emptiness. Not even the wild celebrations and firing of the guns that greeted the news of the Armistice on the 29th.

ɞɞɞɞɞ

Fair Abe read, with a sense of futility, the report of President Pierce's speech on the 11th, in which the President vowed to use military force to quell the violence in Kansas. He knew something had to be done, but it was inconceivable to him that the president would use soldiers to fire upon American citizens.

'That is what would happen, Father, isn't it? If merely the presence of the troops was not enough, or some fool shot at them?'

'Yes, it is possible, my son.'

'I am beginning to feel we are descending a maelstrom where violence can only beget more violence, a downward spiral that is becoming more and more difficult to break. How can it ever be stopped?'

'We can still work for a peaceful solution. A delegation from New England Yearly Meeting is being organised to go to Washington to meet with the President. It is not too late, but I do fear the events in Kansas are reaching that critical point thou didst just speak of, where the violence will only bring more of the same.'

'Now, this is too much, Father. The editorial today is using our *Resolute* to fan the flames of their warmongering against Britain! They call the British refusal to relinquish rights to her salvage as '...adding insult to injury.' Fair Abe handed the paper to Father and watched his face turn red with anger as he read.

'Isn't there something we could do with *Resolute* to defuse this situation?'

'If the money from the salvage only went into my pocket, Fair Abe, I would give the ship back to England today. But we owe our allegiance to the brave men, thyself included, who risked all to bring her home. Captain Buddington, his officers and men, not only depend on us for their livelihood, but also to defend their rights. My ire has been raised by this article very much indeed. That this man could use our right to *Resolute* in such a way as too support his sabre rattling is offensive in the extreme.'

Fair Abe watched his father read and began to realise just how difficult it must be even for Father to keep the Quaker Peace Testimony when it seemed clear that he could be just as capable as the next man of succumbing to the desire to take a punch at a man. He was beginning to understand that it can take more courage to refuse violence, that there were times like now, when it was much easier to get swept up in the fever: the angry fever that was spreading throughout Kansas, the war fever that was building against Britain.

169

CHAPTER THREE
APRIL 1856

Ambassador Crampton made several clandestine visits to Commodore Kellett after the very favourable meeting they had had at the end of January. Prior to their meeting Kellett had developed a rather negative image of the man through the press reports, but had been pleasantly surprised to find him a soft spoken and modest man. In the privacy of Kellett's cabin, Crampton had confessed he had never liked the whole business of circumventing the American domestic laws, let alone the international laws of neutrality, to set up the five recruitment stations in Philadelphia, New York, Cincinnati, Boston and Chicago.

'There are many things we must do in the line of diplomatic duty, but to do something so clearly wrong, well...I was against it, but was told I had to do it. I believed in the idea of allowing men who may want to serve the opportunity to sign up, but only if it could have been done legally. And now it looks, at the very least, as though it will be the end of my career. The evidence against me was presented very clearly in the Hertz trial. The fool kept letters that he was instructed to destroy and I signed several of them! As a consequence, your government has requested my recall. I am returning to Britain in several days' time, and the Embassy will be closed. The diplomatic relations are drawing to a close. I will not try to avoid the personal consequences of my actions, but I want to do all that I can to avoid the human costs that will result if America and Britain succeed in using this as an excuse to start a war. I do not want to see my country getting into another war, when our young men are still dying in the Crimea. And from our conversations I believe you share that same desire.'

'If there was anything I could do, I would do it. But what can I possibly do? To be honest, I don't really understand all the issues involved, but from what I can gather, I hardly think the issues are worth the lives of any men and boys. If you know, can you tell me why our government doesn't just apologise and diffuse the situation?'

'This whole story broke when things were looking very dark in the Crimea. Because of the mismanagement and poor logistics, more of our young men were dying from exposure, lack of medical care and supplies, and even food than wounds from battle. For God's sake they were starving! The causes of the war were never understood by the average British subject, but they did understand that their taxes had been raised significantly to pay for it. When they saw those Russell reports from the front, when they saw their brothers and husbands and fathers dying because they had no food or blankets or medicine the British public became angry. And justifiably so! An unpopular war equals an unpopular government. Things got so bad in London that groups began meeting in the pubs, advocating the end of the Monarchy as well as Parliament!

'We were never directly told that the recruiting issue was going to be made a diversionary issue, but in the consulate we viewed it that way. In the name of diplomacy we were instructed to be anything but diplomatic! We could make no apologies; do nothing to smooth things over. In fact, every communication with the American government Downing Street told us to make, and every press release, was designed to make matters worse.'

Kellett shook his head. 'The irony now, if things go well at the Paris peace talks, is that the Crimean conflict is drawing to a close, but this looming conflict with the United States seems to be taking on a life of its own. The Americans see my squadron at its doorstep, and a fully functional navy and army that could be easily shifted from one theatre to another, and they have every right to feel threatened and see us as the aggressors.'

'This brings me to why I am sitting here with you, Commodore.'

The two men talked until the early hours of the morning when Crampton departed just before losing the cover of the night. Kellett sighed as he lowered himself onto his bed. As he drifted off to sleep, he thought of his most recent letter from Alice. The issue of war, all wars, and his career in the Royal Navy was in such direct conflict with her budding Quaker beliefs that she had finally said she could not see a way forward to continue in their marriage. From the number of tear stains on the letter, this awareness was breaking her heart. Tears wet Kellett's pillow as he realised it was breaking his as well. Napoleon, hearing his master crying, put his nose on the pillow next to Kellett's face and whined. Kellett could not keep from feeling comforted as he reassured Naps that all was well while stroking the dog's ears.

If he and Mr. Crampton could succeed in the plan the ambassador had laid out, it might not only stop American and Britain from going to war, but there was a chance that it might also keep his marriage from falling apart.

⚓⚓⚓⚓⚓

Father Abraham called an emergency partners' meeting to discuss the most recent letter from the British Minister Crampton.

'I am gravely concerned, in the temper of these times, that our rescue of HMS *Resolute,* and our insistence in claiming our rights to her, may be seen as an aggressive act. My faith calls for me to live in such a way that, if at all possible, I do not contribute to war or violent conflict, and that I must do all I can to alleviate the causes of war. I do not know if war is inevitable. Our government still has options to pursue with Great Britain which may avert armed conflict. But I fear our ship may be used as a pawn in the game.

'I have called you here to discuss amongst ourselves if there are any possible courses of action open to us, besides the claiming of our salvage rights.'

'Mr. Smith and I have the greatest respect for your faith, Mr. Abraham, but we must consider carefully not only the welfare of the men who brought her back, but also the financial health of our firm.' Mr. Perkins opened the accounts book and found the entry for the month the *George Henry* came home.

'Although the revenues have been good this year, we are only just recovering from several years of low returns. Therefore, I still believe our firm needs the monies from this salvage. What say you, Mr. Smith?'

'I wish with all my heart that we could do something noble like offering *Resolute* back to Great Britain as a gift. This is what you are suggesting, is it not? But, not only do I agree with Mr. Perkins about our bottom line, I believe we owe it to our men to secure the salvage monies for them. They are, after all, the ones who risked their lives for her.'

'Thy answers echo my own thoughts, gentlemen. I cannot see any other course that we can take. I suppose I needed the reassurance from you that we can see no other way forward other than continuing to fight for the salvage rights to *Resolute*.'

The partners left their meeting discussing the latest news from Washington.

'I thought Cass's war speech on the tenth was bad enough, but now the *Congressional Globe* is reporting that President Pierce has called for an increase in military spending, most of it for the navy.' Perkins shook his head. 'Three million dollars worth of increase! War with England would be devastating for our New England commerce. Even though we are not Quakers like you, Mr. Abraham, we were still against the last war for that very reason.'

'Yes,' Father Abraham agreed, 'I saw an article quoted from a Manchester newspaper, where the merchants of England say the same thing. Perhaps we businessmen can put some pressure on our respective governments to let cooler heads prevail.'

'Now there you are, Mr. Abraham!' Mr. Smith smiled. 'That is something we can do. Let us draft a petition for other businesses to sign, and send it to our Senators. We may not be able to give up *Resolute,* but we may still be able to have our voice heard in Washington DC.'

'I can set my Fair Abe to the task today.' Father Abraham nodded in agreement and the men separated, disappearing behind the doors to their respective offices.

ℰℰℰℰℰ

With an overwhelming wave of joy and relief, Alice greeted the news that the leaders attending the Paris Peace Conference had finally signed a peace treaty, and all pundits agreed the ratification would be a mere formality, which could be quickly accomplished. With her peace work done, she had little reason to stay in London, but she was reluctant to return to Clonacody. After her last letter to Henry, she no longer felt Clonacody was her home, but she knew she could not stay indefinitely with her Quaker friends.

However, the letter that came from Margaret made her realise that she had to return to the family home. Margaret wrote she expected to arrive in Ireland on the 16th of April; she would be sailing on a troop ship, with wounded soldiers and other nurses and medical workers. Again in this letter, Alice could discern no emotion and it was almost as though Margaret was sleepwalking through the final days of the war. Her daughter's words, '…if there is a God…' struck fear in Alice's heart. What irony, if the very times that had strengthened Alice's faith were the same times that may have killed Margaret's. Yet, Alice remembered the utter despair she had felt when she had witnessed extreme affliction during the Famine. Her faith had been rocked and almost destroyed then. She knew precisely the difficulty that lay in believing in a loving, compassionate God and experiencing excessive suffering in the world.

If Margaret was in the state of spiritual crisis her mother thought she was, the familiar surroundings of her beloved Clonacody would be an essential ingredient for healing. Alice wrote to the staff that they would soon be coming home. She spent her final weeks in London saying goodbye to the Friends who had been so instrumental in her spiritual awakening, and with whom she had had many joyful moments of fellowship despite the grim work with which they had been involved.

It was during one such farewell, that Alice learned about the latest developments in the war of words against the United States. One of the women showed her a *Telegraph* article which reported a leaked memo from a meeting in Downing Street, wherein the Prime Minister was considering using the moral high ground of Britain's stance on the slave trade to justify war with the United States.

'Oh well, why not scare up another war! The boys are on the transport ships this very moment; just sail them straight across to America and don't bother to bring them home. It's a ready made army and navy, no fuss or mess involved. Such an imbroglio had been made of the fight in the Crimea; maybe the government can rally the people's support if they make a good show of this one. Poor Henry! He would be so upset to think his work stopping the slave ships could be used in such a cynical way.'

'Is thy husband still on the ships that are a part of the naval build up?'

'For all I know, yes, I am afraid so.'

'I shall hold him in the Light and in my prayers that he may not have to be involved in any hostilities.'

Alice Kellett kissed her friend's cheek. 'Thank you. I pray for the same every night.'

ℐℐℐℐℐ

'Senator Mason from Virginia spoke in the Senate, and his speech is reported here. He seems to be the most vigorous spokesman for the warmongers in Congress..."Our honour, our sovereignty, the very soul of our Nation has been threatened..." it goes on and on.' Father Abraham tossed the paper away in disgust. Fair Abe looked across the room at his father, startled by the anger in his voice.

'It seems all the rage, this sabre rattling. I have begun to see, Father, how true what thou doest say is: that violence begets violence, and that it may take more courage to stand for peace in the midst of so many calling for war. I understand more clearly why tempers are fraying in Kansas, but I cannot comprehend why there is so much hostility against Great Britain. Or at least why we are not hearing wiser and calmer voices speaking up. There must be someone willing to settle the differences between America and Britain, rather than allowing this situation to degenerate into out and out war.'

'Thy mother and I have been speaking about this very issue, and one editorial we read seemed to offer one plausible explanation, and I would like to know what thou doest think of it. The editor connected the two issues thou hast just spoken of: the trouble in Kansas, and the stirring up of feelings against Britain. Thou must realise that we are coming into the presidential campaigning season; soon President Pierce will have to work for his party's nomination in order to remain in the White House. His record is not one for him to be proud of. On his watch the country has come much closer to breaking apart. He has tried to please everyone, vacillating between placating the north, then the south, with the result that no one trusts him anymore. At a time when our country needs a strong leader, he has been weak and unable to steer us through this very dark time. And I fear the violence in Kansas is just a beginning.'

'So, if the politicians can scare up a fight with England, a fight that just might appeal to both the north and the south, maybe they will be able to unite the country?'

'Yes, Fair Abe, thou hast seen exactly what thy mother and I have begun to believe is happening here. Perhaps we have grown cynical in our advancing age, but we have learned through the years to strip away the rhetoric when governments are leading their people into a conflict, and have always tried to see what lies behind the patriotic words, to see what each government has to gain by putting its young men in harm's way.'

'Doest thou always believe there is such a hidden motivation, Father? Can't there be times when the cause is truly just?'

'As thou knowest, one of the basic tenets of our faith is that we are conscientious objectors to all wars. But yes, even so, I admit there may be times when, as the world exists now, there may be conflicts based primarily on principles. Yet such un-lofty elements as political or economic gain always play some part. When the cause is truly just, Friends have never shied away from dying for it, but we draw the line at killing.'

'I know, Father! I don't need another lecture…'

'I am truly sorry. I did not want this to seem…' Father took a deep breath. 'In the same way that thou hast said there must be someone out there willing to settle the differences between America and England, I have come to realise that we must do the same with the conflict that has been tearing our family apart and making us strangers to each other.'

'I cannot give up my willingness to fight for the freedom of the slaves, if it comes to that.'

'No, I know thou cannot. Thy understanding of the Light, the leading thou doest feel, must be that which guideth thy feet. I must accept this, Fair Abe, and I do accept this. Mother and I both do. And by doing so, we hope we can work together to restore the harmony in our family. We cannot offer peaceful solutions to the world if we fail to find them in our own home.'

Fair Abe was speechless. Father put his arms out to him, and Fair Abe lost himself to the warmth of his father's hug.

CHAPTER FOUR
JUNE 1856

Commodore Kellett split his squadron and took three ships north, arriving in New London, Connecticut on the 5th of June. His guest passenger onboard was Ambassador Crampton. Two ships stayed out at sea, and only the *Medea* anchored in the harbour. A representative of the mayor's office met them quietly on the quay. With tensions so high, the Mayor had been concerned about the reception the people of New London would give a ship from the Royal Navy. Having his carriage there to meet Kellett and Crampton he felt would diffuse any possibility of the ship's visit being interpreted as a hostile move.

When Crampton and Kellett, accompanied by the faithful Napoleon, arrived at the mayor's office, the Mayor, Captain Buddington, Mr. Perkins, Mr. Smith, Father Abraham, and Fair Abe were already assembled there. The Mayor held out his hand, 'Welcome Ambassador Crampton and Commodore Kellett. Please, follow me.'

When they entered the room Naps greeted his old friend, Fair Abe, with enthusiasm and Kellett addressed him warmly. 'I am so pleased to be meeting you again. You have no idea how many times in the past two years that I have thought of you, and hoped to meet you again. And now, here we are!'

'Commodore Kellett, I would like to introduce to you my father, Mr. Abraham, and his partners, Mr. Perkins and Mr. Smith.' Kellett shook hands all round, and then introduced the ambassador to the New Londoners.

The men took their places around a large mahogany table. Ambassador Crampton sat to the right of the Mayor, with Commodore Kellett sitting next to him. Father Abraham sat to the left of the Mayor, with Smith and then Perkins following on. Fair Abe and Captain Buddington sat between Kellett and Perkins.

'Welcome, gentlemen. I have called you all here at the request of Mr. Crampton. So without further ado, I will turn the floor over to him.'

'Thank you for taking time from your very busy lives to come to this meeting. As you know, the relationship between our two countries is on the breaking point. Yesterday, your president stood before the Senate and called for the cessation of diplomatic relations with my country. I need not tell you that, if the Congress agrees with President Pierce, and Mr. Buchanan and I are returned to our respective countries, we will truly be on the very eve of war.

Already the Royal Navy, under the command of Commodore Kellett, has amassed a fleet of war ships off your coast. The United States Navy is sailing out to face it as I speak to you now.

'Against this background, my government has chosen to argue with your firm over the rights to HMS *Resolute.* I do not believe, until the actual moment when hostilities break out and the first shot is fired, that it is too late to carry on discussions and negotiations. In that spirit, I also believe a symbolic gesture, no matter how small, may serve to break the tensions between two hostile parties, and help to bring them back to the negotiating table when they have given up hope of a peaceful resolution. Thus, it gives me great pleasure to tell you that, with the support and assistance of Commodore Henry Kellett, I have succeeded in persuading Her Majesty's Government to alter their position regarding their ownership of HMS *Resolute.*'

The partners held their collective breath, not believing what they were hearing, waiting for Crampton to finish. Kellett could feel the tension emanating from his young friend, Fair Abe, and turned to smile at him.

'I have been authorised by Her Majesty's Government to notify you that, as of this morning, all British rights to HMS *Resolute* are hereby relinquished, and the ship is yours for the salvage rights.'

⚓⚓⚓⚓⚓

Father Abraham and Fair Abe were speechless, but Captain Buddington jumped up with a loud 'Huzzah!' He shook hands with Kellett, and then ran around the side of the table to shake Crampton's hand. 'The men will be very pleased, very pleased indeed! They've been worrying some, I have to tell you. You just wait until I tell them; they will be celebrating tonight!'

Martha and Father Abraham talked well into the night, after a celebratory dinner with the partners and their families. Could this be the gesture that might pull the countries away from the brink of war? They were both determined now that *Resolute* would fulfil her destiny by doing just that. And Father Abraham met again with the partners the following morning.

The Abraham family arrived in Washington DC, and checked into their hotel. The children danced around the room in excitement. They had never been to their nation's capital before and they were anxious to go see the sights. Martha and Fair Abe got the family unpacked, fed and dressed for an afternoon outing, while Father met with Connecticut's Senator Foster.

He came back to the hotel hours later, tired, hungry, and disgruntled.

'Didst thou have no luck, Father?' Martha took her husband's coat, and poured water into the basin for him to wash before dinner.

'No, Martha, though he was interested in what I had to say, Senator Foster did not think he would be able to make our idea succeed. And I thought I was at my most persuasive, too.' He smiled sadly. 'I know not who else to approach for I didst think he was the one most likely to work on our behalf. Never trouble thyself, tomorrow will come soon enough, and I will try every senator in Congress if needs must.'

On the fourth day he found as unlikely an ally as he could have imagined. Senator James Murray Mason from Virginia was a southerner who strongly supported the state's right to have legal slavery within its borders. He did not base his stance on the constitutional issue of limited federal power. He had appealed to the federal government to stop the admission of California as a free state, so he clearly believed in the federal government retaining power over the states. He did not even believe in the state's right to determine whether slavery was legal within its borders.

He based his arguments for slavery on the fact that to limit it anywhere in the United States or their territories was to deny equal rights to the men who owned slaves. He was one of the only politicians to thus base his denial of equal rights to black men and women on the issue of equal rights for whites! He was a strong supporter of slavery, and had been the author of the cursed Fugitive Slave Act, an act which again relied upon the federal government for passage and enforcement, and the act that Father Abraham, and other Quakers and abolitionists, had spent the past sixteen years fighting.

Not only this, but Senator Mason had been the most vocal of the warmongers against England: standing in Congress for hours at a time declaring the actions of Great Britain as having been an insult to the sovereignty and dignity of the United States, actions the government could not ignore. He had strongly advocated the ordering of the US Navy to face off against the Royal Navy Squadron that was still stationed off the Chesapeake Bay. With fiery words he said he had '...no fear that war is to follow the apparent collision which has taken place between the two governments; but I confess that I feel deeply the indignity that has been put upon the American people, in ordering this British squadron into (these) seas without notice.'

Yet this was the man who listened with great interest to Father Abraham's proposal.

ÉÉÉÉÉ

Alice waited impatiently for the carriage to arrive. Margaret had made it plain in her last letter that she did not want her mother meeting her at the dock; all she wanted was for her mother to send the family carriage. Alice felt she had to honour her daughter's request, but that did not make the waiting any easier.

She paced from room to room: making certain the flowers in Margaret's room were placed exactly in the middle of the bedside table, the quilts and pillows fluffed, the fire blazing. Returning to the ground floor, she arranged the flowers in the front hallway for the fifth time that morning, asked Sally to bring more coal in for the fire in the lounge, and checked the freshly baked cakes and the table linen in the kitchen. Once again, Sally had to answer Alice's queries about the dinner preparations while the two women walked from the kitchen to the dining room. The crystal chandelier sparkled in the sunlight, the silver gleamed, everything was set just so on the table.

McCaffrey ran into the kitchen just as Alice and Sally returned to check the foods in the ovens. 'She's here, my little lassie is here! The carriage is coming up the drive. She's here!'

'Yes, Mr. McCaffrey, thank you. Now calm down; you are making me nervous.'

McCaffrey and Sally exchanged bemused glances before following their lady to the front door. The carriage drew up, its wheels and the horses' hooves crunching gravel and scattering the chickens, which had escaped from the garden.

Mrs. Kellett's words of greeting died on her lips as her daughter stepped down and extended her hand for McCaffrey's assistance. Her patched and stained clothes hung on her as though draped on a skeleton. Alice struggled to keep the tears from her eyes as she rushed forward and enveloped Margaret in her arms. Alice and McCaffrey guided her into the house, and McCaffrey carried her up to her room.

'Sally! Draw a bath immediately, and bring those clothes down to the garden for McCaffrey to burn. Quickly, lass, don't stand there gawping.'

Alice prepared tea and cakes while Sally bathed Margaret. Bringing them to her daughter's bedside, she fussed with the covers and pillows again, and then tucked Margaret into the fresh sheets. 'Here, my darling girl, let's have tea.'

Tea! Her mother's panacea for all troubles! How good it felt: strong, milky, and sweet as she sipped it slowly. Did it feel good to be home? She really couldn't say. Emotions were beyond her; she could only say that the sensations of being warm, and clean, and tucked in her old bed while drinking Mother's tea felt better than she had imagined possible. The room was perfect, Mother's touch evident everywhere in the fresh flowers and the blazing fire, but she felt none of the feelings she thought she would.

Not even the letters from Fair Abe, which she read over and over again, could reach her. And thus it continued, day after day, and week after week. Nothing touched the frozen core of her soul.

⚓⚓⚓⚓⚓

In America, events continued to spiral out of control. Out in the Kansas Territory proslavery men had attacked and tarred and feathered, kidnapped and killed Free State men. Then they had rioted and burned Lawrence, the free-state capitol. A man named John Brown had gathered his sons and a few other radicals in response to these outrages and attacked proslavery men in Pottawatomie Creek. They dragged five men from their homes and hacked them to death with axes.

The violence had reached Washington DC for the first time in the later half of May. Senator Charles Sumner, an abolitionist, had given an emotional speech, denouncing the violence and crimes 'against Kansas'. He accused South Carolinian Senators Atchison and Butler of cavorting with the 'harlot, Slavery.' Butler's nephew, Preston Brooks, took such offence at Sumner's language that he attacked Sumner while he was sitting at his Senate desk, beating him into unconsciousness with his cane.

Against this background of sectarian violence, the Virginian Senator Mason worked on putting into action the plan that he and Father Abraham had devised. It had been easy for him to convince his brother senators from the south. They quickly made the same leap of logic he had made when Abraham first met with him. States were already threatening to secede, and the recent violence was making that a more likely outcome every day. If the south did secede, there would be no way they could survive without Britain as a market for cotton. And with most of America's factories in the north, they would need Britain for manufactured goods, particularly arms and ships. Once the southern senators began to rally round the cause of sending *Resolute* to Britain, the northern senators quickly began to sign up to the idea. In reality, no one was proud of the way the country had reacted to the Anglo-American crisis, and the purchase and return of the ship was a good way to save face.

On the evening of June 24th, he met with the two Abraham men in his office to report on the day's work in the Senate.

'My dear sirs, I presented this day a joint resolution before Congress for consideration regarding HMS *Resolute*. In the resolution, I have requested the American Government to purchase *Resolute* from your whaling firm for the sum you suggested of $40,000.00. The resolution sets out all that you have proposed: that after the government has purchased the ship, additional monies shall be caused to be set aside for the complete repair and refurbishment of the ship at the Brooklyn Navy Yard. Further, that she then be sailed back to The United Kingdom as a gift from the American people to the Queen and her subjects.'

'We dearly hope that thou canst succeed in getting this resolution passed, Senator.'

'I have good news for you on that score as well.' Senator Mason poured three glasses of wine and set them on his desk. 'I suggest we toast our gallant ship. For the Senate passed our resolution on this very day with an enthusiastic and unanimous vote!'

Father Abraham could hardly contain his joy, and Fair Abe failed entirely in restraining his. He jumped up out of his seat with a loud 'Huzzah!' danced around the room and picked up his glass of wine. 'Father, Senator, I give you HMS *Resolute*!'

CHAPTER FIVE
NOVEMBER – DECEMBER 1856

Commodore Kellett joyfully received the orders to accompany Captain Hartstene on HMS *Resolute* for her return voyage to England. In the months after Senator Mason's resolution, Kellett's squadron had been ordered home. Kellett made Pim the acting captain on board *Medea* and sent the ships home with letters for his family from himself and the Abraham's. He stayed behind to oversee the works on his old ship, travelling back and forth between Washington DC, the Brooklyn Navy Yard, and (as often as he could manage it) New London, Connecticut. The Abraham children loved Napoleon, and the dog tolerated with magnanimity the ear-pulling from little William and the bonnets the girls forced him to wear. Kellett and the children took numerous walks with Napoleon, who was glad to be on *terra firma* for such a long time. Kellett noticed his old friend was beginning to walk more stiffly, but he still ran a good chase when he found the scent of rabbit or fox.

Throughout the summer the refurbishment progressed, and Kellett was surprised and delighted by the efforts that had been put into repairing or replacing even items like the books and instruments. The United States government gave Henry Kellett the honour of delivering the cheque from them to the Perkins, Smith and Abraham offices. And it was during that late August visit that he had invited Mr Abraham and Fair Abe to be his guests on HMS *Resolute* for the trip to England, an invitation they accepted happily. At the launching, the new American ensign, sewn for the ship's return journey under American command, unfurled proudly in the wind, and *Resolute* looked better than he had ever remembered.

⚓⚓⚓⚓⚓

The morning of departure dawned bright with a clear sky. The men's breath swirled away into the frosty air. All of the Abraham family had come down to the Brooklyn Navy Yard to see Father and Fair Abe off. It was a gala affair, with the Marine Band playing and both American and British flags flying. Martha had never seen so much red, white and blue bunting. The excitement infected the children and they ran about with their own small flags, cheering each sailor that boarded the ship. Martha joined in their cheering; making herself almost hoarse by the time she spotted Father and Fair Abe.

The Abraham men waved to their family and the crowds from the deck, causing a surge in the children's shouts. The Marine Band alternated between playing American and British patriot songs, bursting forth with the American National Anthem when Captain Hartstene pulled up to the quayside in a naval carriage, and they continued to play as he was piped aboard. But it was the British anthem of 'God Save the Queen' that they played when Commodore Kellett, and Napoleon, arrived and boarded the *Resolute*. The ship left the quayside exactly on time, at twelve o'clock noon, and it was accompanied for several miles by a flotilla of small boats.

Although the voyage across the Atlantic was uneventful, on December thirteenth *Resolute* anchored at Spithead in the midst of a violent winter storm. Lightning and thunder drowned out the sound of the men's pounding feet as they furled sails, and the clanking of the anchor chain could barely be heard as they let go the anchor. Naps cowered under Kellett's bed and no amount of encouragement could dislodge him. In the pouring rain, the fierce wind whipped the American Ensign straight out, where it snapped and swirled and cracked in the storm.

⚓⚓⚓⚓⚓

Alice and Margaret Kellett had come to Portsmouth, where *Resolute* would anchor, on the tenth of December, anticipating as Henry had written to them, that the Atlantic passage would take about a month. Alice wasn't certain that she had done the correct thing by coming to England for her husband's homecoming. Her last letter to him had borne her news, after all, that she was leaving him. But she had seen the first spark of any life in Margaret's eyes when Henry's letter had arrived saying that Mr. Abraham and Fair Abe would be arriving with him on *Resolute*. Alice felt she had to go for her daughter's sake.

The months since Margaret's return had been difficult ones, and Alice had not been able to re-awaken her daughter's spirit. McCaffrey had tried to get her interested in her horses, but even that had not worked. Alice hoped that seeing her father and the young man who loved her would help break through Margaret's deadness. Thank God Napoleon would be there as well. Naps had always been able to warm Margaret's heart. Maybe he could work his magic again. Everything else had failed.

Yet, she could not honestly say she only came to Portsmouth for her daughter's sake. She needed to know she was making the right decision, and she could not know that without seeing and speaking to the man with whom she had spent most of her life. When the news came that *Resolute* was at anchor she realised she was more nervous than she had been, all those years ago, when she first came to Clonacody. Her nervousness was almost matched by Margaret's when Henry and Fair Abe sent the message that they were in the Hotel's reception room, waiting to be received.

Margaret wanted, more than anything, to feel something when she saw Fair Abe. Anything. If his eyes could warm her again, if his arms could melt what was frozen within her…she could not explain or understand why she had shut down so completely. One day she had still felt the pain of the men around her and the next day, like a lake that had suddenly frozen over during the night, she felt nothing. She had wanted to feel again when she saw her mother, when she saw Clonacody, and when McCaffrey had tried to get her to groom her horses, but she had barely been able to go through the motions of dressing and eating: pretending to be a living person.

When Fair Abe took her in his arms, she tried again to feel. She let him hold her, she even raised her face for a kiss, and she saw her mother and father looking on in concern and approval, but nothing stirred inside her. Nothing. She did not respond to Napoleon's exuberant greeting; she only pushed him away.

⚓⚓⚓⚓⚓

Fair Abe thought he was prepared to see Margaret. Commodore Kellett had explained what had happened to her, and how her time in the Crimea had affected her. Kellett had even shown him the letter from Mrs. Kellett, which detailed her concern for Margaret after her arrival home.

Yet he had to work very hard to disguise his dismay when he took her in his arms. She was much thinner that she had been; her face pale. Even though she let him hug her, and give her a kiss, she felt wooden in his arms. The smile she gave him didn't reach her eyes. But Fair Abe was a patient man. This was the woman he loved. And if he had to walk her through the motions of life and love for a long time before her heart could catch up, then that was what he would do.

Together Captain Hartstene, Commodore and Mrs. Kellett, Father, Fair Abe and Margaret met with the commander-in-chief *pro tem* of the port, the lieutenant-governor, the mayor of the borough and the flag captain onboard HMS *Victory.* On the morning of the fifteenth, all pomp and circumstance accompanied the changing of the ensign on *Resolute.* Captain Hartstene raised the British Ensign and the shore battery fired a twenty-one gun salute, while spectators ashore waved both American and British flags. Then, accompanied by a drum roll, he lowered the American Ensign.

That afternoon HMS *Resolute* was towed to Cowes at the request of Her Majesty Queen Victoria, where Captain Hartstene, Commodore and Mrs. Kellett, Father Abraham, Fair Abe, and Margaret received Her Majesty and Prince Albert on the quarter deck. The ship's company gave three hearty cheers. Hartstene introduced the Kelletts, Abrahams, and all the ship's officers to the Queen and Prince, and in a short presentation ceremony he said,

'Allow me to welcome Your Majesty on board the *Resolute*, and, in obedience to the will of my countrymen and of the President of the United States, to restore her to you, not only as an evidence of a friendly feeling to your sovereignty, but as a token of love, admiration and respect to Your Majesty personally.'

With a gracious smile the Queen responded with, 'I thank you.' Fair Abe followed Commodore Kellett as he led the royal party on a tour through the ship. Kellett had helped to arrange all the officers' cabins, and he was pleased to see that the ship looked even better than when he had left it. The restorers had cleaned and polished all the muskets, swords, and telescopes and had replaced the nautical instruments. Even Pim's old music box was repaired and Kellett had placed it on top of a cabinet in the captain's cabin, where all of the officers' log books sat proudly on a shelf.

Queen Victoria invited Captain Hartstene, the Kellett family and the Abrahams to dine with her and Prince Albert at Osborne House the following evening. During the main course, Fair Abe took Margaret's hand under the table and squeezed it. Margaret held his hand tightly and smiled. And to Fair Abe's delight, he saw that smile dance in her eyes before she discreetly lowered them and continued to eat her meal.

THE END

EPILOGUE

After the return of *Resolute,* all talk of war between Great Britain and the United States ceased. Instead toasts were raised, editorials were written, and kerbside conversations took place, all extolling the natural familial relationship that existed between the two countries. Many claimed that the courteous way Captain Hartstene had returned *Resolute* would live forever in the memory of the people of England. People queued for hours, day after day, in rain and fair weather to tour *Resolute.*

The British and American governments subsequently re-established diplomatic relations. Queen Victoria knighted Commodore Kellett for his service to crown and country, and Sir Henry and his family returned to Clonacody. Fair Abe joined them there in order to court Margaret. With patient persistence he continued to reawaken Margaret's heart. They married in the spring of 1857 and settled in New London, Connecticut, where they raised their family in the Quaker faith.

Sir Henry and Alice worked diligently to reconcile their differences while Kellett continued to serve in the Royal Navy. Despite the real love and affection between them, this proved to be an impossible task. Rather than lose Alice, Sir Henry decided to retire from active service, and spent the remainder of his days ensconced in Clonacody, running his estate and raising horses. Naps died peacefully in 1859.

HISTORICAL NOTES

This is a work of historical fiction inspired by true events. While the majority of the book stays very close to the historic facts, several fictional characters have been added to the cast, and for dramatic effect some events have been changed.

Sir Henry Kellett is an historical figure and his naval career is factually presented, though I take some license with his North American station in making that part of the naval build-up related to the United States and Great Britain going to war. While the Admiralty may have indeed seen him as a resource to be called upon if war broke out, his orders for his station in Jamaica were to monitor and interrupt the illegal cross-Atlantic slave trade which was still in operation. In real life he continued this command until 1859, when he was promoted to Rear Admiral. Later, after reaching Vice Admiral, and being knighted, he served again in China. He retired in 1871, and died at his home, Clonacody, on 1 March 1875. He did go to the Arctic with his dog, Napoleon, though I do not know when Naps died. There is a mystery in Kellett's personal life. His marriage to Alice Fletcher is recorded in the Easington Register, Durham, England, but in his home town of Fethard, County Tipperary, Ireland he was always known as a bachelor, and Alice Fletcher was never heard of. I couldn't bear such a good man living and dying alone, so I made Alice Fletcher his life long and loving partner, and I gave them a daughter.

Sir Edward Belcher is an historical figure as well. He was a sadist. In 1836 he was court martialed for the way he treated his men off the coast of Africa when onboard HMS *Aetna*. While he treated his men badly in the Arctic, and he was known for turning every ship he commanded into a living hell, earning himself the nickname of 'Hell Afloat Belcher', there is no record of his actually torturing them during the 1852 Expedition. Fair Abe is a fictional character and I created Belcher's treatment of him by adapting what Belcher actually did to one of his men in the extreme conditions off the African coast. He was never given another active commission in the Royal Navy after the Belcher Expedition debacle, and he was the only man to have abandoned so many ships in the history of Arctic exploration. Roberts and McCoy are fictional characters, but all the other men I mention onboard *Resolute* were real.

The whaling firm of Perkins and Smith existed in New London, Connecticut, and they owned the *George Henry,* which salvaged *Resolute.* Captain Buddington is also an historic figure. Ironically, the crew of the *George Henry* were never paid, because Perkins and Smith failed before the payment could be made. Buddington went to court to sue for the monies owed, but was unsuccessful. He moved back to Illinois around 1860, but missed the sea and moved back to Connecticut seven years later. In 1885 he entered the Sailor's Snug Harbour on Staten Island, but his restless spirit could not settle and he returned to the sea to sail twice as his son's mate, and to complete one last whaling voyage in 1889. He re-entered the Sailor's Snug Harbour in 1907, and died on the 53rd anniversary of bringing *Resolute* home to New London. The entire Abraham family is fictional.

Senator Mason did base his support for slavery on the issue of equal rights. He became Confederate Envoy to Britain and France after the outbreak of the Civil War.

The British Yearly Meeting of the Religious Society of Friends was involved with anti-war work during the Crimean War, primarily in the forming and distribution of their Appeal, and in the members' examination of their own business dealings to be certain they did not support the war. However, I borrow from the future for the formation of the ambulance corp. This did not happen until the twentieth century. British Friends and American Friends were instrumental in the creation of the abolition movements and the abolition of slavery in both Britain and America.

I come from German-American stock, and my mother went to the Carl Schurz High School in Chicago, Illinois. When I did the research for a ship to carry the Kellett women to America and found the *London* with Schurz on its passenger list, I could not resist writing him a small part in the book. Carl Schurz is an historical figure, who did sail on the *London* in order to emigrate from Germany after his involvement in the 1848 revolution, but he was happily married at the time and sailed with his wife.

HMS *Resolute* went to the breaker's dock at Chatham in 1879, and Queen Victoria had a desk made from her timbers, which she then sent in 1880 to the president and people of the United States. Affixed to the front of the desk is a bronze plaque engraved as follows:

'H.M.S *Resolute,* forming part of the expedition sent in search of Sir John Franklin in 1852, was abandoned in Latitude 74 degrees -41 minutes N Longitude 101 degrees -22 minutes W on the 15th of May, 1854. She was discovered and extricated in September 1855 in Latitude 67 degrees N by Captain Buddington of the United States whaler *George Henry.*

'The ship was purchased, fitted out and sent to England as a gift to *Her Majesty Queen Victoria* by the *President and People of the United States,* as a token of good will and friendship. This table was made from her timbers when she was broken up and was presented by the *Queen of Great Britain and Ireland* to the *President of the United States* as a memorial of the courtesy and loving kindness which dictated the offer of the gift of the *Resolute.'*

The Resolute desk has lived in the White House ever since with only one exception, when in 1963, President Johnson sent it to the Smithsonian, where it remained until President Carter returned it to the White House and used it in the Oval Office.

Appropriately to the fact that the warmongering that took place in the United States towards Britain in 1855 and 1856 had been intimately entwined with pre-civil war politics, the desk was in the Lincoln bedroom for a time. President Roosevelt sat at it while he made his radio broadcast fireside chats throughout WWII, and, poignant to my story, although he did not live to use it, he had a sliding panel added to it so that his braces and wheel chair could not be seen when he sat behind it. President Eisenhower used it when he was doing televised speeches.

Jacqueline Kennedy, when she did her remarkable refurbishment of the White House, was the first person to bring the desk into the Oval Office, where President Kennedy used it through out his presidency. For this reason, it is frequently referred to as the Kennedy desk, and an exact replica was made for the Kennedy Presidential Library. After President Carter returned it to the White House, he also used it in the Oval Office, as did Presidents Reagan, Clinton, and George W. Bush.

The Resolute desk today continues to sit proudly in the office of the President of the United States: the Oval Office in the White House, the ever present testimony to the special relationship between America and Great Britain.

ACKNOWLEDGEMENTS

Many people helped with my research for this book. In England I wish to thank the staff at the National Maritime Museum Caird Research Library as well as the National Maritime Museum's Curator of Ships Plans and Historic Photographs, and the Access Co-ordinator for viewing artefacts; the staff at the Public Record Office in Kew; and at the Chatham Dockyard Historical Society; the Scott Polar Institute in Cambridge; the Durham Record Office; the Plymouth Library; the British Library and the Library of the Religious Society of Friends in London.

In Ireland I wish to thank the staff at the County Tipperary Museum, the Dublin City Library and Archives, the Carrigan family who allowed me to spend two glorious weeks in Captain Kellett's home, Clonacody, in County Tipperary, and Tony Newport, the Fethard historian who shared his photographs and stories of Kellett's home village with me.

In America I wish to thank the staff at The New London, Connecticut Historical Society; the G. W. Blunt research library at Mystic Seaport, Connecticut; the New Bedford, Massachusetts Whaling Museum; the Library of Congress; and the Naval Base in Washington DC; The Glen Ellyn, Illinois Public Library; The Wheaton, Illinois Public Library; and the President Hayes Memorial Library; The Wheaton, Illinois Public Library.

Many individuals made it possible for this book to come to fruition, and I hope you won't hold me in contempt if I forget to mention you here. I wish to thank Richard, James, Linda, Kim, Scott, Deb, Mike, Fiona, Ted L, Judy, Johnathon C, Bradd, Randee, and all my friends and family who encouraged me and believed in this project. And last but not least thanks to Brian: for a room with a view, and regular infusions of Yorkshire tea.

ABOUT THE AUTHOR

Elizabeth Matthews was born in Chicago, Illinois, and became an avid sailor in the 1980's. With a life long interest in history, it did not take long for her to combine history with her love of sailing, and begin a lasting, ongoing passion for maritime history.

In 1993, after she had completed her first year of law school at Georgetown University in Washington D.C., she was involved in an automobile accident, which resulted in a severe back injury. After a year of being completely home bound, her doctor prescribed a reclining wheelchair for her. While this chair would give her more freedom, she was saddened by the fact that she would have to have a wheel chair in her life. In order to overcome that sadness, and to celebrate the arrival of her chair, she decided to have a wheel chair launching party. Much like a ship launching, Elizabeth needed a name for her chair so she could christen it with champagne. She chose Resolute, naming her wheelchair after the 1920 America's Cup winner. In addition to the dictionary definition of the word resolute and knowing she needed to be resolute to continue with her painful physical therapy, she also liked the story of the 1920 America Cup race. *Resolute* had lost as many of the early races as she possibly could without being disqualified. And then she started winning. She came up from behind to win the silver.

When Elizabeth progressed with her therapy, and it looked as though she might someday be able to own a sailing yacht and sail again, she researched what other ships had been named Resolute, and found this story.

She and her husband split their time between living in London and on their Halberg Rassy, S/Y *RESOLUTE*.

Printed in the United States
111738LV00004B/9-14/P